FOLIES D'AMOUR

FOLIES D'AMOUR

ANNE-MARIE VILLEFRANCHE

Carroll & Graf Publishers, inc.
New York

First Carroll & Graf paperback edition 1986

Carroll & Graf Publishers, Inc.
260 Fifth Avenue
New York, NY 10001

Manufactured in the United States of America

ANNE-MARIE VILLEFRANCHE AND HER FRIENDS

When I first began to translate into English the unpublished memoirs of Anne-Marie Villefranche it did not seem probable to me that these accounts of the intimate concerns of the people she knew would interest more than the few who take pleasure in scandalous gossip about the past. In this I under-estimated the appeal of tales of Paris in the 1920s, for there proved to be for that first volume, *Plaisir d'amour*, a large readership, not only in Britain but also elsewhere in Europe, in the United States – and even in far-off Japan.

This unexpected interest led to a request for more of her work and a further selection of her stories was published under the title of *Joie d'amour*. The demand for that book has resulted in a third collection, here presented as *Folies d'amour*.

The title of the present volume, as of the two former, was not chosen at random. As the reader will discover, the persons concerned in these stories involve themselves in extraordinary predicaments through their pursuit of illicit sexual pleasure.

To quote Anne-Marie's own words from *The fortune-teller*: 'The truth of the matter is that we each carry our destiny within us, for destiny is the outcome of character.' Seen from Anne-Marie's point of view, it may be said that events, whether fortunate or indecent, do not happen

1

by chance; they are the logical result of personality in action and, in that sense, they are deserved.

This can be seen plainly in the story of Marie-Claire Fénéon, whose devotion to narcissistic pleasures brings its own curious reward. Or again, in *The emancipated Madame Delaroque*, a man complicates his life by the pursuit of a fancied ideal which, when attained, proves comically different from his expectations.

Follies indeed! But it is the human capacity to be easily diverted from the path of social convention into the secret byways of pleasure that provides Anne-Marie with her material. She invites us to smile at the quirks of human nature, not at simple virtue.

How much of these memoirs is fact and how much should be attributed to Anne-Marie herself is not an easy question to resolve. As I reconstruct her method, she extracted from her friends as much of their adventures as they were willing to disclose. After that, her own knowledge of those concerned was used to fill in the gaps. Thus, in the narrative of Christope's disgraceful behaviour at Cannes, her confidant was obviously Christophe Larousse himself, who appears in the two previous volumes and seems to have been a favourite of hers. In the crystal room misadventure, Anne-Marie's source of information could only have been Marie-Claire Fénéon – presumably at a time much later than the events recorded, when she had perceived the truth about Giles and could take a more detached view of the whole episode.

Anne-Marie's own comments on the characters and motives of her friends are frequently wryly humorous. From them it is possible to form the view that she found the human comedy, particularly the pleasures and follies of love, endlessly amusing.

Jane Purcell
London 1984

2

MARCEL LEAVES HIS VISITING CARD

After the Bolshevik revolution in Russia and the establishment of a most monstrous tyranny by Lenin and his band of cut-throats, all who could fled the catastrophe that had overtaken their homeland. To be seen in public wearing a pair of clean shoes was a crime against the proletariat for which one could be shot against the nearest wall! In making their escape from this proletarian paradise Monsieur Diaghilev and the Ballets Russes brought to Paris a revolution of their own – the transformation of the classical dance into a colourful and vibrant spectacle.

The achievement, heralded throughout the whole of Europe, held little interest for Marcel Chalon, who did not find the ballet entertaining in any form, old or new. Yet he endured performances with good grace for the sake of his mother, who greatly enjoyed them. Since the tragic death of her husband a dozen years before, Madame Chalon had found no other male companion – indeed, she had not even sought one. Marcel, who still lived with her even though he was approaching thirty years of age, escorted his mother to the ballet whenever she wished.

One fine spring evening, events took an unusual course soon after the lights went down and the music started. As was her invariable custom, Madame Chalon insisted on occupying a seat next to the aisle – for what reason Marcel had never known and thought it impolite to ask. On the other side of him sat a pretty young woman and, beyond

3

her, an older woman whom he took to be her mother. Marcel surrendered to her the seat-arm between them – a courtesy she did not even acknowledge. Since his mother had already taken possession of the seat-arm on his other side, Marcel had nowhere at all to rest his elbows.

When the dancing began, Marcel amused himself by admiring the uncovered thighs of the female dancers on the stage. They were extremely beautiful, these thighs, shaped to perfection by years of hard practice – long, slender, gracefully muscled – how delightful it would be to have them gripping one's waist in the throes of passion!

But pleasant as it was at first to contemplate those thighs, it was inevitable that Marcel's interest diminished after a time, until eventually he was bored. The seats were not particularly comfortable and he had to make an effort not to disturb his mother's enjoyment of the spectacle by fidgeting. He fell back on his customary trick to keep himself amused – he recalled in as much detail as he could remember the most recent intimate encounter between himself and a beautiful woman – in this instance a certain Madame Bataille, two nights before. She was the wife of a friend of his and, needless to say, the friend knew nothing of his wife's excursions with Marcel. The memory of that encounter was a pleasant one and it served to arouse Marcel. The pressure of his trousers on his upright part diverted his attention from the stage and with a little luck would retain his interest until the intermission. Ah, dear friend, he silently addressed the source of his masculine pride between his legs, what charming adventures you have led me into!

He glanced down with affection into his lap, trying to discern in the darkened auditorium the long bulge he knew to be in the front of his trousers. He was embarrassed to see that, in sitting with his legs apart to accommodate his enjoyable stiffness, his left knee was touching the thigh of the young woman in the seat next to him.

4

How very rude she must think me – that was his first response, to be followed almost at once by a more pleasing thought – she had not moved her leg away! By way of experiment Marcel withdrew his own knee from contact with her, waited for a moment or two and then moved it back. She did not flinch away from the pressure – but nor did she return it. Could it be that she was so engrossed in the spectacle on the stage that she was unaware that a stranger's leg was pressing against her own?

Slowly, for he had no desire to attract the attention of his mother, Marcel half-turned his head to look at his unknown neighbour. She was hardly more than twenty years of age, he thought, dark-haired and wearing a short evening frock which, in the dimness of the auditorium, he took to be a shade of pale blue, with a narrow belt of the same colour. The frock was short enough to show her knees as she sat. It was also sleeveless, displaying slender arms with a gold bracelet on each wrist to match the gold chain round her neck. Most exciting of all to Marcel, needless to say, was that the frock was décolleté to a point between her breasts. Even if it had been possible to wear a chemise beneath so deep-cut a neck-line, Marcel knew instinctively that no woman with any pretention to style would have considered it for a moment. He gazed fondly at the gleaming skin of the upper curve of a breast as the young lady moved slightly and so caused her bosom to roll a little under the thin material of her frock. If he could but reach out and place his hand on that delicious rounded swelling nearest to him, he knew that he would be able to feel the warmth and softness of a tender little breast through the pale blue material.

Marcel's upstanding part bounded in his underwear at the very thought! It was urging him to carry out his wish and touch that tempting breast – to feel gently for the little bud through the frock – even if the action brought instant public disgrace upon him. The perfume she wore

5

was delightful – light and fragrant as befitted one so young – yet with a subtle promise. Marcel studied her profile as best he could out of the corner of his eye. Her hair was beautifully cut and left the lobes of her ears uncovered, and they were innocent of any jewellery. Her forehead was high and smooth, betokening intelligence. Her eyebrows were plucked to a fashionably thin line. Her little chin, under a brightly painted mouth, was firm and showed decisiveness of character, in Marcel's estimation. Altogether a most charming person to be seated next to – how was he to make her acquaintance, that was the question. In other circumstances he would have introduced himself and hoped for the best, but with his own Mama at his side and the girl's Mama at her side, so bold an enterprise was impossible.

His hands lay on his thighs, for without the benefit of arm-rests, the only other choices were to fold his arms across his chest or to clasp his hands in his lap. Marcel let his left hand brush against his neighbour's silk-clad knee, so lightly that it might be accidental and he would be able to apologise profusely for his clumsiness if she raised any objection. She made no move at all. He let his hand lie along his thigh, down near the knee, in such a way that the whole side of his palm was in light contact with her knee. He thought that he detected a tiny quiver of her leg at the touch, but she did not pull away from the contact. The delicate warmth of her flesh through the silk stocking made Marcel sigh with pleasure.

Up on the distant stage the dancers were flinging themselves about in a creative frenzy that went totally unremarked by Marcel. His attention was concentrated on the silken knee which his finger-tips were now caressing without pretence. A cautious half-glance at its owner's face showed him that she was still looking directly ahead at the stage, though even in the dim light he could perceive that her eye-lids were nearly closed and her red lips were a little open. Who could she be, he wondered,

6

this enchanting young woman who allowed him the exquisite pleasure of stroking her leg in a public place?

By now Marcel's hand had moved beyond its starting-point – had dipped slowly between her slightly parted knees and up under her frock a little, to caress the tender inside of her thigh. Again that delicious little tremor! This time he thought that she gave him a quick glance from the corner of her eye. Marcel was enraptured by having the boredom of sitting through a ballet performance dispelled in so unexpected and exciting a manner. If all the female dancers on the stage had, at that moment, stripped themselves and continued the ballet stark naked, he would have ignored them for the secret little delight of his hand lightly stroking his unknown neighbour's thigh.

When his fingers moved higher still and touched her garter, she reached out almost furtively to pull her frock down towards her knees again, for it was riding up toward her lap. But she accomplished this without impeding him in the slightest. At last he touched her bare thigh above her stocking-top and was rewarded with an unmistakable little tremor the length of her leg. The skin under his fingers was smooth as satin and warm to the touch – a combination of delights which so aroused Marcel that he felt a prickle of perspiration start in his arm-pits.

Ahead of him lay the incredible moment of discovery when, his fingers gliding slowly up that stretch of bare thigh, he would encounter her underwear – a hem of soft lace first, no doubt. After that – his mind reeled in sensual anticipation!

But it was not to be as he imagined. Her warm thighs closed on his hand, forbidding any further exploration of her secret charms! While he was trying to understand this sudden disappointment, she took hold of his wrist and pulled his hand away from her completely. A moment later the dancers froze into immobility, the music stopped and the audience applauded.

7

'Magnificent!' said Marcel's mother to him as she clapped her hands together, 'superb!'

'Superb,' Marcel agreed at once, though his compliment was intended for the young woman in the pale blue frock sitting next to him, 'the experience of a lifetime!'

Madame Chalon looked at her son as if he had lost his senses.

'I have never known you to be so enthusiastic before about the ballet,' she said, 'are you feeling all right?'

'The experience was enthralling – there is no other word to describe it, Mama.'

He said this loudly, to be overheard by his neighbour.

'Really?' Madame Chalon commented. 'You had better have something to drink, in this strange mood of yours. A small cognac, perhaps. Come along, Marcel.'

During the intermission Marcel thought furiously about how he was to make the acquaintance of the enchanting creature who had provided him with a most memorable interlude. He caught sight of her once or twice in the crowd, talking to the woman he was sure was her mother. But how? He could hardly walk up to her and pretend that he had met her before – not with that formidable mother standing at her side.

'Mama,' he said, 'that lady over there – the one in the black frock and the jet bead necklace – she looks familiar to me in some way. Is she not an acquaintance of yours? Perhaps I have seen her visiting you.'

Madame Chalon turned to look.

'The lady talking to the pretty young girl in blue, you mean?'

'Yes, that's the one.'

'No, I don't know her. She has a very unsympathetic look – I'm sure that I wouldn't want to know her.'

Marcel excused himself and, in the privacy of the men's toilet, scribbled a few words on the back of one of his visiting cards. It should not prove impossible to slip it into her hand unnoticed when the performance resumed.

The second part of the ballet was sheer delight for him. No sooner were the house lights lowered than his hand found its way discreetly under the pale blue frock. A most ingenious plan had presented itself to him during the return to his seat. In his palm, held flat by his thumb, was his visiting card! With infinite caution he slipped the thin card down the top of her stocking until it was held against her thigh by the pressure of her garter. That accomplished, his eager hand sought the smooth bare flesh between garter and underwear. What joy, what incredible joy surged through his heart at the touch! What wild thoughts whirled through his mind! More than anything in the world he wanted to be alone with this marvellous girl, to take her in his arms! He was on fire to kiss her trembling lips, to caress the sweet little breasts he half-discerned under her frock. Above all, he was full of an insane desire to press his lips to the warm and tender flesh of her thigh where his hand now rested!

As before, to his infinite sorrow, her legs clamped firmly together when he tried to reach her secret citadel, though not before his questing little finger touched the lace that hemmed her underwear. He was at the very threshold of success – his stiff part was quivering deliciously within the confines of his trousers. He risked a glance at her face in the dark, his eyes imploring her to relent and let him touch the summit of his desire. But she did not return his look – she stared fixedly at the stage, even though her pretty mouth was open in what Marcel believed to be faint sighs of pleasure.

All too soon she pushed his hand gently away. The orchestra reached a climactic finish and the audience applauded the end of the performance. With regret that his joy had ended, Marcel helped his mother into her fur wrap and took her arm to lead her out of the auditorium. The girl in pale blue gave him not one look as she and her mother made their preparations to depart. Yet seeing her full face and so close, Marcel was struck by the exquisite refinement of her appearance and the air of slight haughtiness in the cast of her features. Yet she had permitted him, a stranger, such intimacies! Between her appearance and her actions there was so great a contradiction that Marcel was unable to understand it – yet he intended to do so.

He caught sight of her back in the foyer before she disappeared into the slow-moving crowd – just a glimpse of pale blue, a sable stole about her shoulders, going out of the main entrance. Impatient as he was to keep her in sight for as long as possible, Marcel could do nothing – his mother moved slowly, having a touch of arthritis in one hip, or so she claimed, so that it was impossible to hurry her along. Outside the theatre, there was no sign of the blue frock. Marcel shrugged in resignation and set about getting his mother into a taxi.

That night he dreamed about Mademoiselle Blue-frock, as was to be expected, for her charms had made a formidable impression on him. And besides, this was the third night since he had last enjoyed the company of Madame Bataille. In his dream Marcel was with the girl and together they were climbing the steps to the summit of the Eiffel Tower – an undertaking too daunting in waking life for Marcel ever to have considered. Yet here he was, clambering up the endless steps inside the cast-iron latticework of one of the legs of the giant edifice, the blue frock a step or two ahead of him. Under her frock the enchanting cheeks of her bottom moved up and down in turn as she climbed upwards.

'Can't you keep up with me, Marcel?' she asked over her shoulder.

'Let us not rush this ascent,' he answered.

'Are you tired already?'

'No, I can go on forever with you!'

'Put your hand between my legs, that will help you.'

He reached under her frock and felt his vertically-held hand clasped between the bare flesh of her thighs above her stockings. In this remarkable posture she seemed to draw him onwards and upwards, until the ground seemed a long way below when he looked down.

'How much further before we arrive at the summit?' he asked in wonder.

'There are one thousand six hundred and fifty-two steps to the top,' she answered sternly, as if surprised by his ignorance of so elementary a fact.

'But how many have we ascended so far?'

'Fifty-two,' she said, 'why didn't you count them?'

Marcel turned his hand sideways between her legs and clasped her tender mound, only the thin silk of her underwear between his palm and her soft fur.

'Let's stop and do it here,' he suggested.

At this moment he woke up. He lay thinking about his dream, trying to prolong for as long as he could the pleasant memory of his hand between her legs. But the remnants of the sleeping fantasy faded and left him with the reality of his male part at full stretch and no one in the bed with him.

The little ormolu clock at his bedside indicated that it was not much after three in the morning. Marcel pondered his predicament. He could dress and go out – fifteen minutes fast walk through the silent streets of sleeping Paris would bring him to the Bataille apartment, where Georgette would welcome him and offer a warm lodging for his homeless part – except that her husband had returned home the day before. It was too late to visit a private establishment Marcel held in esteem not far from the Opera – visitors were not admitted after two in the morning, so that the girls could sleep off the ravages of the evening and restore themselves for the following day's work.

Of course, there were still women offering all-night services in the streets around the Place Blanche and at the St Lazare railway station, which was even nearer. There were women available in the little cafes around

11

Les Halles market, looking for business from the market-porters just starting their day. But all that was repugnant to Marcel, the women to be encountered in such locations being ugly and coarse.

His hand was inside his pyjamas to fondle his stiff flesh. In his condition of high arousal a dozen or twenty strokes at most would be enough to bring about the emission which would relieve his emotions and allow him to go back to sleep. But to Marcel that course of action was an admission of defeat and unacceptable to his pride. A woman had caused this stiffness – a woman must provide the means to make it limp again. There was nothing for it but to risk a visit to Annette's room. He got out of bed in the dark, put on his long striped dressing-gown and opened his door with the utmost caution.

Annette was the younger of the two servants Marcel's mother employed. She was about thirty, plain but clean and well-fed. Marcel had availed himself of her willingly-rendered services on various occasions during the five years she had been with them – occasions when he had been in dire need of a woman's company, as now. But he had a fear that his mother might find out one of these times. That would be disastrous! Annette would be dismissed instantly, of course, and Marcel would be subjected to an angry lecture and his mother's contempt.

Nevertheless, dear Mama, he thought as he went silently towards the maid's room, sons have particular needs which mothers fail to understand sometimes. And not only sons – he wondered, not for the first time, if his mother had understood his father's particular needs, or whether his father had been driven to seek solace elsewhere.

Annette was fast asleep and snoring lightly when Marcel entered her room and closed the door carefully behind him. She had not drawn the curtains close and there was enough light through the window to guide him to her bedside. She was lying on her back, her hair tousled

12

over her forehead. He smoothed it back with a gentle hand, then stroked her cheek until her snoring stopped and her eyes opened. At once he pressed his hand delicately over her mouth to stop any exclamation of surprise which might disturb the household.

'Annette – it's me,' he whispered.

She stared at his face briefly and then nodded. He removed his hand.

'I awoke in a condition of loneliness,' he explained softly, 'will you comfort me a little, Annette?'

Her answer was to throw aside the bedcovers to make room for him. Marcel slipped off his beautiful dressing-gown and pyjama trousers and got into the narrow bed with her.

'I knew that you would understand,' he sighed, his hand feeling for her breasts.

Annette, as has been said, was well-fed – and well-fleshed as a result – broad of hip and solid of bottom. Her weighty breasts bore no comparison to the chic and pointed little breasts of women of fashion, naturally, but Marcel thought no worse of her for that. After all, she was a servant, a simple daughter of the people.

He helped her to pull her ankle-length cotton nightdress up round her neck so that he could roll her big slack breasts in his hands, and he noted that, as on previous occasions, their sheer size stimulated him in a strange way. She, meanwhile, had taken hold of his projecting member and was squeezing it clumsily but enthusiastically.

'I always say you've got a good one on you, M'sieu Marcel,' she whispered. 'You know I'm always ready to take care of it for you.'

What Annette's usual arrangements might be was not a subject to which Marcel had ever given more than passing consideration. With only one half-day free a week, it seemed improbable that she enjoyed much in the way of

13

the pleasures of love. Naturally, she welcomed Marcel's infrequent and furtive visits.

'You mustn't be too long about it,' she whispered, spreading her plump legs for him, 'and be careful about making the bed rattle. Old Louise next door is a light sleeper and you don't want her to know your business – she might tell your mother if she got suspicious.'

In spite of the limitations imposed upon him by her admonitions, Marcel positioned himself in great anticipation on Annette's broad and warm belly. A long push and he was well inserted where he wanted to be.

'God, what a ramrod,' she gasped, 'do it hard!'

Marcel plunged vigorously, closing his mind to the contrast between the elegant young woman whose thighs had so excited him and the hot and plain maidservant on whose body he lay.

'That feels good!' Annette exclaimed 'Harder!'

It did not take long before physical sensation overwhelmed Marcel and he fountained his climactic release into the maid's receptacle.

'That was quick,' she said as he withdrew from her and got out of her bed to dress himself.

'And most agreeable,' he said. 'Thank you, Annette.'

'Then if you are satisfied. . . goodnight, M'sieu Marcel.'

'On second thoughts,' he said, taking off his dressing-gown again, 'one should not stint oneself of the pleasures of life. If the meal is good, a second helping never comes amiss.'

He got back into bed with Annette, lying on his side, and told her to turn to lie with her back to him. In this position, like two spoons together, her big soft bottom pressed against his belly, he put his arms round her to fondle her breasts until his musket was reloaded – a process which never took him long. This time he adopted a more leisurely pace, ignoring Annette's gasps and sighs of pleasure while he imagined that it was Mademoiselle Blue-frock whose body he was enjoying. In this manner the affair was concluded to the satisfaction of both participants.

'Thank you, M'sieu Marcel,' the maid said when he dressed for the second time, 'be careful going back to your room – there's a creaking floorboard that needs fixing just outside my door.'

Back in his own bed Marcel slept soundly, with no more dreams to disturb him, and woke up at nine o'clock feeling refreshed and full of hope for what the day might bring. Annette served his breakfast in bed – café au lait, two croissants still hot from the baker, with butter and apricot preserve. She winked broadly at him when she placed the tray across his lap and he gave her a handsome tip for her compliance.

That afternoon he took a taxi to the corner of the Place de la Bastille and strolled up the short and narrow rue de Birague into the Place des Vosges, timing himself to arrive there at five minutes before three o'clock. By common consent the Place des Vosges is one of the most beautiful squares in the whole of Paris and, on a fine spring afternoon, a perfect setting for a rendezvous. But would the young lady keep the assignation Marcel had scribbled on the card he had left under her garter?

He entered the little garden in the centre of the square and stood near the stone fountain to admire the elegant old mansions of red brick and pale stone that surrounded the square – buildings from the days of King Louis XIII. At the level of the street they were gracefully arcaded in stone, above that they rose two more stories to their steep roofs of grey slate broken by dormer windows. The sun was shining brightly and the little trees that fringed the garden were just showing their pink and white blossom – the scene could not have been improved upon! But would she come? Marcel made himself stroll slowly about the garden, trying to contain his rising agitation of spirit.

At ten minutes past three exactly he caught sight of her entering the garden on the other side from him. He

15

uttered a great sigh of relief and strode quickly towards her. She was a very picture of elegance in a charcoal grey spring coat that fitted closely down to the waist and then flared out into a fuller skirt to her knees. It was trimmed with a little collar of grey fur, matched by cuffs of the same fur. Her little grey hat had a turned-back brim and in one white-gloved hand she held a square handbag of ultramarine blue. Marcel's heart bounded in time with his steps as he hurried towards her, a welcoming smile on his face – though her own expression remained tranquil.

They met close to the fountain. Marcel removed his hat and kissed her gloved hand. He stared with affection into her face, remembering each feature with pleasure. She was beautiful, no less, and her air of slight disdain enhanced her beauty enormously.

'I cannot tell you how enchanted I am to see you again,' he said, investing the commonplace words with a wealth of meaning.

'Your invitation was so unusual that it was difficult to refuse,' she replied, 'shall we walk together a little?'

Her words and her manner were cool, Marcel noted, but the mere fact that she had come to the assignation gave him hope.

Side by side they strolled at a leisurely pace around the Place des Vosges. Marcel was oblivious to the passers-by and the children playing under the stone arcades. He had his wish – he was with the marvellous young woman of his dream. But how ought he to proceed? On what terms were they? At the ballet she had allowed him certain intimacies, perhaps under the influence of the music and dance. But here and now – in the light of day? It might be that she regretted the generosity of her response to his advances the evening before and would repel him with indignation if he made reference to what had passed between them. Yet on the other hand – she had undoubtedly accepted the invitation on the back of the visiting card he had tucked down her stocking-top.

16

He decided that frankness was the least dangerous approach to the delicate situation.

'My name is Marcel Chalon, as you already know,' he began, 'I am unmarried and of independent means. I live at the address you have seen on my card, with my widowed mother, whom you saw last evening at the ballet.'

'You have told me nothing I did not know or could not guess,' she answered distantly. 'What then? Are there not certain improprieties on your part which require an explanation?'

'Without doubt,' said Marcel, 'and I must thank you with all my heart for giving me this opportunity of explaining my actions.'

'I am waiting.'

'My story is soon told. When I saw you sitting next to me yesterday evening I was so totally captivated by your beauty and elegance that I behaved with more boldness – one might even say rashness – than ever before in my life. I hope that you can understand and appreciate the formidable strength of the emotions which impelled me to do what I did.'

'I see,' she said, 'then it is not customary with you to put your hand up the clothes of women to whom you have not been introduced?'

Her directness took Marcel aback.

'No,' he answered, 'I was swept off my feet by the emotions you aroused in me.'

'What a pity,' she said, glancing at him thoughtfully.

'What do you mean?'

'I mean that I hoped to have found in you a man of spirit. The truth is that my life is dull, has always been dull and promises to always remain dull. I wish it to become adventurous and unpredictable. For a brief space I thought that you might be the person to make that happen, but I see now that I was mistaken. *Au revoir*, Monsieur.'

17

'Wait – don't go!' Marcel exclaimed urgently, putting his hand on her arm, 'I am exactly the person you are looking for. What I said before conveyed a false impression. Permit me to explain.'

'Then you do put your hand up the clothes of unknown women?'

Marcel smiled at her, beginning to appreciate her directness.

'Only give me the opportunity and I will transform your life, which you say is dull, into a veritable Arabian Nights adventure.'

She thought that over for a little while as they strolled along.

'Are you really capable of keeping that promise,' she said with a note of doubt in her voice, 'or does it mean no more than that you wish to take me to bed a few times for the sake of a quick thrill? That's not my idea of adventure.'

Marcel could hardly believe what he was hearing. Her appearance was so refined, her manner so well-bred – and yet her words implied a secret desire for incredible sensations. Perhaps this was the greatest moment of his life – perhaps he had accidentally encountered the one woman in the whole of Paris with whom he could realise his own desire to escape from the boredom of conventional society. He took her hand gently and raised it to his lips.

'You shall have no reason to complain,' he assured her, 'yesterday you experienced an unpredictable pleasure when I touched you. You cannot deny this, for I felt the delicate tremors when my fingers caressed your thigh. But that was no more than a modest overture. You shall enjoy remarkable sensations in improbable settings, I give you my word.'

'I am half-persuaded to give you an opportunity to prove that you mean what you say. But. . .' and she halted to turn and look him full in the face, 'disappoint me once and you will never see me again.'

'I understand. Now, tell me your name.'

'Marie-Madeleine. That's all you need to know.'

'No family name? No address? No telephone number?'

'If you attempt to discover any more about me I shall disappear forever.'

'Then Marie-Madeleine is enough for me,' Marcel said fervently.

'Good. Now, Monsieur, it is well after three o'clock and I must be home by six thirty to dress for dinner. Be so good as to begin the adventures you promised me.'

Marcel thought furiously. She had made it quite clear that to be taken to a hotel to be made love to was not her conception of an adventure. But that was what he had planned for! One false step now and he could lose this marvellous creature forever. What to do? Naturally, Marcel was not without extensive experience of women, married and unmarried. Most of his experiences had been fairly brief – affairs of a few weeks only – but twice in the last seven years he had formed deeper and longer-lasting liaisons with women, to the extent of maintaining them in an apartment which he visited several times a week – to the great disapproval of his mother every time he spent a night away from home – a disapproval no less ferocious because it was never spoken in words. The fact was that Madame Chalon fully expected her only son to marry, bring his bride to live in the family apartment and quickly produce grandchildren for her. Marcel had no inclination to fulfil these expectations.

'Well?' Marie-Madeleine demanded, 'are we to walk here all afternoon? Astonish me!'

'Certainly,' said Marcel, with more show of confidence than he felt at that moment, 'I intend to bath you in champagne.'

Her jet-black eyes opened wide and her mouth trembled. The disdainful expression was replaced by one of geniune astonishment. Marcel knew that he had struck the right note.

'In champagne!' she murmured.

'Before the War, in the days of the Belle Époque, so I have heard,' said Marcel, 'every great beauty of Paris was bathed in champagne by her special admirer. These famous devotees of Venus, whose glorious names are enshrined forever in history and legend – they bestowed their divine favours not on ordinary men of the sort one meets every day. No, they admitted to their intimate friendship the grandees of their day – Archdukes from Germany, Princes from Russia, Kings even, from Belgium and England.'

'Ah, yes,' Marie-Madeleine sighed, 'how magnificent!'

'Within the hour you shall be enrolled in this pantheon of great beauties worthy to receive this ultimate accolade. It will be my sacred privilege to perform for you, Marie-Madeleine, the most sumptuous rite of love.'

'Yes, yes,' she breathed, her eyes almost closed in delight, 'you are more marvellous than I could have imagined.'

The private hotel to which Marcel conducted her was not a hotel at all in the usual sense of the word. It was located in the rue Réamur, completely anonymously, with a discreetly unmarked entrance door on the street that led directly to a flight of stairs to the first floor. It provided, for those who could afford the cost, elegantly furnished bedrooms and even more elegantly furnished suites of rooms, to lovers who desired to entertain their beloved for a few hours in luxury and in privacy. Naturally, establishments of this type are popular with men entertaining other men's wives – that most Parisian of pastimes!

From a small café only a short walk from the Place des Vosges Marcel telephoned ahead to ensure that a suite appropriate to his needs was immediately available. He also ordered a sufficient quantity of unchilled champagne for his purpose to be placed in the suite before his arrival.

As every man of distinction knows, it requires a minimum of eight dozen bottles to fill a bath of average size to a depth sufficient to impress a woman of quality. And remembering that the baths in the house to which he was taking Marie-Madeleine were of the large old-fashioned type, he ordered ten dozen bottles to be in readiness. To skimp on a few bottles at a moment like this might ruin beyond repair what promised to be a great adventure. The person to whom he spoke expressed not the least surprise at his request, as was to be expected in one who was accustomed to purveying special services to persons of adequate financial means. Marcel was a valued client, after all, and he was assured that the house would not charge him for any unopened bottles that might be left over.

The room in which Marie-Madeleine disrobed, with Marcel's expert assistance, had a certain fin-de-siècle charm which pleased her – long curtains of dark-red plush with tassels, a vast bed ornamented in white and gold with an oval plaque of porcelain let into its woodwork painted with a small and chubby Cupid about to let fly an arrow from a tiny bow. But for all the carefully-preserved pre-War finery, Marcel had eyes only for the beautiful young woman he had brought there – which was as it should be.

Her outer clothes removed, she stood gracefully, one hand at her cheek, so that Marcel could admire her slender figure in silk camiknickers of damson-red, an exquisitely flimsy garment which covered her from just above the point of her breasts to just below the join of her long thighs. Marcel sighed in delight at this vision of desire.

But then – an unimaginable shock caused him to gasp loudly! He caught sight for the first time of a ring on her finger – not a wedding-ring, for that would have meant nothing. But this!

'You are engaged?' he asked incredulously.

Marie-Madeleine raised her hand and frowned slightly at the offending ring. 'Does it matter to you?' she replied.

'No – but doesn't it matter to *you*?'

She shook her black-haired head gently.

'No, he's a boring man and I don't love him.'

'Then why are you engaged to be married to him, whoever he is?'

'I told you when we met – my life is dull. My parents are worthy, kind, dull people. They chose my fiancé for me and how could I refuse? He too is kind, worthy and dull – and most suitable, of course. Our marriage will be ideal in everyone's opinion except mine. We shall live in a large apartment, entertain a great deal, go to the most boring part of the country each summer and have two children. And that's it.'

'But this is frightful!' Marcel muttered.

'To you, perhaps. To me it is normal because that is the way I have been brought up. Now, Marcel. . .' and she used his name for the first time, 'you give every indication of becoming boring yourself. I am disappointed in you. I did not expect this conventional attitude. I shall dress and leave at once.'

'Don't go! It was only a moment of surprise and is now forgotten. Your first adventure is about to begin – let me kiss your knees.'

'That's better,' said Marie-Madeleine, smiling at him, 'no one has ever kissed my knees before.'

'Not even your fiancé?'

'I forbid you ever to mention him again.'

Marcel sank to the floor and kissed her pretty bare knees, his finger-tips lightly caressing the backs of her thighs. She gave every indication of enjoying what he was doing to her and by stages his hands moved up the loose legs of her silk *chemise-culotte* until he could squeeze and stroke the tender cheeks of her bottom. She let him continue this for some time before she gently pulled away and suggested that they might move into the bathroom together.

The bathroom was spacious and ornate, as befitted the establishment. Marcel opened a bottle and poured two glasses of champagne to drink with her a salute to the beginning of their adventures with each other. Marie-Madeleine sat on a chair, her bare knees gracefully crossed, sipping her wine and watching in total fascination as Marcel discarded his jacket and set to work popping corks and pouring fizzing champagne into the big and old-fashioned pink onyx bath. The delicate fumes of the wine filled the air, making Marie-Madeleine's eyes sparkle.

'But this is quite mad!' she exclaimed, laughing.

'Yes,' Marcel agreed, laughing with her as he stood, a bottle in each hand, champagne streaming into the bath.

He worked quickly, tearing open the packing cases, unwiring corks with a deft twist, until he had emptied the contents of eight dozen bottles and the floor was littered with corks, wires and empty bottles.

'Now,' he exclaimed, 'your bath is ready, my princess.'

Marie-Madeleine giggled and stood up, her arms stretched out towards him. Marcel kissed both hands and the insides of her wrists, then took her gently in his arms to kiss her adorable mouth. 'Oh Marcel, I think I am falling a little in love with you,' she breathed.

He slipped a hand between her warm thighs to undo the tiny mother of-pearl buttons of her camiknickers, then pulled the damson-red wisp of silk slowly up her body and over her head.

'You are truly beautiful,' he said, stepping back to look at her naked.

'Truly?' she asked, as if unsure – though no beautiful woman ever is.

'Utterly and breathtakingly beautiful,' he answered. 'Give me your hand.'

She put her hand in his and with great courtesy he helped her into the bath. She lay back in the pale gold champagne, a sight to dazzle the senses of any man.

The delicate pink tips of her breasts showed above the surface and the rest of her long svelte body and legs were visible through the wine. Marcel gazed in wonder at the good fortune which had made it possible for him to attract the interest of a woman as exquisitely beautiful as Marie-Madeleine. Those breasts of hers were works of fine art in their perfect proportion, as much a delight to the eye of the connoisseur as to his sense of touch – though Marcel fully intended to explore the truth of that with his hands in due course. For the moment he was content to regale his eyes! That elegantly curved little belly, with its circular navel, lay cradled between her slender hips in so artistic a manner that Marcel's heart missed a beat. To kiss it would be enchanting! And there, at the join of her long thighs, her neat triangle of fur was of thick curls that invited the fingers to comb through it!

'How the bubbles tickle!' Marie-Madeleine exclaimed with a little laugh, 'I love it.'

'Let them burst against that most sensitive part between your legs,' Marcel suggested 'open your thighs a little.'

A slight pinkness touched her face at the frankness of his suggestion, but only for a moment, then she moved her feet as widely apart as the bath allowed.

'Oh!' she cried a few seconds later. 'Oh! Marcel – the sensation is incredible !'

He watched her for a while as her eyes half-closed in her enjoyment of the tiny tickling of the champagne bubbles against the tender flesh between her thighs. Then, throwing off with reluctance the spell of her naked beauty, he tore open another case, popped two corks and let the frothing wine pour down over her breasts.

'Oh yes, yes!' she squealed, 'Oh, Marcel – how marvellous!'

She sat up and cupped her hands under her enticing

little breasts, holding them to receive the cascade of pale wine, her expression one of surprise and pleasure. Marcel opened two more bottles quickly and poured again from as high as he could hold the bottles, directing the two streams of champagne onto the pink buds of her breasts, where the wine foamed and sprayed out in a great torrent. The expression of her face had changed, he noted – the surprise had been replaced by that look of slight hauteur he loved so well. Her thinking had adjusted to the situation, he surmised – she now felt herself to be one of the great courtesans of the past receiving her rightful homage from an admirer. Her words confirmed his thought.

'Again!' she commanded, when the bottles were empty.

Again he cascaded foaming wine onto her pink buds, now engorged and firm. Her mouth slowly opened wide as if she were screaming, though no sound emerged. Her eyes stared at nothing, her long legs kicked abruptly, sending a deluge of champagne over the side of the bath onto the floor, then she sank back and lay trembling.

Marcel set down the bottles and reached for a large pink towel. In a few moments Marie-Madeleine's eyes opened and she looked at him with tenderness.

'Oh Marcel!' she murmured for the third time, her voice a little shaky this time.

She stood up and let him wrap her in the towel, which was big enough to cover her from shoulders to knees. Marcel picked her up and carried her into the bedroom, laid her on the broad bed and unwrapped her with a delicacy bordering on reverence. His clothes were off in seconds and he was beside her, kissing and caressing her. She sighed in great contentment as he kissed the tips of her breasts and tasted champagne.

'I believe that I am already a little in love with you,' she murmured.

'And I with you, Marie-Madeleine,' he replied, his lips moving over her belly, his hand between her thighs,

25

touching at last the warm treasure she had denied him at the ballet the evening before. He pressed his lips to the damp curls that tasted of champagne and to the soft folds of flesh the curls concealed.

They were both a little drunk from the fumes of so much wine. Marie-Madeleine's hands grasped him by the shoulders and pulled him towards her. At once he slid on top of her and, as her legs moved apart, brought his stiff projection to the voluptuous entrance to her enclosure.

The thought had been in his mind earlier, after what she had told him of the dullness of her life, that she might well be a virgin still. He pushed hard to overcome any such obstruction to pleasure, but the ease of his entry proved her to be otherwise. However boring a person her fiancé might be, at least he had displayed enough initiative to have relieved Marcel of any difficulty in that respect.

At this supreme moment Marcel tried to rein back his passion and to proceed at a canter rather than a gallop – to prolong the uniqueness of his first lovemaking with Marie-Madeleine. But her beautiful face so close to his expressed pure delight at what he was doing to her and the feel of her enchanting body under him was so stirring that, try as he might, nothing could restrain the sensations that were running away with him. His loins bucked wildly, Marie-Madeleine cried out in pleasure, and his passion erupted hotly within her.

In the weeks that followed their first encounter Marcel devised adventures to astonish her – he led her into erotic episodes unguessed at in her hitherto predictable life of prim conformity. Their meeting-place was always the Places des Vosges, the scene of their first rendezvous, and their arrangement was that he would wait for her by the little fountain at three in the afternoon. If she was not there by a quarter past the hour, then she would not come that day. Not knowing her family name or where she lived added to the uncertainty of when he would next see her and made the affair extraordinarily piquant for him. It was a veritable Arabian Nights story for him, a story in which he was the lover of a beautiful unknown – a mysterious princess who slipped away from the Caliph's harem at enormous danger to herself in order to be with the young man she loved! For Marie-Madeleine it was the same – she escaped for a few hours from the boring routine of life at home and with her fiancé into a world where the most improbable things happened to her.

One afternoon when a light spring rain was falling Marcel took her for a ride on the Metro, saying that he intended to show her something deliciously shameful. The words caught her imagination.

'But how can anything shameful be delicious?' she asked as they went down the steps from the street to the underground station.

'You will see,' he answered cryptically, purchasing two tickets.

At that time of the afternoon the trains were relatively little used and they were able to board an empty carriage. Instead of taking seats, Marcel led her to the end of the carriage and pressed her to the partition and, as the train jerked forward, slid his hand under her coat and skirt to rest for a moment between her thighs above her stockings! But only for a moment - then he had found his way into the loose leg of her knickers and was stroking the soft curls of her warm mound. Her face turned up to stare at him in amazement from under the brim of her little cloche hat.

Her red-painted mouth opened as if to protest, but showed instead the tip of her tongue as Marcel's fingers slowly parted the tender lips between her legs. It seemed to him that she gasped as his caressing fingers found her little bud of pleasure, but whatever sound she made was lost in the rattle of the train.

They had boarded the Metro at the Bastille station, heading westwards. By the Hôtel de Ville stop she was clinging tightly to him and he could feel her legs trembling against his own legs. Someone got into the carriage and sat down, but Marcel and Marie-Madeleine were too engrossed by then to pay any attention and he continued to caress her secret bud with great delicacy. Before they reached the next stop he felt her body convulse in passion and saw her eyes go blank in ecstasy. Still he kept his hand there, up her clothes, hiding what he was doing by his own body between her and whoever entered or left the carriage.

She was smiling up at him now, enchanted by the effrontery of his action in a public place.

'Deliciously shameful,' she whispered, just loud enough for him to hear as the train left the station.

Her smile broadened as his fingers began to move inside her again, wet now with the dew of her climactic emotions. This time she responded very quickly to his caress, rubbing herself rhythmically against his hand. The shuddering that announced that she had again reached the zenith of delight coincided with the train's arrival at the Étoile stop. Marcel stroked her quickly until she was still again, then removed his hand at last and kissed her cheek. They rode on to the Porte de Maillot and waited until the two or three other passengers had left the train before getting out themselves. On their way out of the station they passed an elderly couple. The woman glared at them and called out loudly that they should be ashamed of themselves, while her husband winked lewdly at Marcel.

Marie-Madeleine's cheeks were fiery red as they hurried away from the couple who had obviously shared the Metro carriage with them. As they entered the Bois de Boulogne she said:

'But suppose it had been someone who knows me!'

'Who, for instance?'

'My fiancé – what then?'

'But it wasn't, and you enjoyed the ride.'

'Marcel – you are impossible! And I adore you for it.'

'You adore me because I am unpredictable.'

'And without shame,' she added, 'I find that exciting.'

The spring shower had long stopped, the air in the Bois was fresh and sweet, Marcel led her off the road and under the trees, until he judged that they were out of sight of any but other lovers seeking privacy for their own pleasures. He stood Marie-Madeleine with her back against the trunk of a large tree and, without another word, opened the jacket of her spring costume – an elegant creation in peach-coloured silk of matching jacket and skirt. She was wearing a blouse of red and yellow stripes with a little collar that tied in a bow at the neckline. Marcel ran his hands over her breasts, then eased the blouse out of the waistband of her skirt, to find under it a chemise made wholly of fine lace. That too he pulled out of her skirt and up around her neck to bare her pretty breasts.

'But people like us don't do this sort of thing in the park,' she whispered as he fondled the marvellous little breasts he had uncovered.

'You and I do,' he replied, 'we are not like other people.'

'Marcel!' she murmured when he unbuttoned his trousers and brought out his hard part.

'Hold it in your hand,' he instructed her, 'until I find somewhere to put it.'

The touch of her white kid gloves on his sensitive protruberance was extraordinary, causing it to leap impatiently. Meanwhile, Marcel had lifted her skirt and pulled aside the loose leg of her flimsy underwear to reveal her black fur.

'There!' he said 'the ideal place for it. Put it in, Marie-Madeleine.'

Her lack of skill in effecting the conjuncture was ample proof that Marie-Madeleine's fiancé was a prosaic person who did no more than to arrange her on her back and penetrate her beautiful citadel of love with a brutal push. Nevertheless, in spite of her inexperience in handling a man's proud part, she persevered until matters were arranged to their mutual satisfaction. Marcel smiled at her in delight at the warm clasp of her flesh.

'Marie-Madeleine, I adore you,' he said, and meant it, 'hold up your clothes so that I can see your breasts.'

She leaned back against the bole of the tree, her gloved hands holding high the delectable creations of expensive couturier and lingerie-maker, so that he could have his wish. Marcel held her by the hips and slid his engorged part to and fro in an access of tranquil delight, intent on her changing expression as her composure disappeared under the impact of arousal.

'Marcel – I adore you too!' she exclaimed, as well she might at such a moment.

There ensued an interlude of sensual bliss, but all too soon Marcel reached the critical moment. His legs shook, he gripped Marie-Madeleine's hips strongly enough to bruise her delicate flesh, though she gave no sign of discomfort and surely felt none in her state of high excitement. He stared at her naked breasts bobbing up and down to the rhythm of his thrusting, then gasped out her name as he paid her his passionate respects.

To dress properly again afterwards she had to drop her peach-coloured skirt and smooth down chemise and blouse. Marcel went down on one knee on the still-wet grass and pressed a fond kiss to the warm lips between her thighs, breathing in the warm scent of her sensuality, before adjusting her knickers for her. When all was set to rights, they strolled back to the Place de la Porte Maillot arm in arm, where he put her into a taxi and waved goodbye as it sped away along the Avenue de la Grande Armée towards the Arc de Triomphe. She had said nothing to the taxi driver which offered a hint as to which part of Paris she lived in, only 'that way', accompanied by a nod of her head.

On one occasion she told Marcel that she was free the next evening and that she would like to be taken to the Opera. They met in the foyer and Marcel was pleased to see that she was wearing the pale blue evening frock in which he had first seen her – that marvellous evening when he had stroked her bare thigh. She looked charming, of course – and more than that, elegant. Her air of slight disdain when Marcel bowed to kiss her hand was enchanting!

Naturally, he had taken a box for the performance, a box for four, well-placed to give a perfect view of the stage. He was extremely attentive to Marie-Madeleine, moving the chairs a little to suit her, disposing of her fur wrap, obtaining a programme, using all his charm to keep her amused. He waved briefly to a man he recognised in a box across the other side of the auditorium, his vivacity conveying itself to Marie-Madeleine, so that she too smiled and talked more than usually. She had a habit of silence, he had observed at their previous meetings, the result no doubt of a dull home life.

As soon as the lights were lowered he put his hand on her knee, let it rest there for a moment or two, then moved it up under her frock until it rested on the bare flesh of her thigh above her garter – this with far more confidence than on that first occasion at the ballet. Her face turned towards him in the half-light and he saw that she was smiling, as if in reminiscence.

Needless to say, on this instance Marie-Madeleine did not press her legs together to restrain his hand from mounting a little higher, not even when his finger-tips reached her soft groin. She stared at the stage, so that it might be surmised that she was enjoying at the same time the intellectual pleasure of the performance and the sensual pleasure of the delicate touch between her thighs.

The presentation that evening was of *Manon Lescaut*, a favourite piece with Parisian audiences since its first production a little before the turn of the century. This

31

version of Prévost's romantic novel telling how the beautiful young Manon abandons everything to run away with her lover, leaves him for a richer one and then returns to the first to die in his arms in distant America – all this is so essentially French in spirit that its success was guaranteed from the first performance. It did not occur to Marcel, sitting in the darkened box, that Marie-Madeleine had asked him to take her to this particular opera because in her mind she perhaps identified herself with the heroine!

Be that as it may, Marcel's hand under her frock undid the tiny buttons of her silk camiknickers so that he could cup her furry mound and rub the curls lightly. He was, of course, an averagely selfish young man, intent on his own pleasure and he regarded others as means to that end. In due course his middle finger found its way between the succulent petals of her rose to touch the tiny stamen at its heart. She sighed and trembled, this well-bred young woman who was engaged to be married to a man of worth and substance – sighed not with outrage but with pleasure at the manner in which Marcel was handling her intimate parts. And he, his male stem achingly hard, took equally intense delight in flaunting public decency in this way. A sense of triumph suffused his being when Marie-Madeleine's hand clutched almost painfully hard the bulge inside his trousers and her whole body jerked as she attained the peak of her sensation. Not even the music of Puccini could compete for attention against that.

At the beginning of the second act Marcel led her silently to the rear of the box and seated himself on one of the chairs placed there. He turned her to face the stage, her back towards him and pulled the pale blue frock up over her bottom, then put his hand inside her opened underwear to fondle the elegant cheeks. She understood his intention at once and sank down onto his lap astride his legs and impaled herself neatly on the fleshy spike he had freed from its place of decent concealment.

For a time Marcel was content to remain like that, enjoying the warm clasp of her body on his most sensitive part while he caressed her belly and breasts through the fine georgette of her frock. And Marie-Madeleine sat quiet, listening to the singers on the stage and savouring the feel of the hard intruder within her intimate enclosure. How ravishing such moments are, so tremulous with anticipation – though more usually experienced in private than in a box only just out of sight of two thousand people in evening dress! Eventually Marcel was impelled to take matters further – for once the fuse had been lit, to prevent the spark from reaching the gunpowder and causing an explosion is exceedingly difficult. Not that either of them had the least desire to pinch out the spark travelling the length of the fuse – far from it, the explosion was what they wanted. In his confined position and in circumstances requiring the greatest discretion, Marcel did not attempt to thrust himself into that exquisite aperture. By clenching and unclenching the muscles of his belly he was able to make his sturdy champion slide a centimetre or two inside her and this, continued for long enough, proved adequate in his emotional condition to precipitate the natural crisis.

To anyone other than Marcel and Marie-Madeleine these secret meetings of theirs would have seemed little more than the stages of a love affair. Perhaps not an ordinary love affair, in that Marie-Madeleine was engaged to be married to another man. There was also the fact that even after three months of demonstrating his passion for her, Marcel still did not know the identity of his beloved. That their love-making was often conducted in highly unsuitable places and at some risk of discovery - this also made their affair abnormal, not to say indiscreet. For persons of the status of Marcel and Marie-Madeleine there was no need for their amours to be discovered and her beautiful bottom to be seen by the public, for example, under the colonnades of the Palais-Royal while Marcel stood close behind her and admired the view over her shoulder at the same time as he penetrated her under her raised skirt! Nor for her to play with his stiff part as they stood leaning over the parapet of the Pont des Arts, staring down into the Seine, into which the affectionate movement of her hand in due course made a libation of his vital essence. Behaviour of this sort might well have attracted the attention of the guardians of the law, with calamitous result for both. And worse than that, behaviour of this sort was, to say the least, in questionable taste. Yet to Marcel and Marie-Madeleine it seemed that they were living in a fairy-tale world of enchantment – a world of inviting doorways, arches and secret corners – where they would pause on their way to some high adventure devised by Marcel – adventures in improbable surroundings to put a keener edge on their appetite for each other.

Marie-Madeleine never spoke to him of her life with her family and from her silence he concluded that it continued to be boring and that he provided her with an escape route into delight.

For Marcel it was a marvellous time and also a difficult time. To plan the adventures they would share and then to live through them with Marie-Madeleine was exhilarating – more than that, it was intoxicating. But there were many afternoons when he waited for her in vain at their private rendezvous. She never afterwards explained why she had not been there, but joined enthusiastically in whatever he proposed. So the good days and the bad days alternated for Marcel, the days of utter sensual fulfilment and the days of bitter disappointment, when he paced for half an hour round the Place des Vosges and turned away at last, knowing that he would not see her that afternoon.

Naturally, his frustration at these times had to find release. He made his way to one of the better establishments to make use of the services of the prettiest young woman available. But it was never enough. The charms of a compliant professional were no adequate substitute for the delirious excitement which Marie-Madeleine aroused in him. These professional services relieved his immediate anguish, but only temporarily. After a disappointing afternoon of this type he would dream of Marie-Madeleine that night - usually half-dressed and in some impossible setting. In her flimsy silk underwear, for instance, at a table on the terrace of the Cafe de la Paix, or standing completely naked and embracing with both arms the tall obelisk in the Place Vendome. Or dancing with him, clad only in her stockings, in some back-street cafe concert - his feverish imagination devised a hundred ways of disturbing his sleep.

On these sleepless nights there was nothing for it but to make his way silently to the maid's room and bestow upon homely Annette the passion due to Marie-Madeleine. The frequency of his nocturnal visits increased as Marie-Madeleine, for reasons left unexplained, came to meet him less and less often. Eventually Marcel found himself in the most unsatisfactory position of making love to Marie-Madeleine no more than twice a week and getting into bed with Annette four or five times a week.

If Annette was surprised by the frequency of his visits to her bed she said nothing about it to him and always made him very welcome. For her, perhaps, these weeks were a period of regular gratification such as she had not previously enjoyed and she made the most of it, guessing that it would end as inexplicably as it had begun. Nowadays she awoke the moment Marcel set foot inside her small room and turned back the sheet for him while he was removing his dressing-gown and pyjamas. In the dark his questing hands found her cheap nightdress already up round her waist to give him instant access to her broad thighs and the fleshy mound between them.

Eventually, as his visits became almost a nightly occurrence, Annette ceased to trouble herself with night attire at all. Marcel would slip into her bed and find her totally naked, her big soft breasts ready for his hands. Sometimes he played with them and sucked her firm nipples for a long time, on other nights he squeezed them only briefly before rolling onto her wide belly to push inside her. Throughout all these encounters, whether his hands were full of the soft flesh of her breasts or his stiff projection was deep inside her hot inlet, in his imagination he was making love to Marie-Madeleine – slim-thighed and small-breasted Marie-Madeleine, the mysterious princess of his adventures!

He was waiting one afternoon in the little garden of the Place des Vosges, almost distraught with expectation. It was five days since he had last seen Marie-Madeleine – and on every one of those days he had been at the appointed place at three o'clock, aching to see her walking towards him – only to creep miserably away in savage disappointment when it was evident that she was not coming. For five nights he had transferred his desperate passion to Annette, belabouring her big body to the point of exhaustion. She made no complaint, of course, but last night, when he rolled her onto her side and pressed his belly against her big bottom to make his third entry within an hour – he thought that he had heard her sigh, perhaps in pleasure, but perhaps not. Whichever it was, by the time he relieved his despair into her very wet interior, she was asleep!

This is ridiculous, Marcel said to himself morosely as he paced round the little garden – I am madly in love with Marie-Madeleine and I am making love night after night to my mother's maid! This must stop at once! If Marie-Madeleine is not here today, I shall never come here again, never! It will be finished! I will not continue this absurd affair!

If she did arrive, what then? He thought about that and the conclusion he reached surprised him. If she came today, he would ask her to marry him! He would refuse to listen to any objections about being engaged already. He loved her, he wanted her, he would have her! He would drag her into the nearest taxi and insist – absolutely insist – that she took him to her home at once to be introduced to her parents. He would inform them in the clearest terms that he intended to marry their daughter at the earliest possible moment - certainly by the end of the week at the very latest, with or without their blessing. Then he would take Marie-Madeleine to the Ritz Hotel and bed her in their finest suite. He would make love to her all afternoon, have dinner served in the suite, take her back to bed and keep her there until midday tomorrow! After all, there were five days to be made up for.

They would be married by the end of the week and she would be with him day and night! They would travel to beautiful places in an endless round of pleasure – Venice, Florence, Rome, Athens, Constantinople – a year-long honeymoon of the adventure she craved. He would make love to her in gondolas, in palaces, beneath the Acropolis in the moonlight – inside the Great Pyramid, even! When they were alone together in their hotel, he would never let her be fully dressed. After long nights of love and a refreshing sleep in the cool hours of dawn they would breakfast together in their suite before huge open windows overlooking whatever the local sights happened to be – the Grand Canal, the Black Sea, the Adriatic – Marie-Madeleine's beautiful body tantalisingly half-revealed to him by an open peignoir of delicate silk – or perhaps she would be naked except for a brightly coloured silk bandanna draped loosely around her slender thighs. . .

He was so lost in his fantasy of married bliss that he started at a light tap on his arm. He half-turned – to find Marie-Madeleine standing beside him. An explosion of joy in his heart rendered him dumb for a moment. Of course, she was exquisitely dressed in a summer frock of sunflower-yellow crepe satin cut with a cross-over bodice and a pleated skirt – and a matching little cloche hat! But Marcel had no eye for clothes just then – only for Marie-Madeleine herself.

'I adore you,' were his first words.

'And I adore you,' she said with a little smile.

'Before we move one step from this spot,' said Marcel, 'there is something of the utmost importance I must say to you.'

'Perhaps,' she replied, 'but first there is something I have to say to you, my dear. Walk with me down to the rue Saint Antoine – I told the taxi to wait for me there.'

'Excellent,' he said, for that fitted in well with his plan, and he took her arm as they strolled out of the square.

Her next words stopped him in his tracks.

'I have come to say goodbye, Marcel.'

'What? Goodbye? What do you mean?'

'This will be a shock to you, I know, but the fact is that I am to be married next week. Our adventures are over, my dear friend, and I must return to my dull and ordinary life.'

'But this is impossible! You cannot marry someone else!'

'Why not? You have always known that I was engaged. You must have realised what that implied – or did you think that my engagement would last for years?'

In his utter bewilderment he let her guide him gently forward along the narrow rue de Birague towards the main road.

'I forbid it!' he exclaimed. 'You must marry me – at once!'

'That is out of the question, Marcel. Everything is arranged.'

'You do not love this man – you told me so!'

'What of it? He will be a good husband.'

'I will be a better one!'

38

'No, you would be a better lover, Marcel, but not a better husband. I know you well enough to be sure of that. Be content, chéri – we have enjoyed some marvellous adventures together and now it is time to return to the real world.'

'Marry me and your entire life will be an adventure – I swear it!'

'Adventures must end sometime. I shall remember you with love and delight all my life, Marcel.'

To his horror he could see her taxi waiting at the end of the street, on the corner of the rue Saint Antoine.

'I cannot accept this parting,' he said firmly, 'I will not let you go.'

'Neither of us has a choice now.'

'Why do you say that?'

'There is something you do not know. I am pregnant, Marcel. Now you understand why it is necessary for me to be married quickly.'

The revelation took away Marcel's power of rational speech. He made gobbling noises as they continued down the street and reached the waiting taxi. Marie-Madeleine got in, closed the door and let down the window to speak to him.

'Goodbye, Marcel,' she said fondly.

'Tell me.' he stammered 'is the child mine?'

'Probably – but how can I be sure?' she answered calmly.

Marcel stood dumbfounded on the pavement, his mouth hanging open, as she spoke to the driver and the taxi pulled away. The encounter had totally deflated him. He made his way like a sleep-walker to the nearest bar and drank three glasses of cognac in quick succession.

'How can I be sure,' she had said. In other words, she had been allowing her stupid fiancé to make love to her all the time that she had been enjoying the most exotic and incredible adventures with Marcel! Yet why should that be a surprise, he asked himself bitterly – fiancés

39

usually have certain privileges with the women they are to marry. Nevertheless, so cruel a reminder of that simple fact had dealt his feelings a vicious blow. He must put Marie-Madeleine out of his mind – even if she was pregnant by him. She had made her choice and if she was content to father Marcel's child on another man, so be it! But the perfidy of it – that was what hurt so deeply.

It was after six o'clock when he left the bar, about three-quarters drunk, and took a taxi home. The apartment seemed to be empty. He poured himself another glass of cognac and with that in his hand, made his way to the kitchen, staggering slightly. Annette was in the kitchen, scrubbing a saucepan at the sink.

'I thought I heard you come in, M'sieu Marcel,' she said, looking over her shoulder at his flushed face, 'will you be in for dinner this evening?'

'I don't want any dinner. Is my mother out?'

'Madame is visiting her sister and staying there to eat.'

'Yes, I think she mentioned that this morning,' he said vaguely.

'It's Louise's day off,' the maid added inconsequentially.

In his state of shock and fuddlement Marcel could concentrate only on the big bottom which filled out Annette's skirt. The sight, together with the amount of cognac he had drunk, aroused him.

'I've got a present for you, Annette,' he said, smiling foolishly.

'Really? What sort of present, M'sieu Marcel?'

He put his glass down on the kitchen table, unbuttoned his jacket and trousers and exposed his firm-standing part. Annette dropped the saucepan into the sink, wiped her hands on her apron and turned to face him.

'It's for you,' he said, advancing towards her, 'take it.'

She clasped it in her hand, still warm and slightly wet from washing up.

'It's like an iron bar!' she said with a little sigh.

By then Marcel had his hands on her breasts and was squeezing them through her frock.

'Are you sure you haven't had too much to drink?' she asked, her hand gliding up and down his proud champion, 'I've heard that it stops men from doing it.'

'It never stops me,' he answered, 'you'll see – turn round.'

He took her by the shoulders and moved her round to face the sink again, her back to him, then bent her over until her hands were in the soapy water, supporting herself.

'What are you doing?' she teased as he pulled her black skirt up over her backside and her plain knickers down her thighs.

He made no reply. There, below the twin melons of her bottom, in the fork of her solid thighs, lay the big split mound he had for so many nights made use of to relieve his unslaked passion for Marie-Madeleine. His thumbs dug into the soft flesh and dragged the brown-haired lips apart until he could stab his hard projection into her. His tipsy state caused him to drive so forcefully into the unprepared entrance that she gasped loudly in discomfort.

Once embedded, the frustration and anger of his dismissal by Marie-Madeleine that afternoon boiled over like an unwatched saucepan over a fire. Marcel rammed hard and fast, not even hearing Annette's cries for mercy, until at last the volcano within him erupted and gushed out his lava in frantic jets, until he was drained.

He pulled away from the maid, took a few short steps backwards, hardly knowing what he was doing, bumped against a wooden kitchen chair and collapsed into it. He stayed slumped there for a time, his eyes closed and his wet apparatus still protruding from his open trousers. Annette straightened up from the sink, dried her hands and turned to face him, while she adjusted her underwear and skirt.

'Do you feel better now, M'sieu Marcel?' she enquired.

He nodded briefly, all emotion spent in the brief and violent act.

His head was still spinning from the effects of the drink and the fierce purging of his emotions when she bent over him and he felt her wipe his softening projection dry and tuck it away.

'There is something I must talk to you about,' said Annette, fastening his trouser buttons for him.

'Yes?' he answered listlessly.

'The fact is, M'sieu Marcel, I am going to have a baby.'

The words were like a slap in the face. Marcel's eyes jerked open and his face turned pale as he sobered up fast.

'But that's impossible!' he blurted out.

'No, it's not,' she said firmly, 'it's a certainty.'

'But. . .'

'It's no use saying *but*. You've been doing it to me practically every night for three months – sometimes two or three times a night. What did you expect?'

'Oh my God!' he exclaimed, 'what will my mother say!'

'She'd be very angry, you can be sure of that. But there's no reason for her to find out, if we both behave sensibly.'

'What do you mean?' Marcel asked, grasping at the least hope, 'you are willing to get rid of it?'

Annette's face flushed dark red.

'How can you say such a wicked thing! That would be a terrible sin. What do you suppose Madame Chalon would say if she heard of that suggestion?'

'No, no!' Marcel gasped, distraught at the very idea. 'She must never hear of that, never! But what are we to do, then?'

'It's like this,' said the maid, seizing the advantage. 'I'm thirty-eight years old now and I've been a servant in one family or another ever since I was sixteen. I've had enough of it. What I want is a little house of my own in the country and enough money to keep me and the child – it wouldn't be a lot.'

'I see. You think that I might provide that?'

'If you don't, M'sieu Marcel, I'm sure that Madame Chalon will – she's a very proper person and she wouldn't let a grandchild of hers beg in the streets.'

'Grandchild!' he echoed, dismayed by the word.

As indeed he might be! He knew his mother to be capable of insisting that the child be brought up in the family, right there in the apartment, whatever disposition was made for the maid. It was unthinkable – as also was the moral obloquy that his mother would heap upon Marcel's head. His life wouldn't be worth living!

'You are right, Annette,' he said, shuddering, 'I know where my duty lies. Tell my mother that you have been left a little house somewhere by a relation and give up your job here. Then go and find a place and I will buy it. You may rely on me.'

'Thank you. Excuse me for saying it, but it would ease my mind if you took me to a lawyer's office first and I got a signed piece of paper saying that I would have the little house and so much coming in every month to live on. That's reasonable, isn't it?'

Whether it was reasonable or not was not important – Marcel knew that he had no choice. He agreed to take her to see a discreet lawyer. While Annette, smiling now, made him a cup of strong coffee, he sat wondering if any man before had ever been presented with two unborn children on the same day. There seemed to him a sardonic cruelty in this accumulation of disasters that made him ask himself seriously whether Providence had arranged the world as well as it could be arranged. To leave one's visiting card carelessly was, he thought, an expensive business, emotionally and financially.

43

RAYMOND AT THE CIRCUS

There are those who will go to extraordinary lengths to acquire a reputation as a joker and usually it is those who have little else to commend them. One such was Georges Bonfils, a person whose predatory business practices might well have made him an outcast from decent society, except that his talent for devising the most elaborate farces somewhat softened the opinion of him which those who had dealings with him would otherwise have formed.

Knowing the man's reputation, Raymond was not astonished when he received from him a handsomely engraved invitation requesting the pleasure of his company at a performance of the Circus Émile. The formality of the wording on the card made him chuckle. Clearly it was one of Bonfils' jokes, something to astound and amuse those invited, something they would talk about for weeks afterwards. Undoubtedly the company would be small and carefully selected, that being Bonfils' style. As with all of these things, there would be a secret purpose – something to Bonfils' own advantage – but no one would mind that. Raymond wrote a formal note of acceptance and then asked around among his friends to discover who else had received an invitation. Quite a few had, the others looked at him enviously and said that their own invitations must surely be held up in the mail and would arrive shortly.

On the day specified, Raymond set out by car after lunch to arrive before three, the time on the card. It

44

was no easy matter to locate the scene of the proposed entertainment. The Circus Émile was not one of the large international circuses which toured the major towns and cities. Far from it, it was a small and down-at-heel venture which had pitched its threadbare tents on a piece of waste-land in a remote eastern suburb of Paris. That was only to be expected, Raymond reflected as he drove through dismal and depressing streets, for how otherwise could Bonfils have hired the facilities of the circus for whatever entertainment he proposed to stage?

When at last, in this unknown territory, he found the spot, Raymond saw that the main tent was small and shabby, the banner carrying its name was so weather-worn and battered that it was almost unreadable. The site was bounded on one side by a railway line along which a freight train rattled asthmatically, and the ground itself was strewn with rubbish that no one had troubled them-selves to clear away. A bankrupt enterprise this, Raymond thought, a few families all related and banded together to make a poor living. It was doubtful whether Bonfils had paid them very much for the use of their facilities for an afternoon, yet however little it was, it was probably more than they would make in a week of their regular performances in so poor a neighbourhood.

The main entrance to the big tent was closed off by a flap of stained canvas, in front of which stood a muscular man with a big moustache. He was wearing a striped jersey and shapeless trousers and looked strong enough to cope single-handed with any sort of trouble which could conceivably arise. Not a person a sensible man would choose to quarrel with, Raymond said to himself as he parked his new Renault a few yards from the tent and walked across the littered ground. There were seven or eight big cars parked there already – evidently he was not the first to arrive.

The bruiser favoured him with a hard stare. Raymond responded by nodding pleasantly and handing him the engraved invitation card. The wording of it was formal in the extreme:

'Monsieur Georges Bonfils, a Commander of the Legion of Honour, requests the pleasure of the company of Monsieur Raymond Provost at a private performance of the Circus. . .' and so on. The man in the striped jersey – perhaps he was Émile himself – took it from him and glared at it briefly. The thought crossed Raymond's mind that it was improbable that striped-jersey was sufficiently literate to read what was printed on the card. Whether he was or not, he at least recognised it as the correct passport for the afternoon. He lifted the canvas flap and gestured Raymond through with a slight inclination of his head.

Inside it was stuffy. There were benches round the sides that would seat not more than a hundred and fifty spectators packed closely together. The sawdust-strewn ring in the centre was large enough for only the most modest of performances – a juggler or two, perhaps, a fire-eater, a dancing-bear with a ring through his nose, a knife-thrower with his board and unattractive wife as living target – the usual banalities. None of which would be presented today, of course, Bonfils must surely have made special arrangements for the entertainment of his guests.

The stuffiness in the tent was partly due to the lighting – hissing gas-flares from containers set in the corners. But the atmosphere was already convivial – about twenty well-dressed men were assembled on one side of the tent, chatting away, glasses in their hands. Two or three servants were busy with the refreshment – champagne bottles cooling in a row of dented zinc buckets and tubs filled with ice and water. The buckets at least looked as if they were circus property, the long-stemmed glasses the servants were handing round obviously were not.

Bonfils detached himself from the little crowd and came forward to shake Raymond's hand and welcome him. He was dressed very formally in a long and elegant morning-coat, cravat and black silk top hat. The monocle he affected was dangling on its thin gold chain against his white waistcoat. The whole attire, Raymond decided, was itself a part of the joke. Perhaps he should have dressed formally himself, but another glance at the other guests reassured him. They wore normal suits, though of mainly dark hues.

'How very pleased I am that you can be with us,' Bonfils exclaimed. 'You missed my last little circus entertainment, as I recall. It was so popular with everyone that I felt I had to arrange another. Come and have a drink. I think you know everyone here.'

'It was kind of you to invite me,' Raymond replied. 'Yes, I know many of your other guests.'

'Good, then there is no need for introductions.'

Raymond had already recognised a number of business associates, a few acquaintances from the Stock Exchange, a couple of important politicians, even a famous author he had once met at someone's reception – a man who had made a surprising amount of money from his boring sagas of tormented family life in the provinces. Glancing round the conservatively-dressed group of men, all wearing hats, Raymond smiled as he thought for a moment that the gathering could almost have been for a deceased colleague's funeral. The only jarring note was a vivid green tie worn by the writer, presumably as a sign of his creative ability.

Glass of champagne in hand, Raymond plunged into the throng, shaking hands, exchanging greetings, on easy terms with everyone there.

'Were you at Bonfils' last circus performance?' asked a friend, Xavier de Margeville, whom Raymond had known would be there. 'I can't remember.'

'I was away from Paris at the time and missed it. I've heard about it, of course.'

'It was the talk of Paris for a month afterwards. It inflated Georges' notoriety enormously.'

'But it didn't do him any harm, as I understand it,' said Raymond.

'Of course not! His invitations are so sought after that the most unlikely people do him favours in the hope of being added to the list, but he is very selective. Why, I was told just before you came in that Georges has disappointed a Minister of State today because he didn't regard him as useful enough. But that may be no more than one of Georges' own rumours to make himself more important. The gossip last year was that he had turned away a certain Eminence of the Church who wanted to be present, on the grounds that dignitaries of the Church knew so much about these things that he would find it boring.'

Raymond laughed and emptied his glass. At once a servant was at his side to refill it.

'On the other hand,' he said cheerfully, 'both tales might well be true, Xavier. Is today's performance to be a repetition of what I was told took place last autumn?'

'No, Georges has promised us something entirely different.'

The drinks flowed freely, the conversation became more animated and the gestures more expansive. Eventually the clanging of a handbell silenced the party. It was Bonfils, standing in the middle of the sawdust ring, his tall hat pushed to the back of his head.

'Gentlemen!' he bawled, 'your attention, please! You are about to witness the most amusing, the most daring, the most original circus performance ever to be presented in Paris – or anywhere else!'

'Since last year, you mean!' someone called out.

'No previous performance can possibly equal what you are to see today, you have my assurances,' Bonfils replied at once, greatly enjoying his role of ringmaster. 'This is the genuine, the unique, the once-in-a-lifetime performance, brought to you regardless of expense and trouble. Take your seats, if you please! The attendants will circulate among you with refreshments during the performance.'

With late arrivals the company now numbered about thirty. Everyone wanted to sit on the front row, of course, and the benches were rapidly filled round the edge of the sawdust ring.

Bonfils resumed his comical introduction when they were quiet again.

'Gentlemen, it is possible that in a gathering of important persons so distinguished in the fields of finance, commerce, politics – and the arts – there might possibly be one or two who have visited certain establishments in this city. Entirely for the purposes of study and observation, I need hardly say. In such establishments there is a remote possibility that you have been compelled to witness actions of a particular nature performed for the instruction of those present.'

'Shameful!' said someone who sounded very far from ashamed at this thought.

'Shameful indeed!' Bonfils continued. 'For I must inform you that these acts to which I refer are faked. They are fraudulent. They are deceptions! But today there will be no deception – you will be privileged to observe the real thing. Gentlemen, I give you, I proudly give you. . . Bonfils' *cirque erotique*!'

He paused and bowed to acknowledge the applause from his audience.

'Thank you, gentlemen – your appreciation is the only reward I seek. And now – for your entertainment, for your amazement, for your delectation, the Circus Bonfils – for one performance only – proudly presents. . .'

He clanged his handbell loudly, a threadbare curtain strung across one end of the tent was pulled aside by an unseen hand, while all eyes turned to catch the first glimpse of what was to be presented.

'Mademoiselle Marie!' Bonfils bawled.

Amid cries of emotion from the small audience a totally naked woman rode into the sawdust arena on an ordinary bicycle. She was in her twenties and reasonably pretty. Her breasts jumped up and down as she drove the pedals round energetically with her bare feet.

'Mademoiselle Jeanne!' Bonfils announced when the first rider was part way round the ring, and another equally naked young woman rode in, smiling and waving with one hand to the admiring little crowd on the benches.

'Mademoiselle Marianne!'

A third rider joined them, this one standing on the pedals and so giving a clear view of the patch of dark hair between her legs.

'Mademoiselle Sophie!'

There were four of them cycling round the small ring, smiling and acknowledging the applause, keeping their distance from each other. They were all about the same age and averagely attractive.

'Four of the most outstanding beauties of Paris for your delight!' Bonfils announced with gross exaggeration. 'Observe them as they ride, consider their merits. Estimate as best you can their strength and fortitude. And then, when the contest starts, pick your favourite and give her your whole-hearted support! Whichever of these lovelies you fancy – urge her on, encourage her! And in addition to your moral support, place a bet when the action becomes hot.'

'Surely they're not going to fight each other!' exclaimed Raymond, aghast.

'Of course not – that would be too brutal,' said de Margeville, 'something far more amusing. You'll see.'

'Are you ready, ladies?' Bonfils enquired loudly of the women circling him on their bicycles.

'Ready!' they chorused.

'Then prepare for the signal to begin. The prize to the

winner is a bottle of the finest champagne – and five thousand francs!'

All the women squealed pleasurably at that as they pedalled solemnly round in their circle.

'Go!' Bonfils called abruptly, clanging his bell again.

To Raymond's surprise they did not increase their speed at all – rather the opposite. Knowing that it was a contest between them, he had assumed that it was some sort of race. He turned to de Margeville, sitting next to him, to ask how the winner would be decided.

'Why, the winner will be the last one to remain on her bicycle.'

'An endurance test? Surely not – we'd be here all day and that would be excessively boring. Or are they allowed to knock each other off their bicycles?'

'No, they must not touch each other – that would bring disqualification. It is an endurance test of another kind. The saddles of those bicycles have been very well greased – see how the riders tend to slide a little on them with each thrust of their legs against the pedals.'

'What follows?' asked Raymond, still puzzled.

'My dear fellow – the intimate parts of our pretty bicyclists are being subjected to constant and rhythmic massage by the exertion of pedalling fast enough to stay upright. What do you suppose will be the result?'

'Heavens!' Raymond exclaimed in sudden understanding. 'You mean that the action of riding round will bring on the physical crisis more usually induced in a woman by her lover!'

'Exactly! Now you understand the amusement which Bonfils has arranged for us. As these women ride around under our close scrutiny, we shall observe the signs of their arousal. This one passing us now, for example – she is already pink of face. In a while you will see her little nipples become firm, her legs tremble! At the critical moment, each woman in turn will topple from the saddle, unable to continue to ride in her spasms of pleasure.'

'Until only one is left to claim Bonfils' prize! But what if there is cheating – if one of them should try to raise herself just off the saddle without being observed?'

'There is no chance of that going undetected. All four are watching each other closely to make sure no one wins the prize by cheating. And Bonfils is observing them – see how he stares at each as she passes in front of him! And finally, all of us here have the right to act as judges, to ensure that the rules are followed.'

'Champagne, Monsieur?' said a discreet voice at Raymond's elbow.

He turned to find one of Bonfils servants behind him with a bottle to refill his glass.

'Bonfils is the most salacious person I know,' said Raymond, sipping at the cold wine.

'Oh yes, but always in an original and interesting way,' de Margeville agreed, 'Look at this little beauty!'

It was Mademoiselle Marianne pedalling slowly past them. She was perhaps twenty-two or -three years old, somewhat broad-shouldered for her slender body. Her little breasts were set high, their buds a dark red that was almost crimson in intensity.

'See – she's well on the way,' Xavier de Margeville observed, 'and they've been round no more than three or four times. I shall not bet on her.'

'You intend to bet on this contest? I thought that Bonfils was joking when he said that.'

'It is part of the entertainment. Bonfils will accept all bets, however large, at the odds set by him. While there are four riders, the odds are three to one. Pick the winner and you may win a considerable sum.'

'One thousand francs on Mademoiselle Sophie!' a voice called from somewhere to Raymond's left.

He craned his neck to see who it was and recognised a well-known banker.

Bonfils, his handbell on the ground beside him, now held an open notebook and a thin gold pen. He scribbled the name of the banker, the amount and the name of the woman.

'Well done, dear friend!' he cried so that everyone would hear him. 'She seems a good choice to me – amateur that I am in such matters! One thousand francs is bet on Mademoiselle Sophie. Place your bets, gentlemen, while the odds are still three to one in your favour.'

'I understand,' said Raymond, 'the odds will shorten as we lose contestants.'

'Exactly. I do not think that Mademoiselle Sophie is my choice – look at the generous width of her bottom. In bed that would be a great advantage, but not here. She has that much weight bearing her down on the saddle and it must take its toll before long. No, I shall choose between Mademoiselle Jeanne and Mademoiselle Marianne. But which?'

'Where does Bonfils get the girls from?' Raymond enquired, 'They're too pretty and too clean to be part of the genuine circus.'

'I suppose he hires them from one of the better houses of pleasure.'

'You are wrong there,' said the man on Raymond's other side, 'I am well acquainted with the best houses in the ten years I have been a widower. These young women are unknown to me. Perhaps they are artists' models.'

'No one else is betting,' Raymond observed.

'They are studying form,' said de Margeville.

The most unusual spectacle of four young women riding round on bicycles and displaying their bodies had a certain piquancy, Raymond found. There were some interesting comparisons to make – the relative size and shape of breasts and bottoms – and their respective elasticity as they jiggled and bounced to their owners' movements. The relative length and meatiness or otherwise of all those thighs pumping up and down to turn the pedals! The colour and texture of the hair revealed by the action of those thighs. . .but above all, the interest lay in the expressions on the faces of the riders – that was truly fascinating.

All four had ridden into the arena smiling broadly to make the first lap – smiles that acknowledged the spontaneous applause and welcomed it. After all, these were women, whatever their profession, who experienced not the least embarrassment in displaying their naked bodies – on the contrary, they thrived on the admiration of men.

After a turn or two of the ring the smiles were still there on all four pretty faces – but they were becoming more like fixed grins as important and distracting sensations started to make themselves felt between the riders' legs. One by one even the grins disappeared as these sensations were intensified by the constant rubbing of the slippery saddles. Mademoiselle Marianne, for example, rode past with her mouth hanging open loosely and a faraway look in her eyes as she struggled against the crisis which threatened her.

'Heavens!' said de Margeville as he observed her, 'she won't last more than another time or two round the ring. This is the last opportunity of getting odds of three to one.'

He called out hurriedly to Bonfils in the middle of the arena.

'Five thousand on Mademoiselle Jeanne!'

Bonfils raised a finger in acknowledgment and scribbled in his notebook.

Raymond had also made up his mind by then.

'Ten thousand on Mademoiselle Sophie!'

Plump-bottomed Sophie, hearing her name, glanced over her shoulder and smiled vaguely in Raymond's direction. Her face was very flushed and Raymond wondered if he had made an expensive mistake. Xavier de Margeville certainly thought so.

'Not a hope,' he declared, 'not with that splendid bottom. Go for the thinnest, that's my advice.'

'And also mine,' the man on Raymond's other side

agreed and surprised him by betting fifty thousand francs on Mademoiselle Jeanne.

'Fifty thousand bet by Barras!' Bonfils announced loudly. 'That's more like it. He'll be able to pay his shareholders an extra dividend out of his winnings! Come along now, gentlemen – get your bets down while there's still time.'

At once several voices called out and kept Bonfils busy writing for a while, though no one approached or surpassed Barras' fifty thousand. In so far as Raymond could judge in the confusion of voices, most of the money was going on Mademoiselle Jeanne and Mademoiselle Marie and it was Mademoiselle Jeanne who was the favourite. He heard only one other wager placed on Mademoiselle Sophie, a circumstance which did not inspire him with confidence in her.

'Ah, look at Marianne!' de Margeville exclaimed, tapping Raymond on the knee, 'in a few more moments. . .'

Marianne on the far side of the sawdust ring was riding very slowly now, the front wheel of her bicycle wobbling. She was breathing quickly through her open mouth and her tiny breasts rose and fell with the heaving of her chest.

'She's cheating!' one of the other riders shouted shrilly, pointing at Marianne, 'she's off the saddle!'

Bonfils strode across to Mademoiselle Marianne and delivered a good-natured smack with his open hand on her bare bottom.

'Sit on the saddle properly,' he cried, 'no cheating allowed here!'

Marianne wobbled on, her course becoming more and more erratic. As she approached the bench where Raymond was sitting her head went slowly backwards until she was staring up at the shabby roof of the tent. She uttered a high-pitched squeal and toppled over sideways. There was a long gasp from the audience and many rose to their feet as Marianne rolled in the sawdust and lay on her side, both hands pressed between her legs, her knees drawn up and jerking in the throes of her climactic moments.

'Mademoiselle Marianne withdraws from the contest,' Bonfils announced formally.

He raised his top hat in salute to the fallen competitor, then assisted her to her feet and gave her a friendly pat on the rump as she picked up her bicycle and wheeled it away.

All eyes were on the three women left in the ring as they circled slowly, each bright pink with emotion. The men who had not yet placed a bet were emboldened to do so now that the field had thinned out, though the odds were now at two to one only.

'Did anyone put money on Mademoiselle Marianne?' Raymond asked his friend.

'I think that Foucault over there had a few thousand francs on her. For the wrong reasons, alas. He knows nothing about betting, but he adores women with pointed little breasts like hers.'

'Who doesn't?' said Raymond, shrugging.

A groan of dismay arose from the benches as Mademoiselle Marie veered off course, her eyes closed and her belly shaking – to be followed by a shout of delight as she collided with a bench laden with spectators. The abrupt halting of her machine sent her sailing head-first over the handlebars into the laps of the onlookers – with such force that the bench tipped over backwards, depositing them all on the ground. Then a roar of laughter filled the tent as Marie writhed in ecstasy on top of two or three dark-clad businessmen who lay on the grass with their legs waving in the air.

When he could make himself heard, Bonfils announced that Mademoiselle Marie had withdrawn from the contest and that the odds had shortened to evens.

'That Sophie has more endurance than I gave her credit for,' said de Margeville, watching the two finalists pedalling slowly round, 'but mine will beat her – see how Sophie's thighs are trembling, while Jeanne's are steady and firm.'

In truth, Mademoiselle Sophie looked as if she was very close to the end of her ride. The flush of her face extended right down her neck and chest and her entire body gleamed with perspiration.

'Perhaps you are right, my dear fellow,' said Raymond doubtfully, 'but I retain my faith in her.'

'You will lose your money – and I shall win a hundred and fifty thousand francs from Bonfils!'

'You sound very confident,' Raymond responded, 'does your confidence extend to another ten thousand francs?'

'A side bet between you and me? But of course! Ten thousand from you to me when my woman wins – that will be very satisfactory.'

'Or vice-versa,' Raymond reminded him.

The vanquished Marie had not left the tent, Raymond noted. She was sitting on the bench between two of the men she had knocked over. Each had an arm round her naked waist and one of them – a banker named Weber who was nearer to his sixtieth birthday than his fiftieth – was whispering into her ear as he eyed her bare bosom. Mademoiselle Marie may have lost the prize money, Raymond concluded, but she will not return home empty-handed. Looking round the benches, he further observed that Mademoiselle Marianne, the first to be eliminated, had returned without her bicycle and was sitting bare-bottomed on the lap of the man who had wagered on her and lost.

With only two riders left in the arena, the contest must surely end very soon, for both of them appeared to be *in extremis*.

'One thousand francs on Mademoiselle Jeanne!' a voice called out, breaking the silent concentration of the spectators.

All heads turned to see who it was that had waited

until the final moments before committing himself at short odds. It was the famous author of novels for good Catholics.

'What a cautious fellow he must be!' said Raymond with a grin.

'There goes your girl!' de Margeville exclaimed in triumph, 'hand over the money!'

Mademoiselle Sophie was swaying dangerously from side to side on her slow-moving bicycle, her eyes closed to mere slits and a rapt expression on her red face. With bated breath the audience watched the last moments of the contest as the two women struggled to cling to the last shreds of self-control.

There was a long wail – and Mademoiselle Jeanne clapped a hand to the wet thatch between her legs! Her front wheel turned sideways and she slid to the sawdust and rolled onto her back, her legs kicking in the air as her climactic tension released itself. A long-drawn sigh from the audience acknowledged her defeat.

'Mademoiselle Jeanne withdraws from the contest!' Bonfils cried, 'The winner is Mademoiselle Sophie!'

'Well done, Mademoiselle Sophie!' Raymond called out to her, 'I have a bonus for you!'

He wasn't sure that she heard him because Bonfils' announcement was followed by prolonged applause for the victor. She managed another quarter lap, her swaying more pronounced, then dismounted quickly and sat in the sawdust, her knees drawn up and her arms round them, shaking violently.

Bonfils snapped his fingers and one of his servants hurried to him with a new bottle of champagne. When Mademoiselle Sophie's quivering had stopped, Bonfils tapped her on the shoulder and, as her head came up, he up-ended the bottle. She opened her mouth wide to catch the stream of champagne, swallowing as fast as she could, until she could drink no more. Bonfils poured the rest of the bottle over her bare breasts and belly to cool her off and she grinned.

During this interesting little interlude the spectators were clapping and cheering, all in exceptionally good humour at what they had witnessed in the arena, however the betting had gone. Bonfils had to ring his handbell for a long time to silence them and summon the four contestants to him. Weber seemed reluctant to free Mademoiselle Marie from his grasp.

'Let go of her!' Bonfils cried, laughing at him, 'you can have her back after the prize-giving, you naughty old banker!'

'I don't believe it,' Xavier de Margeville complained, handing Raymond ten thousand francs, 'I was absolutely certain that the one I bet on would last longest. In logic it could be no other way. Why did you bet on Sophie? She looked the least likely of them all.'

'Intuition,' said Raymond with a shrug, 'no more than that.'

Meanwhile the four naked young women arranged themselves before Bonfils in a row. Mademoiselle Sophie took a step forward and Bonfils congratulated her in the most grandiloquent manner on her triumph and presented the prize-money to her with a great flourish, a bow and a raising of his black top hat. For the others he had words of consolation. Not one of them looked disconsolate, from which Raymond deduced that they had established contacts that promised to more than compensate for what they had lost.

As soon as the women left the ring to dress themselves, Raymond went forward to claim his winnings from Bonfils, thinking that he was the only winner. He had forgotten that Desmoines had also wagered on Sophie, though a smaller amount. Bonfils counted out thirty thousand francs for Raymond and handed it to him with a grin.

'Congratulations – you are a shrewd judge of women, my dear fellow.'

'My congratulations to you,' said Raymond dryly, 'By my reckoning you must have made at least a quarter of a million francs.'

Bonfils winked at him.

'Ah, you must not overlook my expenses in arranging this little contest,' he answered, 'and you must agree that everyone has been greatly entertained. Just look – they're all trying to get their money back by drinking my champagne as if it were water. Take my advice – get a glass before it's all gone. I have the pleasant task of collecting all the money due to me before our friends begin to slip away, so you must excuse me.'

Raymond need not have feared that his offer of a bonus to Mademoiselle Sophie had gone unheard. He was standing among his friends, glass in hand, discussing the finer points of the contest they had witnessed – and she appeared at his elbow. She was wearing a plain black skirt and over it a long jumper that came down below her hips and had a zigzag pattern knitted into it.

'M'sieu,' she said, smiling at him.

Her bosom was fuller than was considered fashionable and her jumper emphasised it. But for the first time Raymond found himself looking at her face properly – it was round and pleasant, though her nose was perhaps a trifle broad. Her expression was one of good-nature, not the false friendliness of the professional.

'Ah, Mademoiselle Sophie! Permit me to congratulate you on a magnificent victory against very serious adversaries. I was inspired to bet on you and you did not disappoint my hopes. I feel that it is no more than justice to share my winnings with you – if you will do me the honour to accept this little gift.'

She smiled at him as he handed her five thousand francs of his winnings and – to his delight – she raised her black skirt and tucked the folded bank-notes into her garter.

Perhaps it was the wine he had drunk, perhaps it was the emotional impact of having seen four naked young women in the throes of passion – perhaps it was both – but Raymond at that moment found Mademoiselle Sophie very desirable.

'I have a car outside,' he murmured, 'it would give me great pleasure to offer you a ride back into the city.'

'You are very kind,' she said at once, 'perhaps you could drop me off where I live.'

The offer and the acceptance implied much more than a ride in his car, as they both understood completely. After another glass of Bonfils' rapidly diminishing stock of champagne they took their leave, while that enterprising person was still working his way through the crowd, note-book in hand and his pockets stuffed with bank-notes. Once in the car and on the way, formality vanished quickly. Raymond called her Sophie, told her his own name and drove with one hand, the other on her thigh above her garter – the one which did not hold her money. He was not acquainted with the district where she lived and they were driving back towards the city centre from a direction that was equally unfamiliar to him. After a longer drive than was probably necessary, he found the rue d'Alésia and followed it westwards until Sophie was able to direct him.

The building she indicated eventually was unprepossessing, but that was of no consequence. Her room was on the very top floor, as he had guessed it would be, and that too was of no consequence. Raymond was on fire from the long contact of his hand on Sophie's bare thigh under her skirt, his apparatus was fully extended and uncomfortable inside his clothes. Sophie too was quite ready – she was breathing even more quickly than the long climb up the stairs could be held responsible for.

The meagreness of her room and its poor furnishing made no impression whatsoever on Raymond, for no sooner were they inside than Sophie's hand was thrust

61

urgently down the front of his trousers to give her a grip on the twin dependents below his upstanding part. At another time he might have found the grip a little too forcible for comfort, but in his heightened frame of mind her squeezing of those tender objects merely served to arouse him further.

'I'm dying for it!' she gasped. 'Do it to me!'

Raymond was exceptionally eager to oblige her. Bonfils' *cirque erotique* and the car ride afterwards had exacerbated his emotions to an impossible degree – and if that were not enough, the clasp of Sophie's hand brought his throbbing stiffness to almost the instant of explosion. He pushed her down onto the untidy bed, not at all gently, his hands clenched on her breasts through her jumper while she wriggled her bottom and pulled her skirt up to her waist – for her need and his were too demanding to waste time undressing. She groped between her parted thighs to rip open the buttons of her cami-knickers, while Raymond was treating his trouser buttons to the same violence.

He threw himself on her, catching one brief glimpse of the hair between her legs still plastered flat to her skin with the vaseline which had been spread liberally on the bicycle saddles. His distended member found her slippery channel of its own accord and slid inside. Sophie screamed in ecstatic release at once and thrashed about beneath him, her loins lifting to force him in further. For Raymond the sensation of that smooth penetration was too much – he made three short and rapid thrusts and fountained his release into her, amazed, delighted and dismayed – all at once – at the speed of his response.

'My God, I needed that,' said Sophie when he lay still on her at last. 'Now we can take our time and do it properly. How about getting undressed?'

Raymond slid from her embrace and together they removed their clothes.

'What a sight!' Sophie exclaimed, staring at her wispy

patch of hair, darkened and stuck flat, 'I must do something about that.'

She left him lying on the bed while she made preparations to wash herself.

The facilities afforded by her room were rudimentary – she took a large porcelain wash-basin from a rickety dressing table, set it on the floor and poured water into it from a jug. Raymond rolled onto his side to watch her at her toilet. She straddled the basin and crouched down to wash between her thighs.

'If this doesn't cool me down, nothing will,' she joked.

'God forbid,' said Raymond, 'it all happened so quickly that I feel that I have been cheated. But if that little plaything between your legs becomes chilled from the water, it will be a pleasure for me to warm it up again.'

'There's no fear of it going off the boil,' she assured him, 'when I get started, I can't stop – not even with all that riding round the circus for Monsieur Bonfils.'

She stood up and reached for a towel to dry herself.

'The speed with which it happened to us both is proof enough that the bicycle contest aroused you considerably,' said Raymond. 'It brought on a little crisis, for I saw you trembling and panting as you sat on the ground after you had won the prize.'

'Yes, I couldn't control myself that time,' said Sophie, 'though I managed to stay on the saddle through the others.'

She threw the towel aside carelessly and stood naked for him to see her, hands on her hips and a smile on her face. She was younger than Raymond had first thought, certainly not much more than twenty, but already her full breasts had lost some of their tautness and were a little slack. The slight loss in aesthetic appeal was more than compensated for, in Raymond's opinion, by the gain in sensual appeal, for a man could fondle them endlessly and find the experience rewarding – even hide his face between them – not to mention another part of his body!

63

But without doubt her most fascinating feature was the plump mound between her thighs. Under its covering of thin brown hair the lips were permanently separated by the overdeveloped inner lips pushing through.

'It is obvious why you are hot-natured,' Raymond commented affectionately 'In fact, I am surprised that you were able to endure the ride so long. What do you mean by *the others*? Are you saying that it happened to you while you were riding round the arena?'

'Five or six times,' she replied, getting back onto the bed with him, 'but as I had agreed to win it was necessary to continue.'

'Agreed to win? But what do you mean?'

Sophie grinned at him in a conspiratorial way as she stroked his belly.

'I'm giving away a secret when I shouldn't,' she said, 'but I like you, Raymond. The truth is that Monsieur Bonfils knows about my nature – how I have to go on when I've started. It's like waves on the sea – you must have seen it – the waves come rolling in, quite small ones, and then about every seventh wave is a much bigger one. At least, that's what I've been told. Well, that's how it is with me. I get aroused with a man and these little waves roll over me, one after the other, until the big one arrives.'

'That was when you were sitting in the sawdust?'

'No, of course not – that was a few minutes ago with you.'

Raymond was flattered that it should have been so.

'So there was an agreement between you and Bonfils to win the five thousand francs he offered as prize.'

Sophie winked at him, her hand sliding lower on his belly towards his most important asset.

'I trust you,' she said. 'The little agreement I had with Monsieur Bonfils was that I should receive ten thousand francs to enter and win.'

'But why?'

She shrugged impatiently at his slowness of comprehension and took hold of his awakening part to encourage its growth.

'Who did everyone bet on?' she asked. 'Monsieur Bonfils did very well for himself today, but I liked you straight off because you put your money on me. What made you do that – you weren't supposed to.'

Raymond chuckled at the thought of Bonfils' duplicity, now revealed to him. What a rogue the man was – yet with what entertaining cunning he brought off the coups which gave him his reputation!

'I liked the look of your bottom when you first rode past me on your bicycle,' he said, 'you have those round soft cheeks which indicate an amorous nature, not the tight little bottom of Mademoiselle Jeanne.'

'You think I've got a big bottom, do you?' Sophie asked, her hand sliding up and down his stiff part.

'A generous bottom, not a big one. Your centre of gravity is well down your body, which means that you are more at ease lying on your back than standing up – am I not right? And then those round soft breasts attracted my attention. One of the contestants had little pointed breasts set high on her chest – modish, of course, but disappointing when you have them in your hands. Yours, on first sight, were of a size and texture to please a man.'

He suited the action to the word by taking them in his hands and playing with them.

'Ah, I understand,' she said, 'you bet on me because you wanted to go to bed with me, not because you thought I could win the contest! I knew you were a sympathetic person as soon as I heard your voice calling out "Ten thousand francs on Mademoiselle Sophie"!'

'Now,' said Raymond, 'I wish to observe this interesting aspect of your nature you have described to me.'

His hand moved down her body to touch the soft and permanently pouting lips between her thighs.

'You won't collapse on me halfway through, will you?' she murmured, 'I can't stand it when that happens.'

'You may have every confidence in me,' said Raymond. 'My desire to see the little waves rolling in to the shore is so strong that I shall continue until the big wave breaks over us together.'

'Yes,' she said, 'get me started, Raymond chéri! I'll let you know when the big wave is on its way.'

THE SECRET OF MADAME DUPERRAY

Even in a society of beautiful and elegant women Madame Duperray was conspicuous. Everyone, including those who disliked her, agreed without the least hesitation that she was exceptionally beautiful and incredibly elegant. Her clothes were made for her by the most celebrated fashion designers in the whole of Paris and the effect was always stunning, whether it was a little velvet suit by Chanel for casual shopping, a short evening frock by Patou and a simple necklace of diamonds, or the full magnificence of a ball gown by Poiret – for Madame Duperray did not restrict her patronage to any one fashion house.

She was perfectly formed for the designers, being tall, slender, small-breasted, with exquisitely long legs. Her complexion was very fine and her hair a rich shade of dark brown that looked well with nearly every colour the couturiers decided was in fashion for that season. A further advantage was that she could afford anything they suggested, for she was rich – that is to say, her husband was rich and he allowed her a free hand.

A kind Providence had endowed Madame Duperray with gifts of intellect to match those of her form. She was intelligent, vivacious, well-informed, interested in everything from the classical theatre to American jazz. Invitations to her little luncheon parties – never more than twelve people – and to her sumptuous dinner parties were greatly esteemed as social occasions of particular importance. It was small wonder that her picture, with the charmingly humorous smile for which she was famous, should adorn the pages of the newspapers and magazines with great frequency.

No man who knew her had ever been heard to say a word of criticism of Madame Duperray. But there were women who disliked her, sad to say, and who made their opinions known to anyone who would listen. The worst that they could allege against her was that she changed her lovers more often than was decent for a woman in her position. No doubt there was an element of jealousy in this sort of gossip, for a regular lover can become as tedious as a husband to a woman of discernment.

If Monsieur Duperray was aware of this ill-natured tittle-tattle he seemed not to pay any attention to it. When he and his wife appeared together in public or entertained at home they were always on the best of terms – he most attentive to her and she to him. At fifty, or thereabouts, he was, of course, twenty years older than his wife but he had never been seen to exhibit any indication of the possessiveness of older men towards beautiful young wives. In short, the Duperrays gave every appearance of being paragons of domestic virtue.

Yet rumour persistently linked the name of Célestine Duperray with an extravagantly long list of young men, though without the smallest shred of evidence. Indeed, one well-known lady whose husband's name had been whispered as having been added to this legendary roll of honour had gone so far as to state that if Célestine Duperray were to charge at the going rate for her services, she would in a year or two be as rich as her husband! But that was mere spite, of course, and not taken seriously even by those who laughed at the joke.

Needless to say, men were absolutely charming towards Madame Duperray, and this was partly because it was impossible to be otherwise towards so great a beauty, and also perhaps in the hope that they might be invited to subscribe their name to the list of those who were supposed to have enjoyed her intimate favours. If any were honoured by so delicate an invitation, they kept very silent about it. In the whole of Paris it was impossible to find even one person who would admit to having been Célestine's lover. Very few women of any charm could rely on total discretion of that sort, men being such inveterate gossips. Even the lady who had started the impolite joke that Célestine could become rich by charging a few francs each time – even this lady was known by almost everyone except her husband to have been the very close friend of Charles Brissard for the past two years.

In these circumstances, the astounded delight of Nicolas Bruneau can be imagined when one evening Madame Duperray murmured secretly to him that she would call upon him the next day at three in the afternoon, if that was convenient! He could hardly believe his ears! He looked into her marvellous eyes and asked himself if he had suddenly gone mad, to imagine so fantastic a suggestion. Madame Duperray smiled her celebrated half-humorous smile and nodded and repeated:

'If that is convenient.'

Convenient! Dear God – whatever else he had planned for the next day was as nothing to the promise of a visit by Madame Duperray. To keep that rendezvous Nicolas was prepared to put off anything at all – even his mother's funeral, if she had had the poor judgment to have died just then – even the dignity of attending at the Élysée Palace to be invested a Chevalier of the Legion of Honour by the President of the Republic himself. Not that any such national recognition was due to him then, or ever likely to be. The truth of it was that Nicolas was already twenty-six, had achieved nothing much and had no great prospects before him, in spite of his family name. He was the second son of a good but impoverished old family which was once prominent but now, by reason of various calamities during the War, the nature of which is best

69

forgotten, had receded into obscurity. Nicolas was a school-boy during his father's misfortunes and therefore not to be held in any way responsible, but his subsequent way of life was affected. His father gave him an annual allowance which kept him from starvation but was totally inadequate to permit him to live in the style he regarded as his natural right.

Happily, old times being soon forgotten, Nicolas's family name assured him of being received into the best circles and he supplemented his allowance by sporadic journalism for the newspapers and magazines which took an interest in the social activities of those eminent circles.

In this capacity he had met Madame Duperray more than once and had written suitably charming paragraphs about her, some of which had found their way into print under his name. After one of these pieces had been published, in which he mentioned her attendance at the races in the Bois de Boulogne, she had sent him a little note at the newspaper office, in her own elegant handwriting on delicately scented paper, saying how charmingly he wrote. He had acknowledged it gracefully, assuring her that it was impossible to write otherwise of so elegant a person, but that was the end of their correspondence.

The matter of her imputed lovers was one that had interested Nicolas since the first time he had seen her. Yet even his most diligent journalistic researches, including attempts to bribe servants all over Paris, had never led him to anyone who claimed this marvellous privilege. Nicolas had the inclination to dismiss the rumours as malicious gossip – and here now was an amazing indication of the most direct kind that there might be some truth in the stories after all!

The occasion at which the invitation – or at least, the suggestion – was murmured to him by Madame Duperray was at the Opera ball – a very grand function at which the richest, most fashionable, most glittering and most beautiful people were present. Nicolas was there, elegantly attired in evening tails, to collect enough names and details for a eulogistic column in the next day's newspaper. He knew almost everyone, of course, and circulated freely, exchanging greetings and compliments, even dancing with one or two of the younger women – those who were not overly enamoured of their partners. At a suitable moment he presented himself to Madame Duperray, while her husband was talking to someone else.

To say that she looked magnificent would be to understate matters. She wore a ball gown evidently created for this special evening by the most talented couturier in Paris – which means in the whole world. In its sophisticated simplicity it was stunning! A few metres of the finest tussore silk, no more than that, transformed into a sheath for her body, leaving her shoulders and arms bare – but the cut of it, that was sheer poetry translated into silk! The rich brown of her hair was accentuated by a strand of pearls woven into it by a hairdresser of genius. Nicolas wondered as he bowed over her white-gloved hand and kissed it how he would ever find words to describe the virtuosity of Madame Duperray's ball gown for his column in the newspaper.

Then she spoke, very softly, the words which so astounded him. His breath was quite taken away. He bowed again to signify his acceptance of so tremendous an honour and, before he was required to say anything, friends of hers came up to talk to her. Nicolas retired unobserved from the little group, his mind in a whirl, and made for the bar to fortify himself with cold champagne and gloat upon this incredible good fortune. Tomorrow at three! It was a date with destiny, no less!

In that he was correct, though not perhaps precisely the destiny he envisaged. But if it is destiny that orders our lives, then the next day's encounter with Madame Duperray was to change the entire course of Nicolas's life.

She had not enquired his address and that was in itself of interest. Months before, when he had acknowledged her note of tribute to his writing ability in the newspaper he had replied from his own address, not from the office. He was uncertain what to make of that. It could be that Madame Duperray had even then considered him to be a prospect for her alleged sequence of lovers – or it might mean no more than that she had a large address book into which she copied details of anyone ever likely to be useful in any way at all.

Nicolas's restricted financial means did not permit him to live in the style his family once had. He rented an apartment in one of the old buildings in the rue de Montmorency and, while it was small, he had taken pains to decorate and furnish it well. A number of the ladies he met during his journalistic work had visited him there – nearly all of them married – for an hour or two of diversion and Nicolas did not underestimate the importance of creating a good impression.

Madame Duperray arrived very punctually, a surprise in itself, and conducted herself towards him as if they had been friends all their lives. She allowed him to assist her out of her coat and roamed freely round his sitting-room, commenting in favourable terms on a picture here and a statuette there, as if they were works of art of value. She sat in one of his very modern black and gold armchairs – acquired for a mere song at a furniture auction – and chatted with easy familiarity about the people at the Opera ball. In effect, she conducted herself exactly as if this were an ordinary social call, with no suggestion of any more interesting motive.

This puzzled Nicolas at first. Perhaps she was nervous, he thought, although she certainly gave no sign of it. Eventually he came to realise that she was sizing him up before deciding whether to proceed any further. If the verdict went against him, she would ask for her coat and leave – and it would have been no more than an ordinary social call. Therefore it was up to Nicolas to take the initiative and persuade her subtly that she could, with advantage, trust to his savoire-faire and remove more than her coat and gloves!

Once his course was clear, Nicolas brought into play all his talents to charm and amuse. He made her laugh with little anecdotes about people she knew, incidents from his observation at social functions. He talked about people he knew well who were also known to her – he was a good talker, this Nicolas. When the moment was right, he began to talk about Madame Duperray herself – how exquisitely she dressed, what elegance of appearance she presented in public, how every man in Paris admired and adored her from afar – and so on and so on.

Célestine basked in his praise, her beautiful eyes shining with emotion. In due course Nicolas found himself, in the most natural way in the world, on his knees beside her chair, kissing her hands. Not long after that, sure of himself now, he kissed her silk-stockinged knees, very expertly and in a most flattering manner. Célestine stroked his hair and suggested that perhaps the time had come when he should show her the rest of his apartment.

By that she naturally meant the bed-room. Once in it, she held out her arms to Nicolas and he embraced her and kissed her with enthusiasm. If the truth were told it was rather more than enthusiasm – it was a sense of wonder he experienced. When he began to undress her he was like a man who has bought a lottery ticket for ten francs and learns that he has won a million! The dumb-struck winner stares at the prize being handed to him and cannot believe his luck. This, or something akin to it, was what Nicolas felt then – the beautiful and distinguished Célestine Duperray was in his bed-room, stripped to her stockings and flimsy silk knickers, her pretty little breasts offered to him to caress! He kissed them until their pink buds grew firm to his lips before completing her disrobing – and his own.

Seen naked, Célestine was incredibly beautiful, as he had guessed she would be. The skin of her expensively pampered body was like satin to the touch, its tones warm and delicate. Her breasts – each a delicious little handful! Her navel – a round and shallow dimple of enchanting shape, set in a belly so graceful that there could never be another to match it! The rich brown fur between her slender thighs was trimmed short to display to the best advantage the classical contour of her delightful mount of Venus. In short – though there was no reason in the world why any man should have wished to cut short the admiration of her charms when they were so generously offered to his view – her body displayed such a wealth of sensuous harmony to the eyes, the hands and the lips, that Nicolas, involved in aesthetic appreciation, almost forgot the purpose of Célestine's presence in his bed.

She reminded him, for even the most beautiful woman becomes faintly impatient if abstract adoration continues too long without any initiative to put her charms to their proper use. When Nicolas had sighed over her for as long as she considered sufficient, Célestine took hold of his rigid part and gave him to understand without words, that she could wait no longer for the pleasure of receiving it.

Her directness had the desired effect and when he was mounted Nicolas thought that he would burst with sheer joy! He was in possession of the splendours of that marvellous woman and the sensations were as magnificent as he could ever have imagined. He felt that he had at last entered into his true heritage. A person of his quality had a natural right to enjoy women like Célestine Duperray! It was only the misfortunes of his father that had until now cheated Nicolas of the prizes that were naturally his! Now that was all changed! The gorgeous Célestine had recognised his true worth and had responded in the only appropriate way! How perceptive she was, how refined her sensibilities!

Nicolas's excitement owed perhaps as much to gratified

pride as to physical desire – and it served him well. It called forth all the tender skills of which he was capable and extended the incredible moments of their intimate union into a long and delirious passage of ecstasy which left them both panting and trembling in explosively fulfilled desire.

'That was marvellous!' Célestine said, a smile of gratification on her face 'you really are very good at it, Nicolas.'

There does not live a man who is not flattered almost to imbecility when a beautiful woman praises his skill as a lover. Nicolas kissed her a hundred times at least – on the mouth, face, chin and neck – then changed his position and bestowed another hundred kisses or so on her elegant breasts.

It goes without saying that in the entire world there is no more superb sight than that of a woman lying naked on a bed, her eyes radiant with the love that she feels for the man beside her, her soft white skin delicately flushed from satisfied desire. This is the vision which painters have for centuries attempted to capture on canvas, though few have had any great measure of success. An exception, perhaps, is Edouard Manet's picture of Olympe, lying provocatively propped up on large pillows, a black ribbon round her neck to emphasise the pale sheen of her skin, her breasts thrust proudly forwards and one hand lying lightly across the join of her thighs, as if to preserve this final secret for her lover alone. As everyone knows, Olympe is in actuality a portrait of Victorine Meurent and the lover for whom she was preserving her most intimate secret was Manet himself.

It must not be supposed that Célestine was wholly passive during this extensive adoration of her attributes in the after-glow of emotion. One of her long-fingered hands caressed Nicolas' back and hip – before seeking to roam over more intimate parts of him, until her red-painted nails scratched lightly the sensitive skin of his inner thighs. By the time Nicolas's interminable kissing had descended to the neat little triangle of brown hair between Célestine's legs – the covering to the adorable private entrance through which he had penetrated to ecstasy not long before – his cavalier had recovered from the lassitude which follows active service and was fully alert again. Célestine was, after all, a woman of experience who knew how to obtain what she wanted. She held the head of his risen part delicately between forefinger and thumb, encouraging it to grow to the maximum.

When two people find themselves in these enchanting circumstances, there is only one course of action that can be followed. After another score or two of kisses to Célestine's open thighs and the warm satin skin of her groins, then some moments of exploring with the tip of his tongue the tender interior of the pouting lips between those groins, Nicolas once more positioned himself above Célestine and inserted into its rightful place the part of him which a benevolent Deity had expressly designed for this purpose.

Many men claim that the second amorous bout is superior to the first, their reasoning being that although the appetite is a little less keen, their natural part has been made more sensitive by its first use and therefore the sensations are greater. On the other hand, women rarely make comparisons of this kind, for the female experience is so different from the male experience in intimate concerns that physical comparisons miss the point completely.

Whatever the truth of it, the second turn was very greatly to the enjoyment of both Nicolas and Célestine, as their little sighs and exclamations testified to each other. Nicolas proceeded without haste, her face between his hands and his mouth touching hers in more kisses, until her legs rose from the bed to grip him tightly round the waist, her ankles crossed above his back. Then, the moment being right, he displayed his strength for her pleasure and before long brought them both to a climactic release.

'You're killing me with love!' Célestine sighed as they separated from each other, 'I adore you!'

These few words, spoken thousands of times a day by women in similar circumstances, no doubt, were enough to draw from Nicolas expressions of devotion, admiration, tenderness – he scarcely knew what he was saying.

They lay a little apart from each other to cool down, for they had become somewhat heated during the encounter, as was to be expected. Nicolas' hand lay between Célestine's thighs, just touching the little fur coat that adorned her. He had never been so happy in his life as at that moment – he had made love twice to this famous beauty and she adored him for it!

His happiness was compounded of sensual satisfaction, pride in his achievement and pleasant anticipation of being Célestine's lover for some considerable time to come – months perhaps – or even years!

Célestine rolled over to lie face down.

'How content I am,' she murmured, 'I must rest a little.'

Nicolas was too exhilarated to want to rest. He propped himself up on one elbow and stroked the cheeks of her bottom, exposed to him by the way she lay. They were superb, those cheeks – there was no other word for it – round, smooth as silk, warm and yielding to the touch.

'Ah,' she sighed, 'I see that I shall be given no rest – you are too virile for that.'

It was not until she praised him in this way that Nicolas decided that he must give her a third proof of his masculine vigour. In the normal course of events he found that twice in an afternoon was enough for him. He had the ability to go further, but to do so subjected him to a certain slight fatigue for the rest of the day. Of course, when a woman stayed all night in his apartment he expended himself fully, for then he was able to sleep late the next day.

No matter – now that the idea was fixed in his mind he intended to continue. A bottle of champagne before dinner would raise his spirits for the evening. But to continue meant that he must arouse Célestine, who had said that she was tired, since it would be discourteous to make use of her charming body for his own gratification unless she too enjoyed the proceeding. He knelt between her parted legs and fondled her bottom with both hands – a caress that usually interested a woman, he knew, to the point where she would be ready for the transfer of his hands to her breasts. After that, nature would take its course.

Célestine's bottom really was delicious. He stroked it and squeezed it until he heard her sigh with pleasure. Things were going well! He rotated those smooth cheeks in his palms and in doing so caught sight of the pink-brown little knot hidden between them – no uncommon sight for a lover and in the ordinary way of things wholly unremarkable. Yet on this occasion, to his surprise, he observed that her little fleshy knot was pulsating gently, clenching and unclenching!

A thought suggested itself to him. To test it he slipped a hand between her thighs and probed with a finger into the wet lips there until he touched and then tickled her secret bud. Ah yes – his theory held good! Célestine's external nodule pulsed in rhythm with his stimulation of her hidden bud! It was impossible not to draw the obvious conclusion from his observation – the normally unregarded part of Célestine between the cheeks of her bottom was for her a centre of acute pleasurable sensation. How pleasurable? he wondered – an experiment was called for. He touched the forefinger of his other hand to Célestine's sensuous nodule and caressed it lightly in time with his stimulation of her internal nodule. The effect of so simple a touch was remarkable. Célestine's legs jerked outwards to their widest stretch, her hands clawed at the bed sheet, dragging it up into two creased peaks and she gave voice to a long wail of ecstasy.

Nicolas was not an innocent, naturally, not one of those who knew no more than the simplest form of conjunction between man and woman. He had heard of the mode of pleasure now displayed for him by Célestine – and he had heard it spoken of as the Greek style of love. But that was the limit of his knowledge. He waited for Célestine's delicious throes to cease before he removed his fingers from her and she sighed, her flushed face pressed sideways into the pillow. Nicolas sighed too, the fact being that the paroxysm he had induced in her by his little experiment had aroused him again. So much so that there was no possibility of abandoning the exploration of this unfamiliar byway of love.

He lay over her back, his weight supported on his arms so that he could look down the length of his own body to steer the swollen head of his probe between the cheeks of her bottom and touch it to her sensitive little knot. How strange it seemed to him to be doing this – and yet, why not? There might be much to be learned and gained by so simple a course. Célestine moaned pleasurably and Nicolas could feel a tiny movement against the tip of his tenderest part, almost like a tiny mouth pressing kisses to the object of its desire. Célestine looked up at him over her shoulder, her dark brown eyes wide in wonder – and in loving admiration for the man who was able to give her these exquisite sensations. Even so, on her face was her familar half-smile with a hint of mockery in it! Then she too raised herself on one arm to try to see what was touching her eager nodule. Whether her contortion gave her a glimpse of Nicolas' straight part, poised at so intimate a spot, only she could say, but from their relative positions she knew that it was not his finger touching her but a stronger and more formidable limb.

She collapsed beneath him, sighing continuously, her body shuddering in the onset of passion. Nicolas pressed forward slowly to complete her pleasure, hardly knowing what he was doing, his mind so dizzy with the strangeness of the moment. For an instant or two he made no progress, then that tiny aperture pouted and he gained a centimetre – then another, and it gaped wide to admit him freely. Almost in disbelief Nicolas felt himself sliding easily into her. He lowered himself onto her back, amazed at this extraordinary insertion.

Beneath him Célestine twitched in continuous spasms, moaning all the time in wordless delight. For Nicolas the experience was not merely new – there was an element of perversity in it which made it incredibly exciting. He lay still, not attempting to do anything at all – and no movement was necessary! Célestine's beautiful bottom was bouncing up and down under his belly and the greedy little mouth which held him was pulling at him. In moments it hurried him past the point of return and he too cried out as he delivered his offering into this improbable receptacle of hers. If she had moaned before, she screamed now as she received his jet and bucked so hard under him that he was almost thrown off her back and only kept his place by seizing her bare shoulders!

This time, he dimly understood, Célestine had reached some sort of culmination of desire and a tremendous release, infinitely greater then the climactic experiences he had effected by the use of his male part within her more usual ingress. What had been started as no more than a casual experiment had led him to make an astonishing discovery about her nature. He waited until her throes eased and she lay still beneath him.

'You were magnificent,' she murmured, 'I love you to distraction!'

Nicolas' emotions were more complicated than that.

'I've never before done it *à la Grecque*,' he confessed, wondering if she would think him foolish for saying so.

'And now that you have?'

'I hardly know what to think.'

'My dear, marvellous Nicolas,' she said in the most affectionate way, 'I cannot seriously believe that you are disturbed by so small a variation from the usual.'

'Not disturbed,' he hastened to assure her, his self-confidence returning now that he saw how casually she regarded the incident, 'no, not disturbed.'

'Then what?'

'A little surprised, perhaps – as I said, it was. the first time for me.'

'But not for me, you imply – and you are quite right.'

Nicolas removed himself from her elegant back and lay beside her.

'If I may ask,' he said, 'have you always preferred that manner of making love?'

'Not *always*. When I was a young girl I knew only the traditional way and I found that very pleasant. But I met a man who showed me a different way. His suggestion horrified me at first – it seemed unthinkable! But because I loved him I let him do whatever he wanted – for all I wanted was to please him! And to my astonishment, I must confess, I adored what he did to me from the very first time.'

'You are speaking of your husband, I assume.'

That made her chuckle. She turned to face him on the bed.

'No, not my husband. His tastes are completely traditional. But enough of that – tell me again that you love me, Nicolas!'

Again was pushing matters too far – he had told her several hundred times that she was adorable but he had not gone beyond that. However, the situation obviously demanded a declaration of that type and Nicolas obliged by saying that he loved her.

'Good, good!' she murmured, 'the truth is that I have fallen in love with you – head over heels! Oh, I am so happy! Kiss me, Nicolas!

It was not much more than a week after his first encounter with Célestine that Nicolas found himself an involuntary participant in an unpleasant train of events which taught him that more was involved in being her lover then merely making love to her. He was strolling home very late one evening from the newspaper office when, in the rue Beaubourg, two men appeared from a dark doorway as he passed it and fell into step with him, one on either side. It was an unnerving experience at that time of night in a street devoid of other people – and it became even more unnerving when each of the men took him firmly by the arm. They were both large men, he noted, with facial expressions that did not indicate benevolence towards him. Nevertheless, he remained in possession of his wits.

'I have only a few hundred francs,' he told them, 'but you are welcome to them. I also have a watch, but that is not worth taking, I give you my word.'

That was a lie, as it happened – the watch was an extremely expensive one which had been given to him by Madame Duperray only two days before.

'Is your name Bruneau?' the man on his left demanded roughly.

'It cannot be of any importance to you what my name is. I suggest you accept the little money I have and vanish before a guardian of the law makes an appearance.'

'I want to know,' said the ruffian in a threatening manner.

'But why?'

'To make sure we've got the right man. If you're not Bruneau I'll be so upset that you'll get a good kicking to make me feel better!'

'I am Nicolas Bruneau, I assure you!'

'Then you're coming with us – somebody wants to talk to you.'

'Really? Who might that be?'

There was no answer. They hurried him to the corner and into the back of a car waiting there. Now Nicolas was really frightened – this seemed more like a plot to murder him than to rob him. Perhaps it would have been better to deny his identity and endure the threatened beating! At least he would have survived that.

'Where are we going? I insist on being told,' he said with all the conviction he could muster, which was not much, but by way of reply he was told in the rudest possible way to keep his mouth shut.

He stared out of the window to check the route they were taking. The car turned east along the Boulevard St Denis and then, after a time, north again. The journey was not a long one and it terminated in a deserted street, where Nicolas was pushed out of the car and into a very ordinary looking apartment building.

They walked up to the first floor, one of the captors tapped discreetly on a door, received no answer and produced a key to unlock it. He led the way through an entrance hall into a large and well-furnished sitting-room, the other man prodding Nicolas in the back to move him along.

'Stay here,' the leading captor instructed, 'I'll tell the boss you're here.'

Nicolas waited – he could do no other, guarded by the other man, who in the light he could now see to be a burly young thug in dark clothes with a hat pulled down over his forehead. A particularly unpleasant type, thought Nicolas, somewhat reminiscent of the pimps one saw hanging round the Place Blanche while their women were servicing customers.

He decided to sit down, to give the impression of nonchalance, but at once the guardian thug scowled at him ferociously and made an insolent gesture that indicated that he should remain standing until he was invited to do otherwise.

In not more than five minutes the other ruffian reappeared at the door and stood aside to allow to enter – and Nicolas gasped as he recognised him – Monsieur

Raoul Duperray, husband of Célestine, landed proprietor, businessman extraordinary and a somewhat mysterious figure on the fringe of politics. This looked like being a most unpleasant encounter!

The last time Nicolas had seen Duperray was the night of the Opera ball, looking incredibly elegant in tails, the ribbon of the Legion of Honour on his lapel, his silvery hair most handsomely smoothed back from his forehead. But at this moment Monsieur Duperray's hair was in disarray and he wore only a crimson silk dressing gown and morocco leather slippers on his bare feet. Even so, for all his fifty years and the casual manner of his attire, Duperray looked like a formidable man to deal with.

'Ah, it's Monsieur Bruneau at last!' he said, staring hard at Nicolas, 'I'm pleased that you were able to come. Do sit down – would you like a drink?'

'Thank you, no,' said Nicolas, wondering whether he would survive a leap through a first-floor window to the pavement below if it became necessary to take fast evasive action. Then he remembered that there was another villain outside – the one who had driven the automobile. No, there was no escape that way.

Duperray told his two hirelings to wait outside and made himself comfortable in a striped armchair. To lessen his disadvantage, Nicolas also sat, but he kept his hat on as a gesture of independence.

'Another time of day would have been preferable for our discussion,' said Duperray, 'but it has taken those two idiots until now to find you. You are an elusive man – where do you get to all day long?'

'May I enquire the purpose of this abduction?' Nicolas retorted, his courage returning now that he saw that he was not to be murdered out of hand.

'I believe you know my wife,' Duperray said noncommitally.

'I have the honour of being acquainted with Madame Duperray,' Nicolas replied carefully, his tone neutral, 'as

I have the honour of being acquainted with many of the most prominent social figures, including the wife of the Minister of Justice.'

'I'm sure you do. It is about your acquaintance with my wife that I felt I must have a few words with you. Her happiness is very precious to me.'

'Naturally, Monsieur.'

'I shall speak frankly. You must understand that I am totally devoted to my dear wife. No doubt most men would claim as much, but in my case it happens to be literally true.'

The words had an ominous ring. Nicolas had never before been confronted by a jealous husband and felt himself to be at a loss – certainly when confronted by one with the wealth and influence of Duperray – a man who had shown that he could command thugs to bring people to him. And who, it could hardly be doubted, could issue instructions to break arms and legs, if need be, or even worse! Nicolas felt the situation to be extraordinarily delicate, to say the least.

'Your devotion does you credit, Monsieur Duperray,' he said very sincerely.

'Oh, but she deserves it! She is the most beautiful and fascinating woman in the world – she is worthy of nothing less than whole-hearted respect and admiration,' said Duperray.

'Very true,' Nicolas agreed.

'Our marriage has been enormously successful. We are the envy of everyone we know.'

'Of course.'

'But,' said Duperray, his face darkening and his mouth tightening, 'my wife has informed me that she is in love with you.'

Nicolas gulped. The moment he feared had arrived.

'She has informed you, Monsieur? Why should she do that?'

'Why not? We have no secrets from each other – we never have had secrets.'

'Then there is nothing I can say,' Nicolas murmured.

'There is a great deal you can say which I want to hear! First – is it your intention to try to persuade Célestine to leave me for you?' Duperray demanded.

'Heavens, no!' Nicolas exclaimed, 'nothing is further from my thoughts, Monsieur.'

'I am relieved to hear you say that. In my eyes the bond of marriage is sacred and I will not contemplate its dissolution in any circumstances. Do I make myself clear?'

'Very clear.'

'Think of the misery it would cause your parents, my dear Bruneau, if you were to be found floating in the Seine one early morning with your throat cut. They would be desolate!'

The desolation of his parents seemed irrelevant to Nicolas in comparison to his own misery in meeting so untimely an end.

'My dear parents must at all costs be protected from so profound an anguish,' he muttered.

'Spoken like a dutiful son! Parents' hearts are easily broken by the misfortunes of their children, and Paris can be a dangerous place for young men who are careless. Don't you agree?'

'Monsieur Duperray, have no fear on my account. I give you my solemn word that I shall never see Madame Duperray again. If you prefer, I will leave Paris this very night and take up residence elsewhere – Lyon, Marseilles, wherever you think most suitable.'

'What?' Duperray exclaimed, his face purple with rage. 'Are you insane? Didn't you hear what I said?'

'I don't understand,' Nicolas stammered 'what is it you want?'

'My wife loves you, though God alone knows why! She will be unhappy if she cannot see you regularly. Therefore you will put yourself at her disposal – do you understand me?'

'But you said. . .'

'You are not listening to me! Pay attention – I said that I will not permit my marriage to be destroyed. Have you got that?'

'Yes.'

'Célestine wants you, so she must have you. Do you understand that much?'

'But don't you mind?'

'Of course not – whatever gave you that idea?'

'You want me to be her lover – is that it, Monsieur?' Nicolas asked cautiously.

'At last! I began to think you were slow-witted. Yes, you are to be her lover until I tell you not to be.'

'This is a most irregular arrangement you are suggesting, Monsieur,' said Nicolas, feeling better now that Duperray's anger had subsided.

'Why should you care about that? You love her – she told me that too. Your compliance with your own instincts will make three people content. What more could you wish for?'

Nicolas at last removed his hat and held it on his knees – an unconscious sign of the decreasing tension, perhaps, or even a belated act of courtesy.

'You are looking puzzled,' said Duperray, his manner urbane once more 'let me explain. My marriage is perfect in every way but one – Célestine and I have different tastes in bed. But we are sensible people and we indulge our tastes separately – and with discretion.'

'That is very civilised, Monsieur. I congratulate you.'

'Then it's all agreed?'

'If that is what you really want.'

'It is what I want and it is what Célestine wants. Therefore it is in your best interests to want the same. Otherwise the consequences would be too distressing to consider.'

'You may rely on me, Monsieur Duperray.'

'I knew that you'd see it my way if we talked things over rationally. One more thing, though – you earn a living in a trade notorious for spying through keyholes and bribing servants to obtain material so that you can print malicious lies about people of importance. I don't like that, not at any time, and especially not now that you have become a part of my own life. I suggest that you resign your job first thing in the morning.'

'I am happy to oblige you in every way I can, Monsieur Duperray, but you must realise that it is necessary for me to earn a living somehow and society journalism is the only way I have found.'

'Then you haven't looked very far.'

'I assure you I have. But I was never trained for any of the professions and I have no talent for business. My only asset is that I know everyone and can move about anywhere and be received on friendly terms.'

'Your father was lucky not to go to prison during the War,' said Duperray, 'I remember the scandal well. But that wasn't your fault. How much does it pay, this so-called journalism of yours?'

Nicolas told him, somewhat inflating the figure to preserve a shred of self-esteem.

'Is that all?' Duperray exclaimed 'why, those two employees of mine who escorted you here are paid that much and their only skill is in disposing of nuisances. You shall work for me.'

'I am grateful for the offer, but I must point out that I do not have the physique for their type of work.'

'I can see that. I suspect that you also lack the ruthlessness required to persuade a real nuisance to cease troubling me. What I have in mind is a continuation of your present work, but reporting to me alone, on the activities of certain people I shall designate from time to time – where they go, who they meet, who they sleep with, who

88

gives them money, who they give money to – do you follow my meaning?'

'Spying?' Nicolas exclaimed in dismay.

'Certainly not – just what you do at present, but with fewer people to interest you and with more detail about them. The results will not be published. Or if they are, then it will not be under your name. Agreed?'

'What salary do your have in mind?'

'Twice what you earn now.'

'There will also be certain expenses, of course.'

'Of course – the people in whom I am interested do not dine in cheap cafés or ride around on the Metro. But I do not expect to be cheated on necessary expenses. That would disappoint me greatly, to find my confidence abused.'

'You may rely on me. I accept the offer.'

'That's very intelligent of you. Now that everything is cleared up between us, I need detain you no longer. My men will drive you home. Oh, by the way, forget about this address – it's a secret little bolt-hole of mine.'

'A most pleasant one,' said Nicolas, smiling for the first time since he had been pushed over the threshold of the apartment, 'I suppose you use it for entertaining. The décor is admirable.'

'You like it? Perhaps I'll give it to you if I find myself a better place. If you're good at your job, that is.'

'Which of my jobs, Monsieur? It seems to me that you have given me two jobs.'

Duperray laughed.

'Work hard at both and you will rise in my favour.'

'I shall be extremely diligent in both, Monsieur.'

'I think I'm beginning to see more in you than I thought. Perhaps Célestine has made a good choice this time. We shall see. If we've made a mistake, there are ways of putting it right.'

'I can assure you that I much prefer a warm bed to a cold river.'

'Spoken like a man of good sense! Having been associated with newspapers you will no doubt remember the sensation a couple of years ago when some young man whose name escapes me was fished out of the St Martin canal?'

'I regret that I do not recall the incident – so many unfortunates seek an end to their troubles that way.'

'Yes, the only reason that one sticks in my memory is that a post mortem examination revealed that he had been brutally deprived of the two objects necessary to sustain a love affair.'

'How hideous!' said Nicolas dismally.

'Well, as I told you, Paris can be a dangerous place for careless young men. But you need fear no such danger – you are my employee now and therefore under my protection.'

'Thank you, Monsieur.'

'Now, if you will excuse me, your mention of a warm bed reminded me of something I must attend to.'

Nicolas stood up politely.

'Of course, Monsieur Duperray. I had already guessed that you were entertaining a friend here tonight. I hope that you will accept my apologies for interrupting you at so delicate a moment.'

'Not your fault,' said Duperray graciously, 'it's those two idiots outside – all muscle and no brains. Still, they have their uses. And, to tell you the truth, a short break has not come amiss. At my age it is necessary to preserve one's strength to make it last out – I'm sure you understand me.'

'Then the interruption was well-timed. I wish you good night, Monsieur, and *bon appétit*!'

'Ah, if you only knew!'

Nicolas smiled in his most charming way, his curiosity whetted.

'I cannot even guess what marvellous delights a man of your eminence can command. To me the friendship of

90

Madame Duperray is the highest achievement I can imagine – and that is something you take for granted. I am lost in amazement at what you must regard as appropriate to your pleasure, Monsieur.'

Flattery, as Nicolas had learned well, will usually obtain a reward. Duperray warmed to him.

'Come with me and just peep round the door before you leave. You will see a sight to remember – and on your way home you can imagine my enjoyment. Perhaps that will inspire you to do your duty towards Célestine tomorrow – you are meeting her tomorrow, aren't you?'

Nicolas nodded, no longer in the least surprised that Duperray knew so much of his arrangements – either he had men watching his wife or, as he claimed, they kept no secrets from each other – an unusual state of affairs between married people. He followed Duperray along a passage to another door and Duperray turned the knob and pushed it open silently, just sufficiently for them to see into the room beyond.

It was a large bedroom, of course, furnished in the modern style with a broad and low bed. The covers were thrown back in disarray and there lay two girls entwined. They were both extremely pretty, Nicolas observed, and neither was older than sixteen – seventeen at the most – both of them slender and small-breasted. They were playing at *soixante-neuf*, one girl on her back with her legs spread impossibly wide, the other above her with her thighs clamped lovingly about her friend's head. The game was not a silent one – the room was filled with little cries, gasps, murmurs and even giggles! Nicolas thought it utterly charming – a scene of almost pastoral innocence. The spread thighs of the girl underneath were towards the door and as the uppermost girl raised her head for a moment, Nicolas had a view of the wet and pink little entrance she was holding open with her hands – an entrance which Duperray no doubt would make use of before the game was finished, in addition to the other little entrance not in view, but evidently receiving delicate attention, for the girl who had raised her head was sighing loudly.

'The little darlings!' Duperray whispered to Nicolas, 'they have become impatient without me. I have been away too long, discussing business matters with you. I must join them and take part in their little game. Good-night, Monsieur Bruneau.'

Duperray's ruffians drove him home without a word – except when he got out of the car. The one who had spoken to him before took him by the arm in a grip that made him wince with pain and held him for a moment.

'The boss expects you to keep your mouth shut.'

'You may rely on it,' said Nicolas, trying to pull away, 'after all, I am in his employ now and I am a man of honour. I have given my word.'

The ruffian laughed most insultingly.

'You can be what you like as long as you keep your mouth shut,' he said, 'otherwise. . .'

By way of completing his threat he drew his forefinger across his throat.

When Madame Duperray arrived at Nicolas' apartment the next afternoon, the intervening events caused him to regard her in a somewhat different light. Of course, it was true that she had chosen him to be her lover because she recognised in him certain superior qualities – that had not changed. But he could no longer regard her as an ordinary married woman seeking affection and diversion away from her husband, as he had once assumed. In effect, she was the wife – and partner – of a man who had convincingly demonstrated his ability and willingness to arrange for the most unpleasant things to happen to anyone who annoyed him. During his visit earlier that day to the newspaper office to resign his position, Nicolas had looked back through the files to find the episode of the St Martin canal which Duperray had mentioned casually. And there it was – a young man of good family, taken from the murky water by the police and subsequently discovered to have been maimed, before drowning, in the manner Duperray had described. What he had been doing in so unlikely an area of Paris, what was the motive for the atrocity and who were the perpetrators – these things remained a mystery to the newspaper and to the authorities alike. Nicolas found the report very disturbing and it reinforced his belief that in dealing with Duperray one needed to be constantly on guard.

But for all that, as soon as Célestine was undressed and in his bed, all such considerations vanished from Nicolas' mind, for she was exceptionally beautiful and extremely well-disposed towards him. The feel of her breasts in his hands, the touch of her warm body pressed against him – this left no room in any man's mind for thoughts of caution or anything else except the enjoyment of the pleasures of love.

And such pleasures they were! Nicolas revelled in the beauties of her body and became intoxicated with sensation. In his heart he despised Duperray for taking half-grown girls as his playmates in preference to the sumptuous delight of making love to Célestine!

After the keenest of ecstasies and a gratifying tribute to Célestine's charms, vigorously deposited deep within her enchanting alcove, he lay beside her, holding her in his arms while he told her that he adored her. At that moment his feelings towards Duperray had been mellowed somewhat by the immense satisfaction of what he and Célestine had just experienced together. Although Duperray had forced an unexpected bargain upon him, Nicolas felt that perhaps after all he had the best of it. Not only had he acquired Célestine as a mistress – he was being paid to love her! A most remarkable position, for any young man!

Even when she rolled over onto her face and presented

to him her superb back and delicious bottom, his mood of exhilaration did not change. He stroked those round and satin-skinned cheeks and caressed with his finger-tip the little nodule between them. If that was what pleased her most, then so be it! Célestine gratified meant Duperray pleased – and Duperray pleased meant that Nicolas could advance in his service – away from the daily problem of making a living as a journalist into some position, perhaps slightly illegal, where he could live as befitted one of his background and abilities.

And besides, the first time he had done it to her that way, it had been an extremely interesting experience. So why not?

'Oh, Nicolas,' Célestine sighed 'yes, chéri!'

MARIE-CLAIRE AND HER CRYSTAL ROOM

In the large and elegant apartment of Maire-Claire Fénéon there was a room into which no one but she ever went. Her personal maid cleaned it, of course, when the room was not in use, but that did not count – and none of the other servants was allowed inside. The room was next to Marie-Claire's bedroom, where one would expect in the usual way of things to find a dressing-room. To some extent it was that, perhaps, but with a difference.

Marie-Claire had caused the walls of her secret room to be completely covered with mirror glass – even the inside of the doors and the long windows that opened onto the balcony overlooking the Avenue George V. And, naturally, the ceiling too. To be in this room was to be inside a glass cube, cut off from any contact with the world. The only item of furniture in it was a low and broad divan which stood in the centre of the floor – the floor at least was parquet, though without the usual carpets or rugs – and this divan was upholstered in pale yellow damask and piled with large cushions covered in apricot-coloured silk.

This was Marie-Claire's 'crystal room', though she never uttered its name aloud and spoke of it to no one, not even her closest friends, for to her it was a sacred place, an oratory, one might say, in which the prayers were not in words.

When the mirrored shutters to the balcony were closed

and the glass-covered door from the bedroom fast shut behind her, Marie-Claire was in a universe of her own making, where her whim was law. It was here that her private dreams became real, and her dreams were, to say the least, stirring creations. For example, at such places of entertainment as the Casino de Paris and the Lido, where she had been taken by admirers assiduously paying court to so desirable an heiress as herself, she had been greatly impressed by the verve of the young women who passed across the stage or stood as a living backdrop for the main performers. To be one of them, what a delicious fantasy! To wear those skimpy and outrageous costumes and stand there for all to see! To show off one's body so freely – what bliss! The dream could be made to come true in Marie-Claire's crystal room, for behind one glass-panelled wall was a capacious wardrobe stocked with brightly-coloured creations bought from theatrical costumiers.

When she was in this mood, Marie-Claire would make up her face with exquisite care and then ransack the wardrobe to dress herself in the most outré style. A head-dress of tall white ostrich plumes, high-heeled silver shoes, fishnet stockings held halfway up her thighs by garters of ruched lace! Long white gloves stretching from her finger-tips to above her elbows! As for the rest, the expanse of gleaming skin between garters and head-dress, for that she wore no more than a tiny silver-coloured cache-sexe over the hair between her legs. Her breasts were bare, as she had seen the show-girls on the stage, and so apparelled she would strut gracefully to and fro across the room, humming a song, her arms outstretched, wholly beguiled by the effect in the mirrored walls. The glass on opposing walls threw her reflection back and forth in diminishing perspective, so that to Marie-Claire's delighted eyes it seemed that she was the leader of an endless chorus-line, each of the others following her slightest movement and gesture as she stepped and swayed. The sight was so magnificent that it almost took her breath away. Who else could produce, direct, choreograph and star in her own show whenever she chose?

On another day she would dress in skin-tight trousers of gold lamé that only just covered her hips and left her bare to a finger's breadth above the little patch of hair that guarded her secret place. From the sides, great lengths of the same material draped to her ankles and up again to be held over her forearms as she spread them wide in a ballet gesture. Two or three gold chains about her neck, looping down almost to her exposed breasts, on her head a close-fitting cap on which was mounted a single plume half a metre tall! Or more daring still when the mood took her, a huge Spanish mantilla of black lace, held at the back of her head by an ivory comb and draped elegantly round her in swirling folds. With that she wore nothing at all but black shoes – this being a spectacle she had once seen at the Folies Bergère – and when she swayed across the room, the gleam of her skin through the lace gave her a pleasure so intense that she became giddy after a while and was compelled to rest a little on the divan until she recovered. Even in that position she had the joy of seeing herself reflected full-length in the mirrored ceiling, pink and white through the lace. This vision of beauty she could contemplate in calm delight for a long time without becoming in the least bored.

On some visits to the crystal room her mood was different again and not inclined towards the stage. Then she would dress as if for going out visiting or shopping – a little cloche hat perhaps of peacock blue and a matching summer coat, fine silk stockings, shoes of black shiny patent leather – the effect was incredibly chic. She left the coat unfastened and as she moved about the room, choosing a pair of gloves to wear or checking the contents of her hand-bag, she caught tantalising glimpses of herself in the mirrors that made her utter tiny sighs of admiration

– for beneath the elegant coat she had put on nothing at all. A movement of her arm would cause the coat to part a little and let a pink-tipped breast peep briefly out. A half-turn would give a fleeting view of a lovely sleek thigh above a stocking-top. Marie-Claire was too much a connoisseur of herself to look fully in these moments – she behaved naturally, setting her hat at the best angle, twisting to check that her stockings were immaculate – teasing herself with sudden sly glimpses of some perfect part of herself. She could play this game of dressing to go out for at least an hour without tiring of it.

However prolonged or bizarre her games, they were in the end only preludes to her real intention – the adoration of her own naked body. Ah, the slow care and the controlled emotion as she approached this central act of worship! She stood before a mirrored wall, regarding herself full-face and at full-length, her gaze calm and steady as she removed one by one whatever garments she was wearing, until the glory of her beloved body was revealed to her eyes.

Time had no meaning while she observed in turn each part of herself from head to toe. Her hair, deep brown with just a hint of chestnut, so expertly cut to shape her head with soft waves and just show the lobes of her little ears! She ran her finger-tips over it very lightly to feel its soft texture without disarraying it in the slightest. How well its colour set off the flawless skin of her face and complemented her velvet-brown eyes under the high-arching and meticulously plucked eyebrows! But that face – classically beautiful, the cheek-bones slightly high and the nose firm and very straight! Her mouth was a poem in its expressiveness – the slightly pouting lips, painted a vibrant red, parting to show her small white teeth. It was a face to fall in love with at first sight, and many a man had done so, though none with the impassioned devotion of Marie-Claire herself.

Her neck was faultless, not short, not long – and not a

shadow or a trace of even the most microscopic of lines anywhere on it. The milky white luminescence of pearls or the bright cold fire of diamonds – both looked marvellously right against the skin of that neck. As for her shoulders – if an artist had carved a statue with shoulders like hers, Jean-Antoine Houdon at his best perhaps, or Antonio Canova at his most inspired – the work would have been instantly hailed a masterpiece.

In Marie-Claire's private opinion the much-admired sculpture by Canova of the Emperor Napoleon's sister Pauline had shoulders not as fine as her own. But then, presumably the artist was copying his model faithfully and if Pauline Bonaparte's shoulders were not as good as Marie-Claire's that was not Canova's fault.

At this point Marie-Claire crossed her arms over her breasts so that she could caress those gorgeous shoulders of hers. What good fortune that the fashion was for evening frocks that left the shoulders bare and so afforded her the opportunity to show off so dazzling a sight in restaurants and theatres around Paris! She took care not to look directly at her hands, for if there was any part of her less than perfect, she felt it was her hands. They were excellently well cared-for, of course – her maid manicured them and massaged them at least three times a week. The nails were coloured the same shade of bright red as her toe-nails – and yet, by the standards of beauty set by the rest of her, the hands failed a little. The fingers were just a little too short, the palms just a little too broad. Once it had vexed her, now she simply ignored this tiny flaw.

By turning herself a little to the side and looking over one shoulder Marie-Claire could see, in the mirror on the wall behind her, the elegance of her own back. It was long and narrow, curving in at her waist, then swelling out again to define her hips and the flawless globes of her bottom. She contemplated this dorsal aspect of herself with awed respect, as well she might, for she was certain that not even the ancient Greek statues of goddesses in the Louvre Museum could be compared with it. If only she could arrange matters so that, at the time when the Museum was empty, she could convey herself and a long mirror into it – and then strip and compare her own back reflected in the mirror with the view of those over-rated statues!

When she had stroked her shoulders and viewed her elegant back to her great content, Marie-Claire uncrossed her slender arms and gazed in rapture at her breasts. The sight of them never failed to bring a small sigh of deepest approval to her lips. They were such miracles of symmetry in their delicate size and shape that she could find no words adequate to praise them. The gentle pink of their tiny buds – the effect against her satiny skin was completely captivating. No man who had ever been so greatly privileged as to see those breasts could prevent his hands from reaching out to touch them.

For Marie-Claire herself, it was equally impossible not to let her hands stray towards them as she stood before the mirror in profound appreciation of them. Her finger-tips slid very tenderly over the blush-pink tips, as lightly as a butterfly's kiss. Even so light a contact caused her to tremble with sheer pleasure. The little buds blushed an even more enticing shade – if that were possible – and stood up firmly.

How could anyone describe the beauty of Marie-Claire's belly? To say that it was smooth and most exquisitely curved, with a round navel set in it like a dimple – the words say nothing! Only the eye of a true connoisseur could appreciate the subtle beauty of that belly – and such a connoisseur would be inspired by his own admiration of it to trace its gentle curve with trembling finger-tips, as did Marie-Claire at this moment. At its base, where her impeccably rounded thighs joined, there was a small patch of deep brown hair, neatly trimmed into the shape of a heart! And what very superior hair it was – as silky as the hair on her head and with just the same hint of chestnut in it. Marie-Claire's fingers played in it, delighting in its adorable texture, until at last they touched the soft little lips it covered. She moved her feet apart so that she could see the reflection of the pink folds her fingers had opened like the petals of a superb rose. By now she was too giddy with pleasure to do more than stare at what she had revealed, as if hypnotised. She was in the same state – dare one say it? – as a female saint in mystical contemplation of the divine!

When the giddiness passed, or rather, when Marie-Claire became sufficiently accustomed to its hold on her to be able to walk without stumbling, she made her way with slow care to the divan in the centre of the crystal room and reposed herself upon it. She lay on her back on the apricot-coloured silk, her legs drawn up, her ankles crossed, thighs flat to the cushions and knees pointing in opposite directions. This was the position which gave her the best possible view in the mirror above her of the enchanting secret place between her legs. She stared with love and reverence, her heart beating a little faster. The spread of her thighs had parted the lips between them to give a view of the pink interior, a piquant contrast with the deep brown of the soft hair. The effect was ravishing!

At last, when her hands found their way to her thighs and then towards the shrine of love between them, it must not be supposed that she did anything so banal as to pleasure herself with her fingers. No doubt maid-servants relieved themselves with work-coarsened fingers in their lonely beds at night, perhaps even women of good family who were too plain to find themselves a man satisfied themselves in that manner. But that was by no means the same thing. That was mere self-gratification, of no more significance than blowing one's nose.

The difference was that Marie-Claire was engaged at this moment upon an act of worship, nothing less! The loving touch of her fingers on the tiny swollen bud within those pouting lips was a heartfelt tribute to her astonishing beauty.

Naturally, there could be nothing hurried or strained in such adoration – that would be completely out of place. Her fingers proceeded at a stately pace, Marie-Claire's eyes intent the whole time upon the reflection above her of her own naked body. Sighs of devotion escaped her as she observed the image of herself responding to her own veneration with little tremors of passion. Soon, very soon, she murmured over and over again '*Je t'aime. . .je t'aime. . .*' When the little tremors became long rhythmic shudders heralding the approach of the natural culmination of her act of homage to herself, Marie-Claire was not tempted to close her eyes and let herself be swept away by sensation. She stared fixedly at the glass ceiling, adoring every centimetre of the body she observed, until she saw her own back arch off the divan at the moment when her body accepted her true worship and bestowed its climactic benediction upon her.

In the profound peace which followed that benediction, she lay with her hands resting at her sides, still rapt in contemplation of her own enchanting beauty in the glass. At this time it seemed to her that she was in a state of grace – though no priest of the Church would have agreed with her on that! Sometimes she meditated for so long on her own loveliness that she dozed off into the sweetest of sleep. At other times, the memory of the blessing she had just received was so rapturous that her hands crept slowly back between her parted thighs to repeat her devotions.

It should not be supposed from this that Marie-Claire had no place in her life or thoughts for men and their love. On the contrary, she had a long-established intention to acquire some day a suitable husband. But *suitable* – that was where the problem lay.

A man must be of a certain status in society to merit even preliminary consideration as a candidate – that went without saying. After that, he must be extremely handsome, for Marie-Claire could not tolerate anything less than that in close proximity to her own beauty. Even her servants were chosen as much for their appearance as for their usefulness in the household.

Alas for Marie-Claire – so many of the best young Frenchmen had lost their lives in the War defending the sacred homeland that her area of choice had become sadly restricted. Admirers she had in abundance, being an heiress as well as beautiful. Of her admirers, the most eligible were permitted to become her lovers – the final test of their suitability! But it was then that her fastidiousness proved to be so insuperable a hurdle – so far not one of the candidates had measured up to the standards she set.

There was one of whom she had been very fond – but when he removed his clothes in her bedroom Marie-Claire could hardly suppress her gasp of horror. There was a thick pelt of black hair on his chest – and on his arms and legs! Even on his back! He resembled a bear, she thought in repulsion. Because of her affection for him, which ended at that moment, she allowed him to continue his love-making, but only in the dark. Throughout it her eyes were tightly closed and her teeth clenched, and although he was skilful enough to bring her to the moment of climax three times that night, she never invited him to her home again.

More often she found that the men who were acceptable in all other ways proved to be inadequate in the most important way of all – they failed to appreciate the immensity of the honour conferred upon them by being allowed to see and touch her magnificent body! Indeed, they were in general so crassly insensitive as to mistake her for an ordinarily beautiful woman whose charms existed merely to inflame their own sensual appetites! They did not adore her body as they should – they *used* it. They squashed her superb little breasts out of shape under their weight when they penetrated her, they beat their bellies in the coarsest of manners against hers in their uncontrolled thrusting. At such times of disappointment and disillusion Marie-Claire recoiled in disgust. It was obvious to her that such men would not have been able to tell the difference if they had been mounted on her maid – or for that matter, on a street-woman. Marie-Claire's body was to them no more than a warm mattress with an accomodating hole!

By good fortune, soon after her thirtieth birthday, Marie-Claire became acquainted with a man only a year older than herself who seemed in every way to meet her exacting requirements. His name was Giles St Amand Mont-Royal and the circumstances in which they first met were much in his favour. In Marie-Claire's grand apartment there were displayed four portraits of her, as was perhaps to be expected, by different artists of whose style she approved. The earliest was a head and shoulders of her aged nineteen, in an evening frock which showed off those splendid shoulders of hers. The most recent was by a woman painter who called herself Monique Chabrol, to whose studio in Auteil Marie-Claire had been taken by her good friend Jeanne Verney. Monique and Jeanne were related by marriage, Marie-Claire learned – Jeanne's sister had been the wife of Alexandre St Amand Mont-Royal who, alas, had been killed in the War. Monique was his sister and Chabrol was her professional name as an artist.

Monique insisted on painting a full-length nude portrait of Marie-Claire. It depicted her lying on a chaise-longue, the merest corner of a Chantilly lace shawl just concealing that most precious part of her where her thighs joined. But for the fact that the finished picture would hang in her salon and be viewed by all visitors to her home, Marie-Claire would have dispensed with the shawl and displayed the rich brown of her heart-shaped little thatch. Throughout the sittings Monique Chabrol showed great and unexpected tenderness of approach to her subject and talked to Marie-Claire with as much affection as if they had been friends for years. At each session she took such care to arrange Marie-Claire's body and limbs in the pose she wanted that her lingering touch was almost a caress. From these indications Marie-Claire formed the conclusion that Monique was a lover of women and wondered what her own response would be if those sensitive fingers touched in an open invitation to love. But they never did and when the picture was completed Marie-Claire understood that Monique's appreciation of her beauty was aesthetic rather than sensual. For the picture was a great masterpiece, in Marie-Claire's judgment – it showed her not merely as beautiful but resplendent! The skin tones were sumptuous, the proportions breath-taking in their subtlety – and in the eyes there was a look of reverie such as Marie-Claire had when she was alone in her crystal room. If Monique had understood her so very exactly, it could only be because she herself in some measure shared Marie-Claire's own self-love.

Monique's younger brother, Giles St Amand Mont-Royal, had seen the portrait in only its half-finished state on a visit to her, but he had asked to be allowed to meet the sitter at once. Monique told him to be patient – her work was far too important to risk having the sittings disrupted in any way. After the painting was finished, she introduced him to Marie-Claire, who found him charming. He had the same glossy dark hair as his sister and the same widely-spaced eyes – though unlike hers, his were a marvellous shade of grey! His clothes were impeccable and the body inside them gave the impression of being robust and athletic. His compliments were well-expressed, somehow giving an appearance of being frank and courteous at the same time.

The first impressions being satisfactory, Marie-Claire accepted his invitation to dine with him. That too was a success, for he proved to be an amusing companion. From then on he arranged a variety of entertainments for her, each pleasing in its different way. He took her riding in the Bois de Boulogne, making sure that they had the best mounts available. He was a magnificent horseman and Marie-Claire, looking utterly radiant in a new riding outfit, was secretly proud to be seen with him – an emotion which surprised her by its novelty! Giles' taste in theatre was for romantic comedy, which Marie-Claire also preferred to the tediousness of serious drama. He took her to only the best restaurants and was extremely exacting in his choice of food and wines – yet he ate and drank sparingly – and this won her approval, for nothing ruins a beautiful body more quickly than over-indulgence at the table.

By talking privately to Monique and to Jeanne Verney, Marie-Claire learned of some of Giles' previous liaisons – and what she heard was entirely to his credit. He had at some time in the past been the lover of the Vicomtesse de la Vergne, Monique related – a woman renowned and respected for her fastidious insistence on maintaining the manners and style of the pre-War era. More recently, according to Jeanne, he had been the intimate friend of Gabrielle de Michoux, the most refined person Marie-Claire had ever met. It was common knowledge among her woman friends that Gabrielle had her maid try out potential lovers for her in order to determine whether their style was adequate to please Gabrielle herself.

Thus reassured, Marie-Claire allowed Giles to become her lover – and he proved to be eminently acceptable. A surreptitious inspection of his body when he first undressed in her presence showed her that he was handsomely proportioned, broad of chest and narrow of waist. The hair on his chest was sparse and soft to the touch, not a bear's pelt to scrub against her delicate breasts. His male part was elegant, neither too large nor too small.

Above all else, it was Giles' manner of making love which won Marie-Claire's heart. He was strong and virile and very much in command of the situation – yet very considerate. When the caress of his hands and lips raised her to a near-pinnacle of delight, he did *not* roll onto her as if she were a living mattress. On their first occasion together he turned her gently onto her side, facing him, put pillows behind her to support her, then moved close and with great tenderness of touch slid his stiff worshipper into her sanctuary. In this way he could continue his reverent caress of her breasts while he paid homage to her – and more importantly, Marie-Claire could look down at her own marvellous body as it was worshipped. His passionate emission seemed to her like a prayer before an altar – a prayer which was answered instantly by her own graceful climax of ecstasy.

As their liaison developed, she learned that he had other postures of adoration. Sometimes he would sit her on the side of the bed in order to kneel between her parted legs and make his offering while contemplating the temple of love into which he had been admitted. Or again, he would lie on his back and seat her over his loins, her body fully open to his view – and to hers – while his trembling part was deep within her. Though satisfactory from the point of view of being able to see her own body in its gentle throes of passion, Marie-Claire did not much favour this position because it required her to make the movements that precipitated the delicious crisis – and her firm opinion was that Giles should do all that was necessary – for herself it was enough to be the inspiration for him. As soon as Giles understood this, he again showed how infinitely obliging he was by demonstrating other and more gratifying possibilities.

Their love affair was so perfect in every way that Marie-Claire eventually began to give careful consideration to the question of revealing to Giles her closely-guarded secret – the crystal room. By this time they had been lovers for three months and all her experience of him was entirely pleasing. In all that time there had not been sounded one false note, there had been not one awkward moment. She was starting to believe that in Giles she had found the love of a lifetime – a man completely in tune with herself, in bed and out of bed. He had not indicated in any way that he was thinking of a more permanent relationship than the one they were enjoying – but then, a man of his unquestioned virtues and qualities could choose almost any woman he wanted when he decided to settle down and take a wife – a thought which brought a tiny frown to her face.

On the other hand, he was so attentive and he assured her so very often of his devotion to her that Marie-Claire became convinced that in his heart a certain love for her must be dawning. A little more encouragement and he ought to be ready to ask her to marry him. Whether she would accept him or not was not finally clear to her, but the probability was that she would, to strengthen her hold on him, if no more than that.

Before that moment of decision was reached, she felt it to be essential to know what his reaction would be on being made aware of her secret. Even if they married, she had no intention of abandoning the pleasures of the crystal room – on the contrary, what she most desired was to have her admirer share those pleasures with her. She debated with herself for a long time – and who can blame her – no one had ever been into that room with her. To allow another person into it was like inviting him into her very soul. He might misunderstand, he might laugh, he might recoil in shock – any unfavourable response would destroy the marvellous liaison they already enjoyed.

Yet for all her misgivings, the day arrived when she made the decision and received Giles in her crystal room. He thought that her maid would usher him, as usual, into her salon, but they passed that door. Could it be her bedroom into which he was being shown? That would be most unusual and, to say the least, irregular. But that too they passed. The maid tapped at the door through which he had never stepped during his many visits to Marie-Claire's apartment. Giles entered and stared about him in blank astonishment as the door was closed behind him. He was in a room entirely lined with mirrors! His own reflection stared open-mouthed at him from the far wall.

Marie-Claire had spent half the day dressing for this momentous visit, trying on all sorts of costumes from her capacious wardrobe, discarding this and that, simple and bizarre. In the end she settled for simplicity – that is to say, for theatrical simplicity. On her head was a tall white toque which covered her hair completely and was draped around with strings of pearls. Around her neck was her diamond necklace, the stones glittering against her flawless skin. A long white skirt was held tightly around her waist by a broad belt of shiny black leather – a skirt with a train nearly a metre long and split up the front so that as she took a step forward to hold out her hand in greeting to Giles almost the whole length of one satin-skinned thigh was revealed. Between skirt and toque, apart from her diamonds, she wore nothing. She had found it impossible to bring herself to conceal her pretty breasts at this supreme moment in her life.

As for Giles, after that one instant of open-mouthed astonishment, he rose magnificently to the occasion. He went down on one knee as he took Marie-Claire's hand and kissed it, as if he were a courtier in the old days saluting a queen. He raised his eyes to her naked breasts and then to her face and told her that she was divine and that he loved her to distraction.

A smile of satisfaction and triumph revealed Marie-Claire's white little teeth. Giles had understood her! As soon as he had entered the crystal room and caught sight of her in her dramatic finery he had in an instant grasped her secret and he rejoiced in this new knowledge of her soul. She had chosen well – Giles was the man with whom she would spend her life in unending adoration of her beauty.

A bottle of champagne and two glasses stood ready by the divan. Marie-Claire herself poured the wine and handed a glass to her lover as he rose from his knee. They drank a toast to each other, then to their future together, then to their incomparable happiness – for both were entirely convinced that no two other people had ever tasted such profound delight together in the entire history of the world. It was a scene so charged with emotion that Giles' voice trembled and Marie-Claire almost wept tears of joy – except that to do so would have spoilt her careful make-up.

'Do you truly adore me, Giles?' she asked.

'I adore you as no woman has ever been adored – I swear it.'

'Then show me how you express your adoration.'

Giles set down his glass and removed her belt with reverence, sighing a little in pleasure as he uncovered her perfect dimple of a navel. He undid the fastening of her long white skirt and let it slide down her legs to the floor. He picked her up as if she were a sacred icon, kissed the pink tips of her breasts and laid her on the silk cushioned divan. In the mirrored ceiling Marie-Claire watched his dark-haired head moving lovingly over her breasts as he kissed them a hundred times and she felt the onset of that familiar dizziness of delight. Then his lips were on her soft belly and the hot tip of his tongue at its entrancing dimple. How he made the pleasure last! What delicacy, what finesse! Eventually, in the mirror above her, she watched him remove her pretty little silver-coloured cache-sexe and she felt his lips kiss the heart-shaped patch of deep-brown hair that clothed her mound of love.

He too must be naked – she permitted him to cease his attentions to her body for the short time it took him to strip. He lay beside her on the divan, murmuring words of love so fraught with emotion as to be almost incoherent. Marie-Claire's hand took hold of the hard stem of flesh standing from between his thighs. Not only was it pleasing to look at, it was a pleasure to hold it and feel its strength and resilience – and the throb of life in it. Yet her firm clasp was less for her own physical enjoyment as for the emotion of pride she experienced in laying claim to it for herself alone.

The many previous passages of love between Marie-Claire and Giles had been marvellously satisfactory but they were not to be compared with the sublimity of this grand occasion in her crystal room. In both her mind and his the importance of what was happening transcended mere love-making to become an act of pure worship. With all the imagination and savoir-faire expected of him, Giles devoted his attentions to her with incomparable though controlled enthusiasm.

At the supreme moment when she desired him to enter her so that she could watch her body while he served it, Giles demonstrated an understanding of her needs and an inventiveness which thrilled her almost to the climax of passion. With a strong sweep of his arms he lifted her from the divan and set her on her feet facing the nearest mirrored wall and only a few hands-breadths away from it. She gazed at her own beautiful naked body and was struck with love for Giles at this moment for affording her so marvellous a sight.

She felt his hands caress down her legs from hips to ankles, as he knelt behind her and showered kisses on the exquisite cheeks of her bottom. He eased her feet apart until he could move forward between them, sitting down on his haunches, until his knees touched the mirror. Marie-Claire's heart sang with joy as she realised his intention was to give her a full view of herself as he made love to her. She waited for his hands, on her hips again, urging her slowly downwards until she was kneeling over his folded legs, her back to him. His mouth pressed against her shoulders and the nape of her neck while she was still intent on her own glorious image, then slowly she looked lower in the glass to see the upright part which was poised to make its entrance.

One of Giles' hands moved lightly to her belly, the other was between her legs, parting the soft lips beneath the heart-shaped brown fur. The touch on her belly urged her downwards again until she felt the smooth head of his upright part within her portal. It was more than Marie-Claire could bear, so exquisite was this moment! Her eyes blinked as ecstasy coursed through her, but she forced them open to view the tremors of her body as it yielded to unbelievable pleasure.

Giles paused, supporting her by the hips, only the head of his quivering part within her. He too was surprised and delighted by her flattering response. He waited in patience until the climactic pleasure had completed itself and Marie-Claire whispered '*Je t'aime!*' Whether she meant that she loved him or loved herself was not a question that even occurred to him.

She was ready to renew that sublime experience in a very short time, stimulated as she was by the sight of her own body with the head of his stiff part lodged in it. She let herself sink fully onto Giles' lap and his patience was rewarded by the soft clasp of her body on his distended member. Over her shoulder he stared at the junction of their parts in the mirror, his eyes full of wonder. Without words – for the banality of speech would have been unthinkable in this meeting of souls – Giles took her wrists and spread her arms out sideways, then showed her how to lean forward until her palms were flat against the cool glass. This lifted her weight a little off his thighs and gave him the freedom of movement he wanted – a slow and rhythmic movement that sent tremors of pleasure through her belly.

For some moments he caressed her matchless breasts, but his hands returned to her hips, so that nothing of her reflection was obscured from his gaze – and hers. His grasp became a little firmer as his thrusts became longer and more probing. Marie-Claire, looking away from her divine self in the mirror and at the reflection of his face, saw that his gaze was fixed upon her heart-shaped treasure into which he was plunged. The delicacy of those open pink lips almost sent her into another spasm of ecstasy – and below them she could see a centimetre or two of the hard stem that transfixed her.

Marie-Claire was in Paradise! Everything was supremely right – the shared adoration of her body – for at last she truly felt that she was sharing that incredible delight with another person. Oh, if these sublime sensations could last forever! But such intensity of emotion, however carefully nurtured, is necessarily of brief duration. Even so, the tremendous thought in Marie-Claire's mind, in so far as she was capable of holding a thought in her mind at that instant – was that this heavenly experience could be repeated again and again, day after day, with dear marvellous Giles.

Deep within her Marie-Claire felt with absolute certainty that what was about to happen to her would be the supreme moment of her life so far – a hitherto unconquered peak which ordinary women could not even see on the distant horizon. The certainty welled up with the divine sensations Giles was provoking in her. As she stared at the mirror image of the tender part of herself from which those incredible sensations emanated, her velvet-brown eyes were round with amazement. To be able to view the erect worshipper in her secret shrine, engaged upon his devotions at the very altar of love itself. . . the climactic ecstasy which swept through her then was totally unlike the gentle waves of gratification she had known all her life. This was a torrent, a tidal wave that engulfed in an instant her awareness of herself. Her eyes were shut tight, her mouth wide open in a piercing scream of unselfconscious delight!

The violence of her release brought on Giles' crisis at once. His strong part pulsed and leaped within Marie-

Claire's shaking body and he poured out his offering. His eyes remained open, and over her heaving shoulder his grey eyes stared fixedly in love and adoration at the reflection of his own handsome face.

CHRISTOPHE AT THE SEASIDE

The twin domes of the Carlton Hotel at Cannes are modelled, it is said, on the superb white breasts of a famous *cocotte* of the last century – one for whose charms men of the highest rank entered into expensive competition with each other. The thought of so graceful a tribute to a woman who had been the inspiration for much pleasure and anguish was pleasing to Christophe as he strolled in the hot sunshine of a beautiful morning, admiring the many delicious women to be seen along the Croisette. Nor was the admiration entirely on his part – he was an extremely good-looking young man and elegantly attired in a striped blazer, white trousers and a straw boater – the very epitome of casual style!

Naturally, before the War no one of any consequence would have been seen on the Côte d'Azur in the summer months. From the end of April the hotels closed down and the Casino was deserted. The season for visiting the southern coast was winter and it went without saying that during the summer months everyone went north to the fashionable resorts of Deauville and Le Touquet. However, all that changed a few years after the end of the War when rich Americans, much given to world travel to escape the cultural and culinary wilderness of their own country, discovered the Mediterranean coast of France. Even then, to go there in the heat of summer would have been regarded in Paris as no more than another eccentricity of an inexplicable nation, but for the whims of women of style. Suddenly Chanel and Schiaparelli were designing the most ravishing and provocative beach clothes and showing them in their Paris boutiques. Every woman of taste wanted to wear these delicious and colourful little garments – it was almost like appearing naked in public to stroll about wearing these tiny shorts or these flimsily transparent beach pyjamas! In consequence, since it is women who rule the world from behind their husbands, within a year or two it was tremendously chic to holiday on the Côte d'Azur in the height of summer.

On his first visit to Cannes Christophe adored all that he saw. The women were so delicious in vivid tunics that displayed their bare brown legs to mid-thigh! And those in flimsy silk beach pyjamas with flaring trousers – marvellous! And in white linen trousers cut tight to display the curves of an elegant rump – exquisite!

Down by the edge of the sea itself, soaking in the sun, the most beautiful women imaginable revealed themselves in no more than skin-tight bathing costumes of thin woollen jersey in the brightest colours, cut to leave their backs bare to below the waist and their legs bare to within a few centimetres of the join of their thighs. What ravishing sights for a young man of Christophe's amorous disposition! He drank in the sight of these beautiful creatures walking barefoot in the sand, the tender buds of their breasts clearly visible through their clinging bathing costumes. The susceptibility of Christophe's nature guaranteed that his male part stood stiffly to attention in his white trousers for the whole length of his perambulation along the sea-shore.

Of course, the beautiful women who had so great an effect upon him were invariably surrounded by admirers, confident young men displaying expanses of sun-tanned skin and muscle. Or older men with receding hair and paunches, who had the appearance of being extremely rich – and to these the young beauties seemed even more attentive than to the young men. Christophe shrugged at the sight – that was the way of the world. His problem was that he was not rich.

Until quite recently he had believed himself to be on the right route to success in his uncle's business, especially when his elegant aunt had admitted him to her intimate friendship. How could such influence fail to guide him by acceptable stages to the very top of the business, with all the accompanying rewards? Alas, Jeanne Verney had ceased to visit Christophe's apartment when she became pregnant. That was the first cruel blow of fate – the second and equally devastating blow came when Verney's business interests were sold and Christophe's employment was terminated. Jeanne, gracious as always, had insisted that Christophe was given a sum of money by way of recompense for his disappointed hopes – a sum sufficient to maintain him for perhaps a year in reasonable style.

'What will you do now, Christophe?' she asked, 'stay in Paris or return to your mother in Lyon?'

'I shall go on a vacation while I think about my future,' he replied, no particular plan in his head.

'Excellent idea. Go to Cannes – I have friends there who will be pleased to see you.'

And there it was! Christophe travelled south on the Blue Train and engaged a room at the Carlton, it being early enough in the summer for that august establishment to be able to accomodate him for a few days. Needless to say, it was most imprudent of him to be staying in so expensive a hotel when the financial resources at his disposal were limited, but one lesson Christophe had learned from his time in Paris was that appearances mattered a great deal. What impression would he make on anyone of consequence if it became known that he was staying in a *pension* in a back-street? The idea was impossible.

On the Blue Train rushing south through the night Christophe had been unable to sleep. So it came about that, at the age of twenty-five, he took stock of himself

117

for the first time in his life. As all the world knows, at three o'clock in the morning, a person alone finds himself face to face with the truth about himself, however displeasing it may be. Christophe knew that he would win no great prizes for his intellectual abilities, but what of it? Intellectuals were those who wrote boring books and lived in the discomfort of the Left Bank. He knew from his service in Verney's business enterprise that he would never become a giant of commerce by his own efforts, for he lacked the application it demanded. The learned professions were closed to him – that had been made obvious at school.

Yet Christophe had other virtues to offer. He was handsome, he wore clothes well, he had an endless fund of small-talk, he was attractive to women of all ages – and, at the top of the list of his qualities, he was an accomplished lover in bed, thanks to the devotion of his aunt Jeanne. He intended to use all these abilities to gain a position of acceptance in society. In short, his plan was to find and marry a rich woman, young and beautiful if possible, older than himself and plain if need be, so long as she was really rich and sufficiently in love with him to let him spend her money freely.

From Jeanne Christophe had an introduction to several friends of hers in Cannes, but he was in no hurry to pursue the matter. There was so much to see, so much to enjoy. Besides, he did not not wish to appear too eager to present himself to any of Jeanne's friends, as that might create a bad impression. Jeanne's friends were all people of importance, that went without saying. One of them even had a title, though there were no real titles in a Republic. To adorn one's name in this way, Christophe considered, indicated a certain nostalgia for the past and was the mark of a snob.

On his second day at the Carlton, he was taking breakfast on the terrace at about ten o'clock and reading the newspaper, when the course of his life changed in a dramatic manner. The lateness of the hour was due to the fact that he had been at the Casino the night before, observing the roulette players and taking stock of the general situation. Naturally, all the rich women there had escorts.

'M'sieu Larousse?' a respectful voice asked.

Christophe looked up from his newspaper to see, in considerable surprise, a tall man in dove-grey livery, a peaked hat tucked neatly under his arm, standing by his table.

'Who are you?'

'I am chauffeur to the Vicomtesse de la Vergne, M'sieu.'

That was the name of the titled lady which Jeanne had given Christophe.

'Madame la Vicomtesse presents her compliments,' the chauffeur said politely. 'She requests the pleasure of your company at lunch today.'

'That is most kind of her,' said Christophe. 'At what time?'

'I am to say, M'sieu, that as the Villa is at some distance from the town, Madame's car is at your disposal. I shall be outside the hotel to take you there whenever you are ready.'

'Very well. I shall finish my breakfast and accompany you shortly.'

'Thank you, M'sieu,' said the chauffeur, bowing as if Christophe had conferred an immense favour on him.

What thoughts passed through Christophe's mind as he folded his newspaper and poured another cup of coffee! Not that he wanted the coffee, but it gave him an excuse to remain at the table and think. A car with a uniformed chauffeur, no less! She began to be interesting, this so-called Vicomtesse. Yet how had she become aware that Christophe was in Cannes? Simple – Jeanne must have talked to her by telephone to tell her that he would be presenting himself in due course. He was confident that

Jeanne had recommended him highly to her friend, since she was still very affectionate towards him even though they had ceased to be lovers over a year ago.

Ah – but how had the Vicomtesse known to which hotel to send her messenger? Christophe hadn't known himself where he would be staying when he left Paris. He had got off the train and told a taxi driver to take him to the best hotel. Evidently the chauffeur had been told to enquire for a Monsieur Larousse at the two or three best hotels. Thank God, Christophe thought, that he had been inspired to make the expensive gesture and had not put up at some cheap *pension*!

Twenty minutes later, when he strolled out of the hotel with careful nonchalance, the sight of the car waiting for him almost made his mouth fall open in astonishment. It was a superb open tourer, the paintwork a gleaming maroon colour, the chrome polished to a degree that made it quite dazzling in the sun. The chauffeur stood at attention by his marvellous machine, his face impassive, and opened the rear door for Christophe – a door on which there appeared a small coat of arms! Christophe seated himself on the soft leather, tapped his straw boater firmly on his head at a jaunty angle and prepared to enjoy the ride.

The Villa was indeed at some distance from the town, as the chauffeur had told him. The route lay in the direction of Nice for some kilometres, then it wound upwards away from the sea. When their destination eventually came into sight it proved to be a large white house perched on a hillside, half-hidden from the road by a white-washed wall. Wrought-iron gates were swung open by a man whom, from his clothes, Christophe took to be a gardener. The long beautiful car entered and passed through a well-tended garden to halt outside the main entrance to the house.

The door opened as if his arrival had been anticipated to the second and a maid conducted him across a marble-floored entrance hall and a large salon stunningly decorated and furnished in the very latest style – all etched glass and sycamore – and out onto a broad paved terrace overlooking a swimming-pool. He stood still for a moment in the bright sunshine, his heart pounding for joy. Everything he had seen so far smelled of money, from the glass sculpture in the entrance hall to the ruinously expensive furnishings of the salon – and especially the people out by the swimming pool. He counted nine – five women and four men – four of them splashing about and laughing in the pool and the others sitting or lying in the sun on long reclining chairs of wood painted white and scarlet.

A young woman wearing the most elegant swimming costume Christophe had ever seen turned her head to stare calmly at him as he descended the broad stone steps from the terrace to the pool level. He guessed her age at twenty-one or two and thought that she might have Spanish or Italian blood, her hair was so dark and her skin so delicately olive-hued. She was so incredibly beautiful that Christophe fell in love with her instantly. He prayed silently to God to let this dazzling creature be the Vicomtesse de la Vergne and unmarried, so that he could marry her himself and live in conjugal bliss with her for the rest of his life. He would have crossed himself to reinforce his prayer, but that would have drawn her attention to him in a way that could not be regarded as stylish.

Naturally, she was not the Vicomtesse. The maid led Christophe to the opposite side of the pool, where a lady in pink reclined on a long chair. Her clothes were exquisite – beach pyjamas of chiffon so delicate that it was almost transparent – two strands of pearls about her neck and slave-bangles on the wrists of her bare sunbrowned arms. But when she raised her head, under the broad brim of her sunhat Christophe encountered a fifty-year-old face, square-jawed and with a little too much make-up.

'You must be Christophe Larousse,' she said, extending

her hand to be kissed, 'I'm so pleased you could drop in for lunch.'

Christophe gave her his most charming smile as he removed his hat and bowed gracefully over her hand, a hand on which there were diamond rings on all four fingers.

'It was kind of you to invite me.'

'I've heard so much about you from Jeanne,' she said with a roguish smile, 'sit here beside me – Marie, bring cold drinks at once.'

She introduced him to the man and woman sitting close by her and while their names meant nothing to Christophe, their expensive casual clothes did. He set himself to make a good impression on his hostess and her friends. He succeeded so well that the shoulder strap of the woman's costume started slipping from her sun-tanned left shoulder in a manner that threatened to expose a breast! Each time she adjusted it she made sure that Christophe's attention was caught by the movement. The man, her husband, ignored her antics and continued to pay court to the Vicomtesse, who permitted a tiny frown to appear on her features the third or fourth time the strap slipped and suggested to Christophe that he might like to refresh himself after his journey by a swim. She dismissed his objection that he had brought nothing with him by waving vaguely towards a long and single-storey building to one side of the pool and telling him that he would find whatever he needed there.

He felt that it was best to do as she said, so as to retain her goodwill. Certainly she wanted him away from the pretty lady having problems with her shoulder strap! Perhaps she feared for his morals if he were exposed to so much temptation!

The single storey building had a veranda its whole length. Inside it was divided into half a dozen small rooms for changing, comfortably furnished and fully equipped with towels, bathing caps for the women and swimming costumes for both sexes. Christophe found a garment to fit him and undressed. Outside again, he stood for an instant on the edge of the pool and dived in, aiming for the life-size figure of a mermaid he could see on the tiles under the clear water.

One of the people now playing in the water was the black-haired girl with whom he had fallen in love. He surfaced beside her, slicked his hair back and smiled.

'My name is Christophe,' he introduced himself.

She returned his smile, then swam to the side and turned, one elbow on the edge to support herself while she looked at him.

'I am Nicolette Santana. You are very white-skinned still – have you just arrived?'

'Only yesterday. There is something I must tell you.'

'What?'

'I love you.'

'You don't know me,' she said, smiling at his impertinence.

'I have seen you – that is enough.'

'Do you usually fall in love so easily?'

'This is only the second time in my life.'

'And the first?'

'That is finished. Will you marry me, Nicolette?'

He said it light-heartedly, but with a touch of sincerity that no woman could miss. Her response was to laugh, but in her amusement Christophe thought he detected a hint of encouragement.

Seen at close quarters, Nicolette was so beautiful that Christophe's heart almost stopped beating. Her glossy hair, as blue-black as a raven's wing, was parted in the middle over an oval face of exquisite proportions, in which large eyes shone like polished jet-stones. Around her neck hung a simple strand of white coral beads – the same colour as her swimming costume, which was of the finest jersey wool and clung wetly to her perfect breasts, emphasising their full roundness.

All this Christophe noted avidly, as a man takes inventory of an apartment in which he intends to live for a long time. In his mind there was no doubt whatsoever – this marvellous girl was going to be his wife and he would never be unfaithful to her throughout his entire life. Unable to resist the impulse, he reached out under the water and ran his hand down her hip in a gesture that said everything that was in his heart. Before anyone could observe his action, before even Nicolette could respond, he said, 'Think about it,' and pushed off from the side of the pool with his feet, to swim at a furious speed across and back. But by the time he had returned, she had climbed out of the water and was sunning herself. After a moment's thought, Christophe returned to the side of the Vicomtesse. The woman who had been troubled by her shoulder strap smiled prettily at him and studied quite openly the bulge under his wet swimsuit, but this time the Vicomtesse chose to ignore her.

'You have made the acquaintance of my niece,' she said brightly, 'a pretty girl – my sister's child.'

'Your niece?' said Christophe in surprise. 'Forgive me, but I see no family resemblance, Madame. You are fair-skinned, while she is dark.'

'Quite right! My sister married a Spanish nobleman. They were both lost on the *Lusitania*, coming back from America, murdered by the Boche!'

'Dreadful!'

'Fortunately the child was not with them on the voyage. I have made it my duty to give her a home and to educate her.'

'You are a very good-hearted person,' said Christophe. 'She is fortunate in having your protection and being brought up in France instead of Spain.'

'What a perceptive young man you are!' the Vicomtesse exclaimed. 'Her father's family wanted to take her after the tragedy, of course, but I refused to listen to any such plan. Of course, her name is not Nicolette – her father insisted that she be called Isobel, but I soon changed that when she came to live with me.'

'You are no great admirer of the Spanish?' Christophe asked.

'Their cuisine is barbarous and their entertainments boring beyond words! Now, you'd better go and change – lunch will be in half an hour.'

In one of the changing rooms Christophe stripped off his borrowed swimsuit and threw it into a container placed there for that purpose. Before he had time to do any more the door opened – he had not bothered to turn the key in the lock – and there stood the Vicomtesse, from whom he had parted only a minute before. He reached for a towel from the neat stack to cover those parts of his body not normally displayed to mere acquaintances, but the Vicomtesse waved her hand in a gesture of indifference as she lowered herself into a chair.

'I have no regard for the idiocies of bourgeois modesty,' she announced. 'Tell me about my dear friend Jeanne – is she happy and well? And that frightful husband of hers – I have heard that he has become insane and has been locked away.'

'The report that has reached you is somewhat exaggerated, Madame,' said Christophe with an ironic smile, 'it is true that Monsieur Verney has suffered a breakdown of his health and requires constant care, but . . .'

'You must call me Régine,' the Vicomtesse interrupted. 'You are a very handsome young man, Christophe. How old are you?'

'Twenty-five,' he answered.

He made no attempt to conceal any part of himself as he rubbed himself dry with the towel – not a lengthy process, of course, for the hot sun had dried his skin by the side of the pool. But he thought it sensible to make a lengthy process of it. He stood facing the Vicomtesse while he raised each arm in turn to rub underneath, then sideways to her while he put a foot up on a white wooden stool and pretended to dry down his thigh and leg. In effect, he was posing for his hostess. He talked lightly of friends in Paris, bringing a smile to her lips, though whether that was the result of his words or the view of his body she was afforded – who could say?

Certainly she demonstrated her contempt for 'bourgeois morality' by studying him closely. Christophe had no misgivings on that account – he knew that he scored highly, being broad of shoulder and narrow of hip. His male appendage, to which the Vicomtesse seemed to be devoting considerable attention, was of pleasing proportions – he had been assured of that by several women of the world in whose experience he had every confidence. In the expert use of it he had been tutored by Jeanne Verney herself, though whether the Vicomtesse had been told that he did not know.

There came a time when he could hardly continue the pretence of drying himself further. His clothes were over the back of a chair close to where the Vicomtesse was sitting. He set aside the towel and reached for his shirt – and she also reached out, to cup his dependents in her palm.

'You have a good body, Christophe,' she said warmly. 'How long were you Jeanne's lover?'

'That is a question I cannot answer with propriety,' he said with a smile. 'You must ask her.'

'I did. She told me that you made her pregnant – a very inconsiderate thing to do.'

'A tragedy,' said Christophe, 'I lost her as a result.'

The Vicomtesse's other hand took possession of his fast-growing stem.

'Did you love her truly, Christophe?'

'I adored her,' he replied with complete honesty. 'My heart was broken when we ceased to be lovers.'

He was wondering if this strange and plain woman had it in mind to invite him to make love to her here in the changing room – and what his response would be if she

126

did. She had brought his accoutrement to full stand by her manipulation, but he felt no desire for her – only for the beautiful niece. Perhaps Madame la Vicomtesse read the expression in his eyes, for her broad face split in a grin.

'Not now,' she said, 'the others will be in to change in a moment. I may despise the common restrictions but I am a strong upholder of the social conventions.'

'And a strong upholder of something else at this moment, Régine.'

She laughed at that, ran her hand lightly up and down his stiff part a few times, then released it with a sigh.

'Dress yourself,' she said, 'we will talk again after lunch.'

She swept out of the little room in a flurry of pink chiffon. Christophe pulled his shirt over his head, hoping furiously that his tumescence would subside before he rejoined the other guests, but knowing from all past experience that it probably would not. As his head emerged through the neck of the shirt, he gasped in astonishment to see Nicolette, still in her tight white swimming costume, looking in through the door her aunt had left ajar – looking at the lower half of his body, still uncovered – looking at his stiff part sticking out like a baton!

Her eyes met his and she pouted at him.

'Nicolette!' he exclaimed, his appurtenance bounding at the sight of her.

He rushed to the door, not knowing what he would do – pull her inside the room and press her to him, tear off her costume . . . but when he put his head round the door she had disappeared into another of the changing rooms and coming along the corridor towards him was the lady who had experienced such difficulties with her shoulder strap. Christophe pulled his head back and closed the door quickly – and turned the key for safety!

Lunch was an enjoyable experience. Everyone was dressed elegantly, the food was delicious and the conversation lively. Afterwards everyone seemed to drift away, until Christophe found himself alone on the terrace. How could he find out which was Nicolette's room? The easiest way seemed to him to ask a servant and, as if on cue, out came the maid who had opened the door to him on his first arrival. But before he had time to make his enquiry, she informed him that Madame would like a few words with him. He shrugged and followed the maid.

The bedroom of the Vicomtesse, to which he was conducted, was large and modern in the most spectacular way. At one end the bed, fully two metres wide, stood in a niche lined with panelling of light beige wood, into which mother-of-pearl had been inlaid in a geometric pattern. At the other end of the room were arm chairs and a long sofa, all upholstered in beige silk. The lady herself, her ample body concealed in a feather-trimmed wrapper of floating chiffon the colour of newly-roasted coffee, sat on one of the chairs reading a letter, for which purpose she wore reading-glasses with tortoise-shell frames. On Christophe's entrance she put aside letter and reading-glasses and smiled at him fondly.

The room impressed Christophe as deeply as the other parts of the Villa he had seen. He knew himself to be in the presence of formidable wealth – wealth used with good taste, for not only did she surround herself with expensive and beautiful objects, but also with fascinating people, to judge from the conversation over lunch. In Christophe's opinion, his hostess was worthy of respect, perhaps even admiration.

She waved him to a chair with a bejewelled hand.

'I like an hour's rest at this time of the day,' she informed him, 'but today I do not feel like sleeping. I need to be amused – I hope you don't mind talking to me, though I'm sure you'd rather be out by the pool with the other young people.'

Christophe assured her that he was well content to be

received by her in so informal a setting. The use of the word 'informal' caused her to glance at the bed.

'To you I must seem a foolish old woman,' she said, 'but I find young people utterly irresistible – the good-looking ones, that is to say. I find it impossible to deny them whatever they want.'

She had said 'young people', Christophe noted, not just young *men*. Perhaps her tastes embraced both sexes. He raised his eyes from the heavy diamond rings on her hand to gaze with as much good grace as he could muster into her pudgy face.

'I am at your service, Régine,' he said, taking the plunge boldly.

'Of course you are,' she replied, 'every handsome young man I've ever met with no money of his own has been willing to oblige me. I have come to expect it.'

'You are very candid,' said Christophe, not at all pleased by the direction of the conversation.

'I can afford to be.'

She stood for a moment to slip off her coffee-coloured peignoir and sat down again, completely naked except for her high-heeled shoes.

'Look at *me*, not at my diamonds,' she commanded, 'what do you see?'

Christophe looked carefully. The Vicomtesse's neck was short and thick, her breasts were heavy, her belly plump almost to the point of being fat. Her thighs were certainly thick and the thin hair between them was so fresh a brown that it was surely dyed.

'I see a woman,' he answered her question.

'I cannot dispute that,' she said, 'but you see a woman who has lived a little too well for a little too long, to the detriment of the beautiful body of her youth. Does the sight repel you, my dear young friend? You are surely used to the sight of pretty young women with firm breasts and flat bellies.'

'I am not repelled.'

'They all say that,' she remarked. 'And for obvious reasons they are not looking at *these*,' – she put her hands under her big and sagging breasts to lift them up – 'they are looking at the rings on my hands instead. When they kiss my nipples, in their minds they are kissing my diamonds.'

Christophe was experiencing a distinct feeling of uneasiness at the outspoken manner of the Vicomtesse. Her philosophy was her own affair and he had no desire to listen to it. Besides, it was unjust – he had asked for nothing, not even the invitation to lunch. She had sent her car for him. Why should he be subjected to this display of middle-aged cynicism?

'When they put their hand between my legs, these charming and obliging young men,' she continued, 'they are in reality stroking one of my fur coats – the sable, perhaps, or the Russian fox – I have a wardrobe full of such coats.'

'Really, Madame!' Christophe exclaimed in a sudden flash of irritation.

'Worst of all,' she went on, as if unaware of his presence, 'when they finally bring themselves to push their stiff little things in *here*,' and she parted her thighs widely so that Christophe saw the thick and pouting lips within the tinted brown hair, 'they are only making love to my bank account. Do you believe that a bank account feels ecstasy when a young man squirts his little spoonful into it?'

Christophe felt that it was intolerable to be insulted in this way. He saw two courses of action that would put an end to it. The most obvious was to walk out and leave the woman to her melancholy victory. The other was to play her at her own game and beat her at it. He got up swiftly and took two steps towards her, seized her flabby breasts and tugged sharply, so that she winced.

'You seem well acquainted with the ways of gigolos, Madame,' he sneered. 'If you had been a little less self-indulgent in the past, perhaps you would have less cause for self-pity now.'

'How dare you speak to me like that!' she exclaimed.

'I speak as I wish,' he replied sharply, tugging at her breasts again, her further expostulations cut off by a little shriek.

'You said that you wished to be amused,' he reminded her, 'then you insult me as if I were a male prostitute you had summoned to give you a quick thrill to occupy a dull afternoon. Your behaviour towards me has been disgraceful and I shall see to it that everyone hears about it.'

'No!' she said quickly, 'I am sorry – it was wrong of me, perhaps. But you let me touch you in the changing room. You let me think that you would not deny me.'

'Courtesy prevented me from taking exception to your uninvited familiarity,' he said, putting anger into his tone. 'But this! You summon me here and bare your body to me as a prelude to a tirade of abuse! It is too much!'

'Forgive me, I implore you,' the Vicomtesse gasped, her face red.

'Your actions have been unforgivable,' he declared and squeezed her breasts so hard that she whimpered. 'Was it your intention to order me to make love to you and then throw me a few francs afterwards? If you were a man I would beat you senseless and leave you sprawled here on the floor.'

Something in his words brought a quick glint into her eyes.

'If I were a man I should not be here naked with your hands on my breasts,' she pointed out.

That was obvious enough, but it left Christophe without words for a moment. Before he could recover, the Vicomtesse slid her jewelled hand up his thighs and began to unbutton his trousers.

'You looked at me and said that you saw a woman,' she said huskily, 'perhaps you spoke truthfully – perhaps you looked at me and saw a woman and not a pile of gold coins. I must know!'

She pulled his male part out into the light of day and, astonished, Christophe became aware at that moment that it was stiff. In spite of the disagreeable nature of their conversation, the sight of her naked body had brought about the usual effect, even though her body had held no particular interest for him – or so he thought. The truth was, though he had never admitted it to himself, that he was so susceptible to women that any pair of breasts, no matter how drooping, could bring him to a state of readiness. That was not to say he threw himself with abandon at every women who gave him to understand that she would not discourage his advances. Certainly he had no intention of allowing the Vicomtesse to lure him into an intimate encounter – she had injured his masculine pride by her words.

'This is too much!' he exclaimed in irritation as she rolled his upright staff between her palms.

He released her breasts to grasp her wrists and pull her hands away. But the Vicomtesse did not wish to surrender her possession of this cherished part so quickly! In the struggle that ensued, she was dragged to the very edge of her chair, then off it altogether, so that she fell sideways to the floor. Even then she retained her double-handed grip and Christophe, to save himself from anguish or damage, was forced to fall to his knees beside her. Still she held on in her ridiculous frenzy of possession, but he was the stronger and at last he prised her hands loose. The Vicomtesse rolled over face down, perhaps to conceal her expression of angry frustration, the tantrum of a spoiled child from whom a favourite toy has been taken. She lay sprawled on the rug and, she being naked but for her shoes, Christophe saw her bottom for the first time.

It infuriated him, that bottom! The rest of her body, which she had displayed uninvited to him during her tirade, was pudgy and unattractive – it spoke all too plainly of years of over-indulgence at the table and lack of exercise. But her bottom! It had escaped the ravages of time and could have been that of a twenty-year-old girl. The cheeks were gracefully rounded, the skin smooth and unblemished! And the colour – a delicate ivory! The golden tan of her legs terminated just below those beautiful cheeks, the tan of her back above them, and this piebald effect seemed to accentuate at the same time the luscious tenderness of her rump and to make it seem somehow more naked than the rest of her.

Christophe found it intolerable that this harpy who expected him to perform on command should be blessed with a bottom that would be the envy of most women half her age. At that moment he hated her and wanted to punish her presumption. Without a thought, directed only by the furious emotion that filled his heart, he straddled her back, facing her feet, and held her pinned facedown to the floor with his weight while he slapped with both hands at the pretty cheeks that had annoyed him so much.

'Stop that! You're hurting me!' the Vicomtesse shrieked, wriggling beneath him to try to escape.

Christophe was deaf to her pleas. He took a fierce revenge for the humiliation to which she had subjected him – and also perhaps for the injustice, as he perceived it, that this middle-aged woman should be so extremely rich and a handsome young man like himself should be without the means to sustain the style to which he felt himself to be entitled. His disappointments in Paris, the uncertainty of his future – he purged all these emotions from his heart by smacking the Vicomtesse's rump until his hands were stinging. By then the ivory cheeks were bright red and the Vicomtesse was sobbing miserably.

After relieving his emotions Christophe felt remarkably light-hearted. His male appendage hang passive and limp outside his trousers as if he had just made love to the Vicomtesse! The change in his mood was so great that he was even well-disposed towards the Vicomtesse herself, she having been the means by which he had attained his happy state of emotional balance.

Her bottom looked painfully red. He touched it lightly and she winced. Something should be done about it, Christophe thought benignly, or she will take her meals standing up for the next day or two. With this in mind, he adjusted his trousers and searched around the room for some means of alleviating her distress. On the dressing-table he discovered a large jar of cold cream – most delicately scented when he removed the lid and sniffed at the contents. With this he returned to the victim of his wrath – still quietly sobbing – and seated himself cross-legged on the rug beside her.

'This will take away the pain,' he said.

He scooped generous quantities of the expensive cream from the jar, one for each cheek, and smoothed it gently into her skin, using both palms. She uttered a little squeal at the first touch, then fell silent as he continued and the emollient cream cooled her fiery bottom.

'Is that better, Madame?' he enquired.

'Yes, it helps. Please continue,' she answered faintly.

He smeared on another double scoop and resumed his light massage. It seemed to him so peaceful, sitting there on the floor, rubbing cold cream into the Vicomtesse's bottom – peaceful and pleasant. Certainly it was a very sensible way to pass an afternoon – much better than baking oneself alive out in the sun by the swimming pool. Nicolette was out there, perhaps, but there was little opportunity of talking to her in private with so many guests at the Villa. Now if it had been *her* bottom he was massaging . . . the thought caused him to sigh gently. With an image of Nicolette in his mind, he stroked the Vicomtesse's rump dreamily, not even noticing when her legs eased themselves apart on the rug, not even aware that his hands were caressing slowly into the divide between the cheeks he had assailed so brutally only five minutes before.

His palms were gliding over warm and supple skin, but his finger-tips were touching short curls, yet still he paid no attention. More cream – the jar was almost empty now – right down between those superb cheeks this time. How pleasant an object was a woman's bottom, he thought as if in a reverie, how delicious to handle! With what genius the good Lord had fashioned the female body in all its parts!

His fingers were in the curls, smoothing cold cream into the soft lips of flesh between Madame's legs. A few moments later Christophe realised with a start that he had the finger-tips of both hands inside those lips! The slipperiness he felt was no longer cold cream but the dew of her arousal! He gasped at the thought, almost stopped, then told himself that to abandon a woman in this condition, after bringing her to it, was out of the question. To leave any woman, Vicomtesse or not, at this point would be the act of a person without manners or style.

Now that he was fully aware of what he was doing, Christophe began to employ the skills he had learned from Jeanne Verney when she and he had been lovers. The most vivid memories of his adult life were of the long afternoons in his little apartment in the rue Vavin, when Jeanne lay naked on his bed and he caressed her elegant breasts and belly, finding out how far she could be aroused before she pulled him on top of her to finish her off. Together they had played this game endlessly and sometimes they had both misjudged the level of her excitement and she had reached a gasping and trembling climax before he could penetrate her wet fleece.

He had been with many women since his affaire with Jeanne had come to an end, but on nights when he slept alone those golden afternoons sometimes returned in his dreams and he awoke erect and disconsolate. It seemed strange to him now that one of Jeanne's friends, the plain and middle-aged Vicomtesse, was enjoying the benefit of those adventures into sensuality.

Of the Vicomtesse's present enjoyment there could be no possible doubt. Her diamond-laden fingers were scrabbling in the rug and she was moaning in delight to his expert touch between her legs. Earlier on, when she had been seated on the chair, she had deliberately parted her thighs to display to him the thick and pouting lips within her brown curls. It had been no more than a glimpse, he staring in surprise at her expression of cynicism, but his close attention to those parts now as she lay face-down on the floor, made it obvious to him that the entrance between the Vicomtesse's thighs was more than usually generous in dimension. Whether that was by nature or by diligent use over many years, who could say? But what in most women of his acquaintance was a shrine of love was, in her case, a veritable cathedral! It would be an extraordinary man who could fill that, he considered, for the eight fingers of his two hands fitted into it without undue difficulty. That being so, he was able to use them all to excite in her such shudders of passion that her feet drummed on the floor until her high-heeled shoes fell off!

Christophe may not have been particularly intelligent, but he was not a fool – no young man in his position could afford to be that. The lady he was pleasuring in so curious a manner was very rich – of that he had seen ample evidence. The private parts to which he was attending might well be the key to his own future happiness and prosperity. With so formidable a possibility to motivate him, Christophe employed all his skill to make the occasion one she would remember with gratitude.

Over a period of perhaps a quarter of an hour his artful fingers brought her a dozen times to the very brink of climactic release, then hesitated delicately, so that she never quite reached the zenith her entire body was straining to achieve. Her moans had long ceased – all that she was capable of was a harsh and heavy breathing through her wide open mouth. Her broad back was shiny with perspiration and she had broken one finger-nail by clawing at the rug.

At last Christophe judged that it was enough. His fingers fluttered wetly within her gaping portal as he applied the final stimulation to her distended bud. The result was dramatic in the extreme – every muscle in her body contracted. Her shoulder blades stood out from her back, the sinews stood out on her neck, her legs stiffened as if they were made of iron and her feet pointed straight downwards. She gave voice to a long wailing shriek as the spasms of ecstasy gripped her and shook her. She was bouncing up and down on her belly and thrashing about with her arms as if she were swimming in her own pool.

'Stupendous!' Christophe said aloud in awe at the effect he had produced.

She lay exhausted for some time after that, as was to be expected. Christophe sat quietly on the floor, his hands resting on his knees, waiting for her to recover.

'Christophe,' she whispered eventually, 'I adore you.'

Of course, it would have been courteous, to put it no higher, to respond with the same words, but that was further than Christophe was prepared to go. His silence passed unnoticed and the Vicomtesse continued, her voice regaining a little strength.

'I did not understand what a very special person you are, my dear,' she said, 'I took you for just another good-looking young man trying to make his fortune with his penis. You were right to beat me – I said dreadful things to you. Forgive me, I implore you.'

'We understand each other at last,' he answered mildly, 'I am glad of it.'

What a stupid woman, he was thinking – all I did was to smack her backside until she wept and then give her a slow feel! And for that she falls in love with me! Thanks be to the divine Providence that set this woman's brains between her legs instead of in her head!

Without getting up from the rug, the Vicomtesse shuffled herself round until her head was towards Christophe. She reached up to lay her hands over his hands.

'Say that I am forgiven,' she pleaded, 'say my name!'

'Régine – we are good friends now, I hope. Let there be no talk of forgiveness. To understand all is to forgive all.'

'Say it again!' she breathed, her eyes on his face in abject devotion.

'Régine.'

She shuffled a little closer until her head was between his knees. Her hands left his and touched his trouser buttons timidly, a look of entreaty in her brown eyes.

'Only if I have your permission,' she murmured, 'but it means so much to me now, my dear Christophe, so very much!'

He made no objection this time as she undid his buttons slowly and extracted his male part. It was full-grown again, naturally – no man can handle a woman as he had handled her without becoming aroused himself. Arousal demands relief, and for this reason he let her have her way, not because he had any desire to become her lover.

Régine fondled him with great respect.

'He is very sturdy,' she said in a hushed voice, 'yet so regal! Yes, he is a king – a king of love!'

To his amazement she slipped one of her diamond rings off a finger and crowned his upright part with it.

'See!' she exclaimed, 'a crown for His Majesty!'

Christophe was tempted to burst into laughter at her ludicrous behaviour but he succeeded in controlling himself. Only half an hour ago his male part had been a mere object of utility to Régine, to be employed for her own pleasure and paid for at whatever rate she decided. Now it had become a royal sceptre, to be adorned with diamonds. That was real progress! Before he could think of any suitable response – not that there was any need of one, for Régine hardly ever listened to what other people

138

were saying – she bowed her head as if in homage and the tip of her tongue swept the diamond ring from its place of honour. Her lips touched His Majesty's crimson head in a respectful kiss. Not content with so simple an act of obeisance, her painted lips opened and at once His Majesty was deep inside her mouth!

Christophe uttered a little sigh of pleasure as her hot and wet tongue applied itself to his most sensitive part. He closed his eyes and instead of the top of Régine's head he conjured up in his mind's eye a vision of Nicolette as he had seen her at the swimming pool. The buds of her beautiful breasts were prominent through her white bathing costume and she was smiling at him in love and desire. He reached out to touch her and his fingers encountered bare flesh – that of Régine's shoulder, of course, but he dismissed that thought from his mind and imagined that it was Nicolette's graceful shoulder under his hand.

His ruse was so successful – and Régine's ministrations so ardent – that it seemed only moments before enormous sensations overwhelmed him and he discharged his passion into her hot mouth. His finger-nails dug into her shoulder fiercely as ecstasy shook him, but she made no complaint.

When it was over she looked up into his face almost shyly.

'Thank you, Christophe, thank you,' she said, 'did I please you a little?'

He nodded, surprised by her humble tone.

'I'm so glad,' she said, 'I've only done that for a man once before in my life, when I was very young, but it seemed the right thing to do to show you my affection for you. I know that you cannot love me or feel for me a tenth of what I feel for you, but I am sure that we can be very close friends.'

The diamond ring with which she had crowned his pride

lay on the rug between them. Régine picked it up, but did not replace it on her finger.

'His Majesty does not wish to wear his crown any more,' she said playfully. 'See -- his head is drooping! Take the ring, Christophe, as a memento of this day.'

'No!' he said sharply, 'I am not to be bought with trinkets. You forget yourself, Madame!'

In truth, he was playing for higher stakes than a ring, valuable or not. If he allowed Régine to believe that she could purchase his favours, as she had doubtlessly purchased young men's favours many times before, then he would be nothing more than an employee.

Her pudgy face creased as if she were about to weep again.

'Christophe – please!' she stammered. 'It was not meant as an insult, I assure you! Just a small present between good friends, that's all.'

'Then I will take your suggestion in the spirit in which it was intended,' he replied, maintaining an aloof manner, 'but I will not take the ring. Put it back on your finger.'

'Yes, Christophe,' she said hastily. 'Please don't call me Madame – it makes you sound so distant and I can't bear that. I want to be close to you, my dear.'

'Régine, you have much to learn about me if we are to be good friends.'

'Yes, Christophe,' she said, smiling at hearing him say her name.

After dinner that evening Régine decided that all her guests should accompany her to the Casino. This journey was not in the open touring car – at least not for Madame herself, Christophe and two others – but in a tall and luxurious limousine, complete with a flexible tube through which Régine could convey her instructions, should there be any, to the chauffeur in front behind his glass panel.

The gaming room was full when they arrived, the men very distinguished in gleaming white shirt-fronts and black

140

tail coats, the ladies – ah, the elegance of their evening frocks and the bright glitter of their jewels! Somewhat to Christophe's dismay hemlines had begun to lengthen a year or so earlier, in response to heaven alone knew what, and by this summer they were at ankle-length. He thought it sad that beautiful women should deprive admirers the sight of their graceful legs in sheer silk stockings – but who could argue against the dictates of fashion? Putting that consideration aside, he felt himself very much at home in this society, proud of his handsome face and good figure. Régine was magnificent in a close-cut frock of the Napoleonic style, bare-armed, the waist-line high up under her bosom, so that the exquisite work of Schiaparelli concealed a certain ungainliness, and the jewels around her neck, wrists and fingers diverted attention from too close consideration of any shortcoming in her physical appearance.

While Régine busied herself at one of the roulette tables, exchanging greetings with everyone – for she knew everyone and they knew her – Christophe tried to attach himself to Nicolette but was thwarted in his attempt by the young man who had elected himself her escort for the evening. He therefore decided to observe everything around him with care – the gambling, the people, the style and, above all else, the women who were gambling. One needed to know the proper way to do things – how to bet, how to win with restrained enthusiasm, how to lose with good grace.

There was a moment when the lively chatter in the salon was hushed, the chanting of the croupiers' '*Rien ne va plus*' was stilled and only the tiny clicks of a ball round a roulette wheel broke the silence as all eyes turned towards the entrance. Christophe turned to see what had caused so great an effect – surely some person of immense importance! There, advancing into the gaming room was a man in his middle years, well-dressed and confident, but in no way distinguished in Christophe's eyes – except

that on each arm he had a small and beautiful woman –
and the two women were identical! Christophe stared
openly at the vivacious twins, whose large dark eyes shone
in their exquisite faces under nearly black hair worn in a
fringe over broad foreheads. The diamonds they both
wore were fabulous in size and in quantity, making Régine
appear almost unadorned by comparison.

The lull in conversation and activity lasted while the
newcomers paraded in grand style the length of the salon
to the end table, then all turned back to their own absor-
bing pursuits, the croupiers took up their polite admonitions and the wheels spun again.

'But who are they!' Christophe asked Régine as she
slid a large plaque onto the red.

'Who?' she retorted, as if she had not noticed the trio.

'The people who just came in.'

'Oh, those! Don't you know? They call themselves the
Dolly sisters – they are entertainers. They used to appear
in the Paris music-halls. They are foreigners, of course –
Hungarian, I understand – probably gypsies, if the truth
were known.'

'I have heard of them, but I have never seen them on
stage.'

'You never will now, not while they have a rich friend
to take care of them.'

'The gentleman with them, you mean. Who is he?'

'An American, of course, what else? His name is
Gordon Selfridge and he is said to own a large shop in
London.'

'How extraordinary!' said Christophe, lost in
admiration.

Régine made it very clear that she did not share that
generous emotion.

'He rarely brings them here,' she said coldly, 'they stay
in Monte Carlo – it's very raffish there, you know. But
perhaps he wanted a change of wheel tonight to change
his luck.'

To Christophe it appeared that, with the delicious twins at his side, Monsieur Selfridge had no need to trouble himself with the banalities of luck.

'They are both his little friends, do you suppose, the Mesdemoiselles Dolly?' he asked, eager to pursue his enquiries even though he was aware that Régine disapproved of the subject. On what grounds he was uncertain, for she had professed herself to be contemptuous of what she called 'bourgeois morality' and by her actions earlier that day had proved it.

'It is said that Rosy, whichever one that is, is his particular friend,' Régine answered, 'the other one is named Jenny. But it is my own view that the two of them are interchangeable.'

Great God! Christophe thought in awe, interpreting her words according to his own disposition – to have two beautiful women in one's bed at the same time!

The splendour of so lavish a feast of warm mouths, soft breasts and silky thighs dazzled his senses and caused to tremble within his evening trousers that part of him to which Régine had paid homage a few hours ago. His interest in roulette, such as it was, and his interest in the people in the salon, evaporated like a thin morning mist when the sun rises. He had eyes for nothing but the two gorgeous women at the distant table. It was not long before Régine noticed his mood. In the hour that they had been in the Casino she had won a few thousand francs and lost them again – not that she was there to gamble, only to be seen in society.

'You are bored with all this,' she said, with a gesture that embraced the salon, 'And so am I. There are other ways to amuse ourselves. Come – we'll leave the others here and send the car back for them.'

In the back of the beautiful limousine Régine sat upright and serene, a strand of diamonds woven into her hair, a costly fur wrap about her bare shoulders, a three-strand diamond necklace around her neck – all this of immense interest to Christophe, far more than the interest he took in her person. Between the passenger compartment of the vehicle and the chauffeur up front there was a thick glass panel, over which a blind of oyster coloured silk had been lowered. Outside it was dark, though not deserted, inside the limousine Christophe felt that he and Madame la Vicomtesse were isolated in a small and luxurious world of their own. If only it had been Nicolette with whom he was making this journey from the town to the Villa!

'You may amuse me,' said Régine, turning to look fully at him, 'but with care – I do not wish to arrive bedraggled, to be an object of derision to the servants.'

Christophe nodded acknowledgment and knelt on the thickly carpeted floor of the limousine to turn up her skirt over her knees. Her legs, clad in the most delicate silk stockings he had ever seen, were not at all bad, he decided on close inspection. Her ankles and calves were well-shaped, in fact, and it was only above the knees that there was rather too much flesh for elegance. But her thighs were warm to his hands, he noted as he turned the Schiaparelli creation further back – and warm thighs are a great encouragement to a man.

Régine raised her broad bottom from the seat so that he could turn her frock right up to her waist. Her stockings were held up by suspenders attached to a corselet, designed to compress her over-abundant belly. Christophe expected therefore to encounter lace-trimmed knickers, but to his surprise she wore no such garment that evening and, when her thighs moved apart on the seat, there was the tuft of bright brown hair he had viewed that afternoon. He stroked it cautiously, not at all sure whether it was her own hair tinted or a tiny wig made to fit over her mound.

'You may continue,' Régine said softly.

He seated himself beside her to let his fingers glide over the object of his attentions. For a time he teased the pouting lips, then reached underneath to gain admission. She was already moist within and as his fingers parted the inner lips and touched her swollen bud, she sighed pleasurably. He stimulated her quickly, intent on pleasing her but wanting it to be over as soon as possible. Régine responded swiftly, her belly and loins rolling rhythmically to press against his fingers – for by this time he had all four of them embedded inside her.

'Oh!' she exclaimed, 'something incredibly nice is about to happen!'

Christophe put the palm of his other hand flat on her bare belly to squeeze in time with his rubbing movements. In another moment or two Régine began to squirm, her legs as wide apart as they would go. Christophe, staring at her face, saw her eyes bulge suddenly, her mouth gape open – and then she was panting hoarsely in her ecstatic release.

When she was finished, he let her rest for a while, his hand lying lightly on her exposed thigh. To impress her he flicked the white silk handerchief from his breast pocket and murmuring 'If you will permit me . . . ' he wiped her gently dry and then rearranged her frock.

They arrived at the villa shortly afterwards. The imperturbable chauffeur opened the limousine door and handed Régine out. An attentive maid opened the house door for her to enter. Régine took all this for granted, Christophe noted, giving not the slightest acknowledgment of any service performed for her – not even the intimate service he had rendered on the journey home.

'Does Madame require anything?' the maid enquired.

'Bring a bottle of champagne to my room,' said Régine, 'with two glasses. And tell Henri to return to the Casino and wait for the others.'

Christophe felt that it was time to assert himself before he slipped back into the role of employee on scarcely a higher level than that of maid or chauffeur.

145

'Bring the champagne to the pool,' he instructed the maid. 'We wish to enjoy the moonlight.'

The maid stared at him, aghast at his presumption in countermanding Madame's instructions. Régine herself gave him a startled look, then nodded her consent.

'You may be right, Christophe,' she said when the maid had left them, 'perhaps I am too much in the habit of telling others what to do. But in the years I have been alone I have been compelled to make every decision for myself. That is not good for a woman.'

They sat on the patio, overlooking the pool, while the maid served wonderfully chilled champagne. It was a warm and cloudless night, a three-quarters full moon in the sky to light the scene – a night ideal for lovers, if they had been lovers. Christophe took up something Régine had said a little before.

'How long have you been alone?' he asked sympathetically.

Alone was not the word he would have used to describe her way of life, with a niece and a house full of guests, but it had been her own word.

'For nearly fifteen years.'

'Your husband, the Vicomte, was he killed in the War?'

'I wish he had been, the callous brute!' she answered angrily. 'But no – he left me. He lives abroad.'

Evidently Christophe had started his hostess along a route which would lead only to unpleasantness. To change the mood, on a sudden whim, he stood up and began to take off his clothes – tail-coat, white bow-tie, patent leather shoes. Régine looked at him in amazement.

'What are you doing?'

'I am going to swim in the moonlight – and you are going to do the same.'

'But I have no swimming costume here!'

'Nor have I,' he said, stepping out of his underpants to stand naked.

146

'How handsome you are, Christophe – come closer and let me touch you.'

'We are going to swim,' he said firmly.

'You expect me to undress here?'

'Why not? This is your house.'

He reached out his hand and she took it. Once on her feet she continued to protest as he undid the bodice of her frock and pulled it off her, revealing a corset in black moiré encasing her body from her breasts to the join of her thighs.

'But this is mad!' she exclaimed as he unfastened her suspenders.

'What of it?'

He rolled her stockings down her legs and undid the corset. She was as naked as he, except that she still had diamonds in her hair, around her neck and on her fingers. Christophe studied her for a moment, his head on one side. Deprived of support, her ample breasts hung heavily and her belly bulged more than could be considered attractive. All the same, the diamonds made a good showing. And if a man liked big breasts . . . Christophe took them in his hands, as if to assess their weight. Régine gave him a pleading look.

'Christophe, do not despise me,' she whispered.

'Why should I despise you?'

'Because I am no longer young and beautiful.'

'You're not so bad.'

He urged her to the edge of the pool with little pats of encouragement on her bare bottom.

'We can be seen from every window in the house,' she sighed.

By way of reply, Christophe put an arm around her waist and jumped, pulling her with him into the clear water. They hit the surface with a mighty splash and went under in a tangle of limbs. When his feet struck the tiled bottom of the pool Christophe released her and pushed upwards, shook the water from his hair and swam slowly round in a circle until Régine broke the surface, spluttering and laughing at the same time.

'You are insane,' she told him, 'but I love you for it.'

As frisky as a young girl, she splashed water at him with her hands and he splashed back at her. They played this game for a long time, laughing at each other, until the water began to feel cool and Christophe decided that action was necessary.

'Time to swim now,' he said, 'five times up and down the pool.'

'It is too much – I shall drown!'

'I won't let you – and the exercise will make you feel good.'

He led the way at a leisurely pace and Régine struggled along beside him, puffing and panting after the first length of the pool. After the fourth she refused to go any further and clung exhausted to the edge. She was a strange sight, drops of water rolling down her breasts and her necklace gleaming in the moonlight. Her once carefully arranged hair was plastered close to her head and the strand of diamonds hung loosely round her ears.

'Let me help you out of the water,' said Christophe, 'and I will get towels from the changing room to rub you warm and dry.'

It was easier said than done. Régine was fatigued by the exertion of swimming so far and it required all of Christophe's strength to hoist her wet bulk up out of the water. But at last they stood on the side of the pool, he half-supporting her with an arm about her waist, she with one arm clinging round his shoulders to ease her trembling legs.

It was at this most vulnerable moment that an unexpected burst of laughter and some impertinent clapping intruded itself upon them! Their heads turned and, horror, there on the patio stood Régine's guests, elegant in evening attire and greatly amused by the spectacle before them.

'My God!' Régine wailed.

Her heavy body swung round quickly to present her back to the unwelcome spectators and so preserve from their curious eyes the sight of her oversize female attributes in their nakedness. Alas, the tiles were wet and smooth. In her haste to protect her modesty she lost her footing and went headlong into the water, taking Christophe with her, her legs thrashing high above her head as she fell, exposing all that she had wished to conceal.

The shock of the immersion, added to that of discovery in so compromising a situation, dazed Régine. She rose to the surface from the depths like a sounding whale, then sank again with no effort to save herself. Christophe, alarmed, flipped over and dived after her, found her on the bottom and got her by the back of the neck. He got her as quickly as he could to the surface and towed her to the side, her breasts and belly standing clear of the water like the superstructure of a sinking ship.

The men in the party rushed forward to assist, still choking back their laughter at these unfortunate circumstances. Régine was hauled limply out of the pool and arranged face-down, where she lay coughing up water. As Christophe got his hands on the edge to pull himself out of the water, one of the helpers accidentally trod on his hand and, with a howl of pain, he sank back into the depths. When next he surfaced he saw that Régine had been turned over and that one of the rescuers had gallantly spread Christophe's discarded tail-coat over her wet bulk – for the sake of decency, of course. In the general solicitude for Régine, Christophe was entirely forgotten. He watched them pick her up and carry her into the house, then at last he felt it was safe to clamber out of the pool. He sat for a time with his arms around his knees, getting his breath back and feeling most uneasy about what had occurred.

149

'You will catch cold if you stay like that,' a voice said casually.

He looked up to see Nicolette standing near him.

'Everyone really is mad here,' he said slowly, 'it must be the perpetual sunshine which boils your brains.'

He got to his feet, ignoring her glance at his male part, shrunk to a diminutive size by the coolness of the water. Without bothering to dry himself he put on his shirt and shoes.

His hand still hurt but there seemed to be no bones broken.

'Shouldn't you be helping to look after your aunt?' he asked coldly.

'She's in bed and her maid is attending to her. She'll come to no harm – she's too tough for that.'

'With that I heartily agree,' said Christophe moodily. 'Goodnight, Mademoiselle.'

'Wait a minute – I want to talk to you.'

'But I want a hot bath and a glass of cognac.'

'Tell me one thing.'

'What?'

'Are you a gigolo?'

'I find that question insulting,' and he turned away from her and made for the house.

Nicolette trotted beside him.

'There's no need to be angry,' she said, 'most of Régine's young men are, you know. What makes you different?'

'The fact that I shall leave this madhouse forever the moment I am dressed and ready.'

'Then why were you invited to stay here?'

She pursued him with her questions through the house and right into the bathroom.

'It can be of no concern to you,' said Christophe, 'but an aunt of mine in Paris informed Régine that I was staying in Cannes at the Carlton. I knew nothing of this, or of your aunt, until a chauffeur arrived with an invitation to lunch.'

He turned on the taps and watched the hot water gushing into the bath. His wet shirt was clinging coldly to his skin and he was shivering.

'Now, if you will excuse me, it is my intention to get into the bath.'

She pouted at him and left. He was lying in the hot and scented water, his eyes closed peacefully, when Nicolette returned with a bottle of cognac and two glasses. She poured a generous measure for him, much less for herself, and perched on the edge of the huge bath to sip her drink. Christophe tasted the cognac and felt its warmth glowing inside him. Why Nicolette should be interested in his relations with her aunt he did not know, nor why she should be here in the bathroom with him, but he put it down to the general eccentricity which seemed to pervade the entire villa.

'That's interesting,' she said.

'What is?'

'When you got out of the swimming pool it was tiny, but now that you're in a hot bath it's grown considerably.'

Not believing what he had heard, Christophe stared up at Nicolette's beautiful oval face and in her large shining eyes he saw a lively curiosity. She was not Régine's niece for nothing, he decided.

'I ask myself whether, if you were naked in this bath and I were sitting there looking at you, you would accept my compliments or tell me to leave at once?' he said lightly.

'Who can say?' she replied. 'It would depend on my mood, I imagine.'

'And at the moment your mood is to observe a part of me which is not usually displayed to young ladies, except in special circumstances.'

'I believe that it's getting bigger still,' she remarked.

'While you sit there it will continue to do so.'

'I can't think why – after all, I am fully dressed.'

'But you are here with me, and that is enough to make it grow bigger.'

'Very much bigger, or just bigger?' she enquired.

'You must judge that for yourself,' Christophe sighed, watching the head of his rapidly stiffening part emerge above the surface of the bath water.

'Nicolette – what would Madame la Vicomtesse say if she knew that you were observing me in this way?' he asked.

'I don't know – or care. Are you afraid of her?'

'Why should I be?' he countered. 'In any case, I'm leaving early in the morning.'

'You said you were going tonight. Why the delay?'

'Because I am at last with the only member of this crazy household for whom I care.'

'Of course – when we first met you declared that you loved me. That was in the pool – you appear to have many adventures there.'

'I told you the truth,' he said, absolutely sincere now. 'The moment I saw you my heart pounded as if it would burst. I knew at once that this was the love of a lifetime – a tremendous and enduring passion – even though I did not know who you were.'

'Very flattering, but I am not at all sure that I need another lover at present,' she said.

'I am not offering myself as *another* lover, Nicolette, but as one who loves you to distraction – there is a world of difference.'

'A bathroom is an unusual place for declarations of eternal love. But then, I never did believe in standing on ceremony. Apart from this great love of yours, Christophe, what else do you have to recommend yourself to me?'

So much sophistication at so young an age – Christophe blinked at the implications and was grateful for the schooling in affairs of the heart which he had received in Paris.

'Only what you can see,' he answered, 'I must tell you openly that I have very little money and no particular prospects.'

'What I can see is not without a certain attraction. It has grown *very* much bigger. Does hot water always have that effect on you?'

'It is not the water, as you well know – it is your nearness that has this effect, and always will.'

'Always is a long time – you should not exaggerate.'

'And love is a rare commodity, Nicolette.'

'So I believe, and God knows that my dear aunt spends enough money trying to buy it.'

Christophe held her gaze, looking into her eyes and willing her with all his heart to recognise the expression of his devotion in his own eyes. After a while she looked away almost demurely.

'I'm going to my room,' she said shortly, 'when you are ready, join me there and we will continue this conversation in more suitable surroundings.'

She was hardly through the door before Christophe was out of the bath and rubbing himself dry briskly. The farce in the swimming pool with Régine was no longer a humiliation, for it had caused Nicolette to take notice of him at last. Then he remembered that he could not present himself to Nicolette wearing a soaking wet evening shirt and creased black trousers – he would have to go to his own room first for something else.

But in the event he need not have troubled himself. When he went into her room she had undressed and was lying on her bed, propped up with big square satin pillows and wearing only a night dress made entirely of Chantilly lace, so short that the hem was only halfway down her thighs.

The next morning, before breakfast, Christophe and Nicolette ran away together. That is to say, before Régine or any of her guests were stirring, they loaded six pieces of luggage into the open tourer – one containing

Christophe's entire wardrobe and five containing a selection of Nicolette's clothes – and had the chauffeur drive them into Cannes to the railway station. There are, after all, ways of doing these things. On the long journey to Paris Christophe, besotted with love though he was, learned with relief that Nicolette was an heiress in her own right and not dependent on the Vicomtesse.

THE LITTLE ANGEL

The gullibility of human nature is such that almost everything that can be eaten or drunk without risk of death – and even some substances with that risk – has been used as an aphrodisiac to intensify desire. In the ancient days, as is well known and recorded, the nobility availed themselves of the testicles of stags and bulls for this purpose, no doubt sliced and lightly grilled in breadcrumbs.

In more recent times celery and asparagus have been considered efficacious, for no better reason than that they have the same general shape as the masculine part in a condition of excitement! Little need be said of the expensive potions and powders that can be obtained from dubious pharmacists, for while some of these are only tinctured sugar to deceive the purchaser, some are known to be truly inflammatory and to carry the danger of death in proportion to their power to arouse. It is less than thirty years since the President of the Republic, Félix Faure, died naked in the arms of his young mistress – of a surfeit of special pills he had taken to stimulate his desires. It was with the greatest difficulty that a public scandal was averted on that sad occasion.

And yet there is an aphrodisiac which never fails to have its effect, which carries no dangerous toxicity, and which costs nothing – the imagination. No one can have failed to observe how a man's imagination can be so stimulated that he mistakes an ordinarily pretty woman for a goddess of beauty, whose favours he must seek at whatever inconvenience to himself. This was the case of André Giroud, who fell in love with a woman before he had seen her, entirely because of what he was told about her. The words he heard wrought such vivid images in his mind that his imagination became instantly obsessed.

It happened while he was dining in a restaurant one evening with a business acquaintance, Adolphe Lacoste, a man much older than himself and with a more extensive knowledge of the private arrangements of persons of importance in the circle of finance and business in Paris. The conversation ranged widely until Lacoste began to speak of the days before the War, when he had first come to Paris to establish himself. He had, he related to André, cultivated the acquaintance of a certain Monsieur Moncourbier, a personage whose financial dealings extended into many areas.

'Moncourbier was a great gourmet,' Lacoste said. 'He employed servants of talent, particularly his chef de cuisine. The first time he invited me to lunch at his private residence, the food was superb, the wines were a connoisseur's delight, the service was impeccable. He was about fifty years old and had no wife. His household was managed by a woman named Cabuchon. She was a small and tireless woman, somewhere between thirty and forty, I estimated, rather plain, one must say. She dressed somewhat above her station, to my way of thinking, though one would not describe her as elegant. A woman of the shopkeeper class who had been translated above her proper place in life.'

'She was Moncourbier's mistress, I suppose, plain or not,' said André.

'I thought for a time that was her station and naturally I was not impressed by Moncourbier's taste in choosing her. But the unfolding of events that afternoon led me to conclude that she was no more than his housekeeper.'

'Another woman was introduced?'

'Not exactly. Picture the scene – after that regal meal

156

Moncourbier and I were sitting at our ease in his impressive salon while the servants cleared the dining-room. Madame Cabuchon was with us and served us coffee – a blend fit for an Emperor. We were comfortably replete and in the very best of humours. To tell the truth, Moncourbier was more than replete – he was jovial from the effects of the wines we had enjoyed with lunch and the magnificent cognac we sipped with the coffee.'

.'He became expansive?' André suggested. 'He confided some private affair to you?'

'He did more than that. He instructed Madame Cabuchon to bring his "little angel" to him. And while she was out of the room, he told me that the housekeeper's daughter was the light of his life. Naturally I assumed that she was his own child by the housekeeper, but he made it clear that she was not, as you will see. To my question of whether she was a pretty child he replied that she was astonishingly beautiful and that he adored her purity and innocence – and much more in that strain. I've forgotten his words after so many years but I remember that he was most eloquent – to the point where I felt embarrassed.'

'He was a gourmet, you said?'

'In everything. And as you would expect, he was grossly fat. I can still visualise him sitting there that afternoon, at ease in his own house, slightly drunk and full of geniality towards the whole world at that moment. His several chins shook as he talked to me and his vast paunch bulged out so much that he had to sit with his legs widely apart to accommodate it. It had been many years since he had last seen his own feet. He had spilled cigar ash down the front of his jacket and made no attempt to brush it off. He had very little hair left, except over his ears, and his bald pate was pink and flushed from the food and wine.'

'You paint a vivid picture,' André commented, 'though not an appealing one.'

'Moncourbier was not an appealing man, merely a very clever one.'

'And the housekeeper's daughter?'

'Ah, yes,' said Lacoste, 'that was a different matter – one in which Moncourbier displayed his gourmet's talent. Madame Cabuchon returned after some time with her daughter, whose name was Lucette, I was informed. I could hardly believe my eyes, I assure you! I saw a young girl of thirteen or fourteen at most, marvellously pretty, slender of form and with long and very light blonde hair.'

André shrugged dismissively and said:

'There are men with a taste for very young girls. I find it pathetic.'

'If it were as banal as that I would not weary you with the story.'

'Then I hope you will pardon my interruption and continue,' said André.

'With pleasure. Lucette entered the salon bare-foot. She was wearing a sleeveless garment cut like a tunic, round at the neck, tied at the waist with a length of golden cord, and ending about halfway down her thighs. The most surprising thing about this curious garment was that while it covered her young body, it did nothing to conceal it at all. It was made, you understand, of some gauze-like transparent tissue. And there was a further surprise – on her shoulders she had small golden wings.'

'Wings? I don't believe it.'

Lacoste nodded and smiled, pleased by the effect he had created on his listener.

'I give you my word. She had small wings made of gauze stretched on thin wire frames, attached to her back by some device or other.'

'She really was dressed up as a "little angel", you mean?'

'Exactly so, except for the indecency of her tunic. My astonishment must have shown on my face because Moncourbier chuckled and shook and spilled more cigar ash down his chest and then asked me if I had ever seen so beautiful a creature.'

'She was pretty, you said.'

'Exquisite, my dear André, in face and in body. Through her transparent garment I could clearly see her small growing breasts and their pointed pink tips. And, though I tried not to look, I observed between her thighs a most enchanting little mound, very lightly covered in blonde floss. When she went to Moncourbier and kissed him on his pink bald head, she presented her rear to me – and it was as adorable as her front view. Below the silly little wings she had a long and sinuous back like a kitten, and a bottom! How can I describe it – the cheeks of her bottom were like two very round and rosy apples.'

'Adolphe!' exclaimed André. 'You speak with such warmth that I begin to believe that you were physically attracted to this child.'

'That was the very question I was asking myself as I sat there, glass in hand, watching Moncourbier fuss over his living toy – for that's what she was, of course. Like you, I have always regarded old men who want little girls as perverse and unpleasant creatures, probably impotent. Yet even so I felt the attractions of that particular child, though with a sense of shame.'

'Was she at all self-conscious in your presence, the girl?'

'Not in the least. She smiled at me prettily when Moncourbier told her that I was a friend of his.'

'A remarkable scene,' said André. 'How did you escape from it?'

'There was no escape for me just then. I was lunching with Moncourbier in private to interest him in a business deal of the greatest delicacy – a matter of enormous importance to me at that time. To avoid giving him offence I was prepared to endure anything.'

'What happened, then?'

'You will find it hard to believe, but I give you my word that it is true. After a while Madame Cabuchon seated herself at the piano and struck a chord. Lucette went to stand in the centre of the salon, some distance from us,

159

in a spot where the afternoon sun shone through the windows to create a long beam of gold across the floor. The effect was highly theatrical, for her tiny wings glittered and her tunic became even more transparent, if that were possible. Then – to her mother's accompaniment – she sang to us!'

'Well or badly?' André asked, the scene vivid in his mind's eye.

'Quite well. She had a pleasing little voice and evidently had been given singing lessons.'

'I hardly dare ask what it was that she sang.'

'You are right to be apprehensive,' said Lacoste, grinning at him. 'She sang the Ave Maria to that syrupy tune by Gounod!'

André laughed at the thought.

'My dear friend,' he said at last, 'the way you describe that scene makes it sound absolutely ridiculous. How did you prevent yourself from bursting into laughter?'

'It *was* ridiculous,' Lacoste agreed, 'a half-naked child warbling away in Moncourbier's salon. Yet the effect on Moncourbier was bizarre! I swear to you that tears rolled down his fat cheeks! Perhaps he was secretly gloating over the sight of her adolescent breasts, perhaps he was moved by the religious sentiment of the words she sang – perhaps both – I could not tell. But to him the experience was evidently sublime.'

'The girl had been trained by her mother to take advantage of Moncourbier's little weaknesses, of course,' said André.

'But of course! And she had trained the child very well. By the end of the recital old Moncourbier was sobbing into a handkerchief the size of a table-cloth. I hid my embarrassment because of my urgent need to get him to back my particular business venture, but there was worse embarrassment to come. After he had dried his cheeks, Lucette went to him and sat upon his knee and kissed his forehead. He called her his little angel a score of times.

He raised his eyes to the ceiling and implored God and the Holy Virgin and all the saints in heaven to protect this dear child – he went on like that for a long time.'

'And the mother?'

'Madame Cabuchon sat primly at the piano, a badly concealed smirk on her face.'

'He was a sentimentalist of some sort, this Moncourbier,' said André.

'Of some sort, yes. But during this lengthy monologue he addressed to Heaven I noticed that his pudgy hands were stroking Lucette's thighs under her short tunic. The question that came into my mind was, that if he did this openly with a stranger present, what familiarities did he permit himself at other times? Lucette was not at all troubled by his caresses – it was obvious to me that she was no stranger to them.'

'The mother's training must have been extensive.'

'All this time,' said Lacoste, 'old mother Cabuchon sat pretending to notice nothing. It was extraordinary. Moncourbier got redder and redder in the face, the child giggled as he stroked her, his arm up her tunic to the elbow. He lowered his head as far as his thick neck allowed and pressed his cheek to her tiny breasts under the thin material. It was only then that Madame Cabuchon rose from the piano and announced that it was time for Lucette to leave so that Monsieur Moncourbier could discuss business with his guest.'

'And that was that?'

'Moncourbier surrendered the child to her mother with reluctance, but he neither argued nor complained at the abrupt termination of his pleasure. Yet there was one thing which stayed in my memory after that day. La Cabuchon held the girl by the hand to lead her out of the room – and instructed her to say "*Au revoir*" to me before she went. Lucette turned her pretty face towards me, said the words and winked!'

André laughed again, but incredulously this time.

'That is imagination,' he told Lacoste, 'perhaps the child blinked.'

Lacoste shook his head, smiling.

'There was no mistake,' he said, 'Lucette winked at me deliberately. It was a tiny conspiratorial gesture that said more than words could. She was letting me know that she and I both knew that Moncourbier was a silly old fool.'

'Then she was a most precocious child, this little Lucette.'

'More than you can imagine – there was also an invitation in that wink.'

'An invitation? No, that's too much – I don't believe you.'

'You were not there to see it, André – but I was. The invitation from that remarkable child was to take her away from Moncourbier and become her playmate, if I had a mind to. And, of course, if I had the means to maintain her and her Mama in the style to which Moncourbier had accustomed them.'

'All that in one wink? Surely not!'

Lacoste shrugged.

'Believe what you like,' he said, not in the least put out. 'There was no intention on my part of accepting the child's invitation, of course.'

'That I believe. How did your business dealings with Moncourbier go?'

'Very successfully. Moncourbier was a clever man in financial matters, however foolish he may have been in other ways. The deal went through and we both made a very good profit out of it. For me that was a turning-point in my life. Until that time I had been successful in Orleans, where I was born, but this venture in association with Moncourbier was my debut in Parisian business circles. The War started the next year and the opportunities for a businessman to make money were unlimited – so long as one was not required for military service.'

'So I have been told,' said André. 'My services were

required and I still have a small piece of Boche shrapnel in my right thigh as a souvenir.'   ·

'Alas,' said Lacoste, 'it was found that I had a disorder of the liver which prevented me from serving France in the trenches.'

'A sad circumstance,' André commented dryly. 'And your friend Moncourbier – doubtless he also found it impossible not to make a fortune during the War years?'

'To my astonishment, he did find it impossible. He made some calamitous investments. By 1916 he was in very deep water and borrowing from everyone he knew. He crashed the year after that – he was bankrupt for an enormous sum. There was even talk of prosecuting him – it seems that some of the means he had employed to try to prevent the crash were uncomfortably close to outright fraud. But in the end he managed to talk his way out of so dreadful a fate and disappeared from the sight of his reproachful creditors.'

'Is he still alive?'

'Certainly. The old rogue saved something from the disaster. He had a secret fund concealed somewhere out of reach. Since he was forced to quit Paris he has lived quietly in Biarritz. He has a small apartment there and a sufficient income to live modestly, or so I am informed.'

'But his great days are over, it would seem.'

Lacoste nodded and smiled sadly.

'Yes, a lesson to all of us to be prudent in business affairs,' he said.

'And Lucette, the little angel, now grown into a woman – did you ever hear of her again?'

'Our paths crossed again after the War, in the strangest circumstances. It seems that old mother Cabuchon also saved something from the wreck. Where she took her daughter to complete her education I do not know. But soon after the end of the War Lucette reappeared in Paris, an enchanting young beauty of about twenty, and soon made her mark in circles where her looks and other talents were of more importance than her virtue. She became the protégé of a Russian Prince for a year or two. He was not one of those Russian nobles who had fled penniless from the Bolsheviks to become a taxi-driver or restaurant doorman in Paris. By no means! He had transferred a good part of the family fortune here long before the War. Lucette was very well off with him.'

'And after him?' André enquired.

'There was someone else, you may be sure.'

'Is she still in Paris now?'

'Why yes, I am surprised that you have not made her acquaintance. Who her present protector is, I am unable to say. Presumably the man she is dining with over there.'

André turned to look across the restaurant at the table Lacoste indicated. He saw a woman of twenty-seven or -eight, her straw-blonde hair cut short and close to her head, framing a delicate profile. Her evening frock was of marvellous elegance – a tight-fitting bodice of white crêpe-de-Chine that left her slender arms bare and was very deeply decollété. Around the long column of her neck she wore four strands of matched pearls – and similar bracelets on both wrists.

'I believe that the jewellery she is wearing was a present from the Prince,' said Lacoste.

What thoughts were stirred in André by the sight of this woman – she who was once in her childhood the 'little angel' of a rich man's fantasy. She had grown into a woman of great distinction. This Moncourbier, her first protector, he who had paraded her almost naked to please himself, what more had he done? André speculated feverishly. He had fondled her thighs in the presence of Lacoste without shame. After Lacoste had taken his leave, no doubt the old Turk had removed the child's tunic to feast his eyes on her body and run his hands over her tiny breasts. Had he gone even further – no, that would have been impossible if he were as fat as Lacoste described him. But he would have devised other little games . . . André was still staring in fascination at Lucette Cabuchon across the restaurant. Those childish thighs which had pleased Moncourbier were now long and sleek under the skirt of her expensive frock. The tiny breasts had rounded out into shapes of elegant beauty.

Lucette realised that she was being stared at, turned her head and looked straight at André. Her face was heart-shaped, her nose long and straight – but the most expressive feature of her beautiful face was her mouth, wide, generous and good-humoured. She returned André's look without embarrassment, until he realised with a start that he was behaving most impolitely in staring at her. He turned back to Lacoste, to find him grinning.

'I know the man she is with,' said André, to cover his confusion, 'his name is Malplaquet and he is a bullion dealer. Strange – I never thought of him as an adventurous man. Quite the contrary, he has always seemed to me to be dull and cautious. Yet there he sits with that marvellous woman, his face beaming with pleasure, as well it might!'

'My dear André – I believe that you are interested in Lucette!'

'Your little story has fascinated me, I admit. I feel that I must make her acquaintance. Let us finish our meal before they do and on our way out we will pause at Malplaquet's table and I will introduce you to him.'

'And in turn be introduced to Lucette,' said Lacoste.

'Naturally. It would give me pleasure to kiss her hand.'

'Her hand . . . of course,' said Lacoste, his knowing smile suggesting that other parts of Mademoiselle Cabuchon's exquisite person were well worth kissing.

'You said that your path and hers crossed again some years ago,' André prompted him, 'that suggests that she had remembered you, which is not easy to believe. It was a good many years after your disreputable friend had let you see her as a half-naked child.'

'Half-naked is so ambiguous a term,' said Lacoste, 'it

seems to suggest that she was naked from the waist up and clothed below, so exposing her tiny breasts – or that she was clothed above the waist and naked below, revealing her girlish charms. In fact, I was privileged to observe all her young treasures through that indecently transparent tunic. She had a tiny oval mole to the left of her dimple of a navel – no doubt she still has, if one were permitted to see her undressed.'

'Enchanting thought!' said André. 'If it is not too indelicate a question, on what terms did you renew your acquaintance with her when she was grown up?'

'It was entirely a business arrangement. I told you that she was under the protection of a Prince for a year or two at the end of the War. Like all Russians he was half-mad, of course. He had moods of black depression at times and then he would drink enormous quantities of cognac and take occasional shots with a revolver at the statues round his house – even at the pictures on the walls. And at his servants, if they were rash enough to intrude on his melancholy. He wounded a footman or two, but he was able to pay them off with large sums of money and so escape the attentions of the police. In short, he was like King Saul in the Old Testament. Lucette was the one who could soothe his black imaginings and restore him to himself.'

'She is brave, as well as beautiful,' said André.

'I think she was very fond of him. At other times the Prince became exuberant beyond reason. He gave vast parties and was absurdly generous. In one such interlude he gave Lucette a handful of deeds as a little present for pleasing him in some way or other. When he died, she consulted me as to whether to retain the property he had given her or to sell it.'

'I find it impossible to believe that she had remembered you, Adolphe.'

'You're quite right. It was her mother who had remembered my name from the days of my successful venture with Moncourbier. After all, it was the old man's last big coup and Madame Cabuchon gave me the credit for it.'

'Was it a valuable property she had been given?'

'Not particularly so. It was a small, neglected and unprofitable vineyard somewhere in the vicinity of St. Etienne. I know nothing about such things so in turn I consulted your esteemed uncle, Aristide Brissard, whom I knew. I understood that he was always interested in the purchase and sale of land, among other things.'

'What did he advise?'

'He said that, unprofitable or not, land of that sort was the best of longterm investments. He suggested that Lucette should keep it and spend money on putting it to rights. Or if she decided against that, then he offered to buy it from her at whatever price she regarded as fair.'

'Did he?'

'Oh yes, little Lucette wanted cash just then, not the problems of vinegrowing. She sold it to him – and paid me a commission for arranging the sale! By now I imagine that your uncle has set his vineyard to rights and is making a reasonable profit on it.'

'I'm sure of it,' said André, 'everything Uncle Aristide touches produces a profit, believe me! And yet no one, not even those inside the family, ever quite knows the extent of his interests. If Mademoiselle Cabuchon was short of money, I assume that the Prince died unexpectedly.'

'The manner of his death was as bizarre as his life. He was roaming the house in one of his black moods, revolver in hand. Lucette had been sent for hurriedly – I think she was visiting her mother at the time. The Prince, at the top of his grand staircase, took a shot at a bust of Napoleon the Third, or some such worthy. The bullet glanced off the bust, then off the marble balustrade and hit the Prince in the leg. He fell head over heels down the staircase and broke his neck. The servants heard the noise of his fall and guessed that he had hurt himself, but they

167

were too afraid for their lives to go near him – after all, they knew he had his revolver and could not be sure that he was unconscious. Alas, he was dead. He lay there at the foot of his own stairs until Lucette arrived much later and she had the courage to go to him. But he had been dead for several hours by then and there was nothing to do but send for a priest.'

'A terrible shock for a young woman,' said André thoughtfully.

'Yes, she was fond of him, as I believe I told you. She stayed with his body until the servants had carried him back upstairs and laid him out on his bed. She knelt and prayed for his soul at the foot of the bed while the priest carried out his sad office. Then, there being no more to be done, she packed her jewels and clothes and sent for a taxi to take her away from there. And if she packed a little more than was rightfully hers – a small objet d'art or two – who shall blame her? She had to face the expense of setting up her own home and maintaining herself in good style until such time as another rich man felt constrained to take care of her living costs.'

'From what you have told me about her,' said André, 'I feel that she is a most remarkable woman. If you have finished, let's call for the bill and go across to Malplaquet's table. I must meet her.'

So he was introduced to her. The next day he telephoned her. Two days later she accepted his invitation to dinner – the brief process was totally uncomplicated because of André's determination to recognise no obstacles or refusals. The truth was that in his mind she had become the most desirable woman in Paris. Reason should have informed him that, like all beautiful women, Lucette was possessed of a head, two arms, two breasts, two legs – and certain other enchanting bodily attributes of the female. But the voice of reason goes unheard when a man's imagination is aroused. If a friend had been disposed to discuss with André the nature and quality of

Lucette's charms, then he – with no direct experience of them – would undoubtedly have been prepared to argue that she had breasts more shapely than those of any other woman, that her legs were more elegant, her skin smoother, her personality more engaging, her conversation more amusing – and this from no more than a minute's formal conversation when he was introduced to her in a restaurant! Lacoste's vivid account of some episodes in her early life had fixed in André's mind the idea that Lucette was a semi-divine creature of love, trained from childhood in the arts of delighting men, immensely skilled in the ways of pleasure and passion.

They dined together, they talked, they danced and drank champagne. It was well after two in the morning when André escorted her back to her apartment in the rue de Monceau, near the park. She unlocked the door herself and went in without a word, André following close behind. It was not until they had traversed the apartment and were in her bedroom that she turned and stared briefly at him, as if in surprise.

'Oh, you're here,' she said with a half-mocking smile.

'But of course,' he answered, sure that he was on the verge of experiencing a night of considerable pleasure with her – or at least as much of the night as was left.

'How hot and uncomfortable I am!' she sighed.

It was a very warm summer night, to be sure, still and airless, even with the long windows wide open. Lucette's elegant frock covered only those areas of her body which decency and good style required, but there was a light sheen of perspiration on her pretty neck and her bare back. André, in full evening attire, was feeling the heat himself – his shirt was stuck clammily to his back and he was wet under the arms.

'I must take a cool bath,' Lucette declared, 'I couldn't stand being touched in this state. It would be inconsiderate to wake my maid at this hour, so you must assist me.'

'With the greatest of pleasure,' André murmured fervently.

Lucette kicked off her high-heeled shoes, loosened something at her waist, shrugged off the shoulder-straps of her cyclamen-red frock and let it slide down her body to the floor. She stood revealed in ivory lace knickers and her stockings – apart from her four-stranded pearl choker, of course. André contemplated her perfectly rounded little breasts, his urgent part rising to attention in his trousers as he tried to imagine the bliss of kissing the delicate pink buds displayed before him.

'Do you think you can take my stockings off without ruining them?' she asked.

He went down on one knee and touched his fingers to her embroidered garters, trying to discern the shape of her mound through the thin material that hid it from sight. Slowly he eased one garter down from where it held her stocking-top halfway up her creamy-skinned thighs, slid it over her knee and all the way down her superb leg and over her small foot. He repeated the performance with the other one, and then rolled her stockings down, finding them as fine as cobweb to his touch.

Before he could reach for the only garment she now wore – the last lace covering of her feminine modesty – she stepped away from him and moved across the room. After a moment of stunned immobility, he leaped to his feet and went after her, desperate not to let her escape him for a second now that he had touched her thighs, though only with his finger-tips and that briefly. She was in her bathroom, bending over to control the taps to produce the cool temperature of water she wanted. It was a very pretty bathroom, the walls a pale gold colour, hung with small pictures and silhouette portraits, but at the moment André had eyes for nothing except the delicious cheeks of her bottom, the ivory material stretched over them as she learned forward.

She took a crystal bottle from a side-table and poured

170

some of its expensive contents into the water. At once the water frothed up and a delicate scent permeated the air.

'Sit there and talk to me,' Lucette said to him over her bare shoulder.

He seated himself on an armchair of wickerwork lacquered gold and attempted to converse as best he could, though his attention was transfixed by Lucette's long and narrow back and the curves of her bottom. He broke off what he was saying and caught his breath as she hooked her thumbs in the sides of her ivory knickers and pushed them down her legs, her back still towards him. He stared at the satin-smooth skin of those marvellous little globes, his heart beating faster. He almost caught a glimpse of blonde fur between her thighs as she stepped into the bath – or did he? Perhaps it was only a trick of his fevered imagination.

Lucette lay in the water, only her head above the scented foam. She rested the back of her blonde head on the edge of the bath, where a Greek key pattern in pale blue traced the outline of the rim. It was only then that André noticed that she still had her choker on – the strands of pearls set off the column of the neck perfectly as it rose from the water.

'Oh, that's good,' she said in satisfaction, 'I was hot enough to burst!'

'That would be a catastrophe of the first order,' he said, smiling at her.

'Well, if not burst, then at least melt away,' she said.

'That too would be a calamity. You are so adorable that not one gramme of you must be lost.'

She smiled at him as if he had said something witty.

'You look very hot yourself, André. Why don't you take your clothes off and get in here with me? There's plenty of room.'

What man could have hesitated over such an invitation? In moments André's black evening clothes were off and

171

strewn across the wicker chair, followed by socks, underwear – everything, and he stepped into the cool water to sit down facing Lucette. She raised her knees and sat up a little to give him more space. The change of position caused her breasts to bob up just above the surface, their pink tips touched with the scented foam of the bath essence.

'Is that better,' she asked.

'Much,' he answered in relief.

'You looked like a boiled lobster in those clothes.'

'I was beginning to feel like one. Though truth compels me to confess that it was not entirely the effect of a warm night. There was another and more important reason, as you must be aware.'

'Truly? What was that?'

'You are laughing at me. You understand very well, dear Lucette, that the sight of you naked in your bath is more than enough to raise any man's temperature.'

He was sitting with his legs outside hers, his feet just touching her hips on either side.

'Thank heaven we cooled you down in time,' she said.

Even as she spoke, she reached forward through the delicately opaque water – he felt her hand touch the inside of his open thighs and take hold of his upright stem of flesh.

'The water hasn't cooled this fellow at all,' she commented with a smile.

'How could it, when you are so close to me?' he murmured.

Lucette's bath essence produced an emollient effect on the water, and no doubt was intended to produce the same effect on her skin. André experienced a sensation of pleasant slipperiness as her hand moved slowly up and down his tautness.

'Oh heavens, it's getting hotter!' she exclaimed. 'How is that possible?'

'Like a volcano, it is building up its forces for an eruption,' he told her.

Lucette rose to her knees and moved forward to straddle his thighs. Under the water he felt her hands positioning him before she lowered herself carefully, her small navel with the oval mole alongside it disappearing back under the surface as she sank down. The mole was as Lacoste had described it, was the silly thought in André's mind at this marvellous moment. He sighed as the cool touch of water was replaced by the warm clasp of soft flesh. His hands moved with gentle appetite up her wet body to cup her little breasts.

'Have you shared a bath with many women?' she asked casually.

She was moving gracefully up and down his embedded pride.

'You are the first,' he admitted, his pleasure immense at what was happening to him.

'Really?' Lucette said. 'Does that mean that you prefer in hot weather to make love under a shower? I've never much cared for that myself – the standing position is not a comfortable one.'

'Yet in a sudden emergency . . .' he sighed, 'even a standing position is acceptable.'

'In circumstances that make it the only possibility, everything is permissible,' she agreed softly. 'Are there many emergencies of that sort in your daily life, my poor André?'

'Not in the ordinary way . . . but there have been occasions . . . '

'How very interesting – tell me of the most recent one,' she teased him as she maintained her slow up and down ride on his imprisoned part.

'Tonight – while we were dancing,' he responded at once, 'you must have been aware of a certain pressure against you as I held you to me.'

'Oh that!' she said lightly, 'that was quite normal. Every

173

man I dance with gives me similar proof of his emotions towards me – anything less would be ungallant and insulting. No, my dear, you used the word *emergency*. That refers to a far more serious event. Tell me of your last real emergency.'

'It was at a ball given by the Marquise de Casa Maury back in the spring . . . perhaps you were also a guest?'

'What caused your desperation at the ball?'

'A woman to whom I was introduced and with whom I danced. I had consumed a great deal of champagne . . . and as we moved to the music I glanced down her frock and saw her breasts quite plainly – at once I was on fire – I can't explain why even now . . . yet I knew that unless . . .'

His words trailed off as the sensations of pleasure through his body intensified.

'Go on – what did you do?'

But before André could find suitable words to describe the events that befell him at the Marquise's ball, an emergency of a more expected kind silenced him – a crisis induced by the slow massage of his stiffness by that marvellous inlet of Lucette's beautiful body which a generous Providence had designed for this very purpose. A series of miniature tidal waves rolled the length of the scented bath water as his body convulsed in long spasms and paid her the compliment due to her talents as a lover.

In the weeks that followed his first encounter with her in her bath, André came to understand and appreciate how remarkable Lucette's talents were. The usual course of intimate events between men and women can be described in a few words – it is to kiss, to remove the clothes, to caress each other, to join bodies together in whichever of the well-known positions seems best to them – and so to induce in each other those sublime sensations that accompany the discharge of passion. With Lucette it was never on any occasion either so familiar or so uncomplicated. There was in her nature, André discovered, a deep-seated desire for play-acting, which made of each act of love a drama pitched in a different mood – tender, comic, sardonic – or whatever her mood dictated.

There was a time in her childhood, he reminded himself, when she had played at being old Moncourbier's 'little angel' while his hand felt between her legs. Now that she was a grown woman she still enjoyed acting out roles, though they had become much more sophisticated since those far-off days. She had another attribute, which he only slowly understood – from seemingly casual conversation she gathered tiny indications and analysed them until she came to know a man's unspoken fantasies. To his astonishment, he would find himself playing them out with her at some later meeting! Astonishment was by no means the only emotion aroused by her on such occasions, of course – there was also intense pleasure and surging desire.

Take, for example, an afternoon not long after André had become established as her lover. She greeted him in her salon looking marvellously chic, her golden hair smooth to her head, her long arms bare – and much else besides, for she was wearing a single garment of crimson silk, much like lounging pyjamas. It was all in one piece – of necessity, for the upper part covered only her pretty breasts, leaving her sides – and her back – uncovered. Even that does not quite do the creation justice, for as André suddenly perceived, the back was cut so low that the beginning of the enchanting crease between the cheeks of her bottom was just visible. The trouser section fitted very closely round her long thighs, then flared out from the knees to give very wide bottoms that hid her feet and showed only the high heels of her white shoes.

'I want to dance,' she said, before he could utter a word, and whirled away from his arms to the gramophone, wound it up and put on a record.

André was instantly ready to indugle her whims, for experience had shown him that the result was always pleasurable. He moved aside a chair or two, took her in his arms and led her, dipping and striding, in the steps of a popular tango across the room. At first his hand rested lightly on the smooth skin of her bare back, up between her shoulder-blades. Inevitably, as the dance continued and he warmed to it – and to her – the hand slid downwards, at first to her waist and, eventually, lower still until his little finger rested comfortably in the crease where her bottom began. Lucette's eyes sparkled at the touch and the half-mocking smile that was so characteristic of her appeared on her face.

When the music ran out, André rewound the gramophone while Lucette turned over the record. He took her in his arms, ready to move off, his hand now thrust down the low-cut back of her lounging pyjamas to rest fully on her satin-skinned bottom – for as he had suspected, she wore no underwear that afternoon.

'Ah, you intend to be impolite, Monsieur Giroud,' she said in mock disapproval. 'You believe that because I asked you to dance with me you can give yourself liberty to handle me at will! Two can play at that game, Monsieur.'

Before he had time to comprehend her intent, she had unbuttoned the jacket of his beautiful blue suit – and the buttons of his trousers! Her adroit fingers flicked his male part out into full exposure, she put one hand on his shoulder, the other on his outstretched hand – and they were dancing again. As they performed the intricate steps, André was acutely aware of the sensation of his exposed part flopping about in this indecent freedom. But not for long – the very sensations he experienced quickly stimulated him to the point where what had been limp before now became firm and upright. After that, each time that Lucette brushed past him, the silk of her garment touching his aroused part, little spasms of pleasure ran through him, until his face was pink with emotion.

They were close to the gramophone when the music stopped.

'Did you enjoy that dance?' she asked him.

'Very much. I think that we should sit the next one out, chérie.'

'Not yet – I want to dance again. Turn the handle while I choose another record.'

This time she selected a slower piece of music, one that made it possible for her to press her body closely against him. The slide of silk over his bared stem provoked such delicious tremors of emotion in André that he hardly heard the music at all. His hand was right down the back of her pyjamas to grasp and squeeze those soft round cheeks.

'Lucette . . . ' he murmured dizzily, 'come, let us sit down . . . '

'I love this tune – don't you?' she asked, her face with its half-mocking, half-sensual smile turned up towards his, 'I often ask the band to play it for me when I'm out dancing. Of course, here at the Marquise's ball one cannot make requests of the band – that would be presumptious and ill-mannered. But I am so glad they are playing it.'

The night of the Marquise's ball! Memories floated up into André's mind, half-dazed as it was by the passion stirring in him. The urgency of his desire that night after dancing twice with Françoise . . . his rapid and fevered search to find some empty and convenient corner anywhere to conceal her and himself while he relieved that tremendous desire she had aroused.

He dropped Lucette's hand and put his arm round her waist. The hand fondling her rump gripped hard and pressed her belly against his throbbing passion. He gave a long sigh and fountained his tribute up the front of her crimson pyjamas. Lucette held him by the waist with both hands, rubbing her silk-clad body against him until he had finished.

'Yes, I see that you do like that tune,' she said, as calmly as if nothing had occurred, though her eyes were laughing at him.

'I find it very exciting,' André responded, trying to match her mood.

'Of that you have provided adequate proof,' she said, breaking away from him. As she stepped back he saw the evidence of his passion in a darkening stain on her pyjamas.

'I must take this off at once and put it to soak before any irreparable damage is done,' she observed.

'I shall replace it,' he offered at once.

'Yes, but in the meantime, dear impetuous André, I can hardly let my maid see me in this condition. Perhaps you will accompany me to my bedroom to assist me in removing this compromised pyjama suit.'

'But of course,' he said, smiling at her.

It occurred to him that his male part, now beginning to loll after its exertions, was still openly displayed. He lowered his hands to put the matter right and Lucette laughed at him.

'No need to hide it away,' she said, 'I'm sure that we shall find a further use for it when you have helped me out of my clothes.'

Naturally they found a use for it, that day and many days to follow. It would not be too much to say that Lucette had a touch of near-genius in finding uses for that interesting part of André's anatomy, making his private visits to her occasions of surprise and delight. In public her behaviour was always correct, whether they were at the races or dining out or attending someone's reception together or at the theatre. At such times she was a lively and amusing companion, but with no hint of her ability to devise unusual and secret pleasures, unless in the half-mocking smile that crept over her pretty face from time to time.

As was to be expected, the once amicable relations between André and Jacques Malplaquet turned sour. Malplaquet had once been privileged to enjoy Lucette's little games and now that he had been displaced in her affections by André he took it badly. He went so far as to ignore André's greeting when their paths crossed, turning his face deliberately away from him, even at social functions. André shrugged and paid no attention – after all, that was life. He felt that Malplaquet might have conceded defeat a little more graciously, but he never voiced this opinion to anyone, not even mutual friends. Since Malplaquet adopted that offended attitude, there was nothing to be done. There was a rumour that came to André's ears that his dispossessed rival had lost a lot of money on an ill-considered business venture and he was sorry for the man – but he felt it best not to approach him to offer condolences, for that surely would have been taken amiss. The rumour also said that Lacoste, of all people, had made money in the same deal, which seemed most unlikely to André, who knew that Lacoste had never dabbled in that branch of business. But it was only a vague rumour, one of many circulating among a certain circle of businessmen and André gave it no more than a passing thought. His life held far more pleasant mysteries to think about – such as what would be Lucette's next whim.

Lucette expressed herself as much impressed by André's abilities as a lover, by the style of his clothes, the trappings of his style of life – by almost everything about him. Her open admiration greatly increased the satisfaction which André derived from his liaison with her. She was even impressed by the fact that he was a member of the Brissard family, through his mother.

'I have met Monsieur Aristide Brissard,' she told him with some pride, 'he advised me over a small matter of business a few years ago. He is a most distinguished man – I could almost have fallen in love with him. And you are his nephew – anyone could guess that – you have the same air of distinction as he.'

'To be precise, I am only half Brissard,' said André modestly, 'my father is also distinguished. The name of Giroud is highly esteemed in certain circles.'

'But of course,' said Lucette.

She was sitting on his lap at this moment, a circumstance which imparted a strange touch to their conversation. They had been to hear Lucienne Boyer sing that evening and were delighted, as was all Paris, by her tender love songs and the gracefulness of her slender figure and pale oval face. Afterwards they had enjoyed a late supper and a bottle or two of excellent chilled Sancerre, before returning to Lucette's apartment for the main event of the evening.

Lucette was looking more than usually elegant that night. Her blonde hair was cut very short and smooth to her head, parted on one side – the effect was boyish, except for the delicately feminine profile and the thin arched eyebrows. Her frock was simplicity itself – the simplicity which only the most expensive of master couturiers can achieve. It was of ivory silk, sleeveless and cut deep between her impertinent breasts and cut even lower down her back – close fitting down to the waist, then a fuller skirt to her knees, showing off her slender and immaculately shaped legs.

André was sitting on the sofa in her salon, while she poured him a glass of cool champagne and brought it to him. The sofa was from the illustrious past, André had thought the first time he saw it, to judge by the shape of its feet and legs and the excellence of the carving on them. But it had been stripped of whatever upholstery its makers had given it and recovered in gold damask to match the style of Lucette's salon. He expected that she would seat

180

herself beside him, but after she had handed him the glass, she asked him to put his feet up.

Most obligingly, André swung up his legs and half-sat, half reclined, the length of the sofa. He raised an eyebrow in surprise and delight as she leaned over him to undo the buttons on his white evening waistcoat – and then the buttons of his black trousers.

'Ah!' he exclaimed in pleasure as she pulled up his shirt-front and released his most cherished part from its place of concealment. From the moment they had entered her apartment it had begun to stir itself in anticipation of what was to follow. The touch of her hand completed the process and it was at full stretch in an instant.

She straightened her back and stood looking down at what she had laid bare. Then with her smile of secret amusement she took hold of her skirt and slowly, centimetre by centimetre, raised it. André was fascinated as the rising hem revealed her garters of pale pink trimmed with tiny white rosebuds, her stocking-tops, then the satin skin of her thighs. Still the hem rose – exquisitely slowly – to the level where he expected to see the lace-trimmed edge of her underwear. But there was only the smooth pale columns of her thighs and his heart was thumping in his breast.

The upward movement stopped and André raised his eyes to her face. She was staring at him with an expression of amusement on her face, her scarlet-painted lips open to display her small white teeth.

'*Voyeur*!' she teased him.

'Yes,' he said, agreeing with her wholeheartedly. 'How beautiful you are, Lucette!'

'You think I've got good legs, do you?'

'Your legs are enchanting – and so is the rest of you.'

'Words are easy enough,' she said, smiling again, 'but the way that great thing of yours is jumping about gives me confidence that you mean what you are saying.'

'Assuredly,' André replied. 'He is nodding his head in agreement with me.'

Her skirt rose another centimetre and André sighed loudly as he spied at last the join of her thighs and the beginning of her blonde floss. It rose higher – and all was revealed to him – her plump little mound and its silky fur coat.

'But you are not wearing any underwear!' he babbled foolishly.

She held the front of her frock up around her waist, so that he half-glimpsed her navel and the little oval mole to the side of it.

'It was too hot this evening,' she answered casually, straddling his lap as he reclined on the sofa.

'You mean that all evening . . . ' André gasped as her hand took hold of his upright part firmly to guide it into the direction she intended, ' . . . you were wearing nothing but that flimsy frock?'

'Ah, now if you'd known!' she said with a smile.

'If only I had known!' he murmured as she sank slowly across him to push his firmness into her soft recess.

'You'd have had your hand up my clothes all evening, I suppose,' said Lucette. 'Next time we dine out together you can amuse yourself by speculating whether I've got any underwear under my frock or whether I'm bare-bottomed. That will keep you in a state of confusion for hours.'

She arranged her ivory-white skirt over her thighs so that he could see nothing of what was happening. But the sensations were more than adequate to keep him informed of her intentions – she was rocking slowly and gently back and forth, a movement almost imperceptible to the eye (particularly the eye made dim with emotion) but the effect on his imprisoned flesh was most gratifying.

'It would be polite to drink a toast to me,' she informed him, her hand gesturing towards the glass of champagne he still held.

182

'Forgive me,' he said, trembling with pleasure, 'you are so adorable and so beautiful that I was struck dumb for a moment. I raise my glass in salute to you, dear Lucette.'

As best he could in the circumstances, he lifted the glass and gulped down the champagne. Her rocking had become a little faster and firmer as she spoke and little spasms of exquisite feeling were rippling through his belly and groins.

Had another person entered the room just then – Lucette's maid, for example – nothing unseemly was to be seen. The juxtaposition of the two on the sofa was most unusual, of course. But apart from that, André was still elegant in his formal evening attire, his white bow tie neatly in place above his stiff shirt-front, his tail-coat on, his black patent leather shoes sticking out of the ends of his trousers. Lucette, astride him, had arranged her full white skirt almost primly, so that not even her knees were uncovered. Yet underneath that silk skirt – ah, what voluptuous sensations were being experienced by the closely joined parts! It was at this moment that Lucette introduced the topic of André's connection with the Brissard family. The conversation was incongruous in the extreme, yet André attempted to play the role required of him in Lucette's game.

'It is a great honour to be so intimately connected with a member of so important a family,' she said dreamily, rocking away.

'As for me, it is a privilege to be on such close terms with so beautiful and elegant a person as you,' André gabbled, hardly knowing what he was saying.

'Ever since I met your Uncle I have wanted to know more about your family,' Lucette murmured, her delicate movements becoming almost jerky.

'You shall! Whatever you want!' he gasped.

'Oh, André – I believe that something delightful is going to happen to me!'

'And to me!'

A moment later she was writhing on his lap as she reached the apex of her passion, her curled fingers digging into his belly through her skirt. André bucked hard as his own critical moments arrived, flooding her with his torrential release.

For a woman like Lucette, a man will do anything she requires – for skills like hers are rare and highly prized. It is not to be wondered at that many a woman who has reached the pinnacle of wordly success as the mistress of a rich and important man is – if her friends spoke the truth – plain of face and undistinguished of figure. Yet in spite of these natural disadvantages she becomes the owner of grand houses, a chateau perhaps, jewels, wardrobes full of the finest clothes, expensive motor-cars – even power, for many will approach her with a fine present in the hope that she will put a word in their favour into the ear of the man she has enchanted by her abilities in the bedroom. So it has always been – the portraits of the mistresses of Kings from our glorious history show them to be only averagely good-looking, even though it is certain that the Court painter flattered them to a considerable extent in his work.

Imagination – that is the unfailing aphrodisiac – and Lucette had it in full measure. One memorable afternoon when André called upon her, she announced that she proposed to give him a body massage. In the ordinary way, a masseur treats the client's body with the hands. Lucette's version was far more interesting than that. She massaged André's body with her own.

'Imagine that you have travelled to the Far East,' she instructed him, 'I am small and have golden skin, black hair and slanting eyes – yes? I am about to demonstrate to you one of the cultural specialities of my country.'

That she was blonde, tall and had alabaster skin was no barrier to André's imagination when it was aroused.

He bowed to her, half-seriously and half-comically, and requested her to be so kind as to proceed.

Her bed had been stripped of sheets and covered with an impermeable sheet of thin black rubber. André undressed completely and lay on it while she covered his body and limbs with sweet-smelling oil. He watched her with great interest as she sat naked beside him and oiled her own body too.

'Face down,' she said.

He turned over, his face cradled on his slippery arms and felt the weight of her slender body on his back. She lay on him and slid herself up and down his spine, her hands hooked over his shoulders to give herself a grip. André shuddered with pleasure as he felt her soft breasts squashed against his skin, rubbing up and down gently – and her warm belly sliding over him. As she moved downwards he experienced the exquisite sensation of the soft hair between her legs rubbing over the cheeks of his bottom.

'Honourable white master like Oriental massage?' she enquired in a mock-Chinese accent.

'Oh, yes!' he sighed, trying to savour all the sensations at once.

By the time she had been on his back for five minutes, André was in a high state of arousal. She pretended to be astonished when he turned over to her command and revealed his male projection at full stretch.

'Honourable white master think bad thoughts,' she said in the sing-song accent, 'maybe massage too much for white foreigners. This person stop now.'

'No, don't stop!' André pleaded.

She sat astride his belly and slithered up and down, massaging him from chest to thighs with that most tender part between her legs. Her eyes were sparkling.

'Slave girl begin to think bad thoughts now,' she said, 'must change massage before this person brings shame on herself.'

She indicated that he should part his legs so that she could lie on the rubber between them and massage him with her small slippery breasts, starting at his navel and working slowly downwards until his upright part was quivering between those pliant delights.

André was near the end of his tether. He grasped at her shoulders to pull her up his body and turn her onto her back so that he could assume the superior position and plunge into her. But she was so slippery from the oil that he could not take hold of her – each time he attempted it she slid easily out of his hands.

'Now honourable visitor understand purpose of oil,' she giggled, 'only way poor girl can be saved from ravishment by every customer.'

André was in heaven – experiencing that sweet frustration and certain of eventual success. His chest heaved to his rapid breathing, his distended part slithered across Lucette's belly as he strove to roll her underneath him, she laughing and resisting to prolong for a few more moments the thrilling struggle.

Yet it was at this supreme moment that their game was interrupted by an insistent tapping on the bedroom door!

'Go away!' Lucette cried out furiously.

'Madame,' her maid's voice insisted, 'it is a matter of the utmost urgency!'

'What is it? Is the building on fire?'

'No, Madame – you must come to the telephone. There is an emergency.'

To André's horror Lucette freed herself from him and skipped off the bed. She leaned over to kiss his mouth, her hand giving his straining appendage a playful tug.

'Be patient for only a moment,' she murmured, 'while I put an end to this nonsense.'

He watched her walk swiftly across the room to the door, still naked, her marvellous body gleaming with oil. She turned for an instant to smile lasciviously at him and was gone. Poor André lay on the impermeable sheet,

hands under his head, staring at his disappointed but still
uprearing limb. So near, he thought, another second or
two and she would have surrendered! And you, dear
friend, would have slid yourself into that soft little slit of
hers! Not all the telephones in the world could then have
prevented you from discharging your duty. But this! To
be almost at the moment of supreme pleasure – and then
abandoned! It is atrocious! As soon as she returns and
you have relieved me of this monstrous burden of desire,
I shall demand an explanation from Lucette, believe me.
Nothing like this shall ever happen again – I give you my
word.

To a man in André's condition seconds are like hours.
He twisted about on the bed in his discomfort, grinding
his teeth and clenching his fists. There was no clock in
the room, his own watch was with his clothes and he had
no way of knowing how much time had elapsed since the
dreadful moment when Lucette slipped out of his hands.
He groaned and rolled over face down – then gasped as
the slide of his sensitive member along the oily rubber
sheet almost precipitated the crisis for which his body was
yearning. Hurriedly he turned over onto his side to avoid
the catastrophe, at the very moment when the door was
flung open with a crash and Lucette rushed in, her eyes
blazing with anger.

'Pig!' she screamed at him. 'Traitor! Deceiver! I never
want to see you again!'

André stared at her in amazement, wondering if
perhaps some bad news conveyed to her by telephone
had rendered her insane. But what?

'What are you saying, Lucette?'

'You have betrayed me!'

'Not so! I have not been with another woman since the
day I met you.'

'I'm not talking about that! You know very well what
I mean!'

She was a magnificent sight, naked and enraged, as she

paced up and down at the foot of the bed, her breasts and belly gleaming with oil.

'I really don't understand what you are saying. How have I betrayed you?'

'The Verney business – you deliberately lied to me to make a fool of me!'

'What Verney business?' André asked, puzzled by her words.

Then his memory stirred and he recalled telling her casually, a week or two before, something his cousin Maurice Brissard had confided to him.

'But anything I said about that is a private family matter,' he said, becoming angry himself at the ludicrous situation he was in.

'Because of your lies I have lost a lot of money,' Lucette said with great bitterness. 'And a good friend of mine has lost millions. I suppose you find that amusing? Get out of here!'

She strode to where his clothes lay across a chair, bundled them up and flung them through the open bedroom door, pointing after them with a shaking finger.

'Get out!' she screamed.

André was seething with rage as he got up and stalked out of the room, hearing the door slam behind him and a key turn in the lock. It did not improve his temper to see Lucette's maid peeping at him from around another door, her hand going to her mouth to cover a grin as she spied his glistening member waving about in front of him. He took his clothes into the bathroom to dress away from the maid's sniggering and realised that he needed to bath to rid himself of the massage oil that covered him from neck to knees. Nevertheless, he had no intention of remaining a moment longer than necessary in Lucette's apartment.

He took a big fluffy towel to wipe himself as dry as possible before dressing, muttering incoherently under his breath as he scrubbed at his shoulders and chest. His anger was not directed against Lucette, as might have been thought, but against his cousin Maurice. André had fitted the puzzle together in his mind – Maurice had intentionally given him information which he had passed on heedlessly to Lucette – and for some reason André did not yet understand, the information had been false. It was Lucette, that marvellous lover, who had incurred a financial loss as a result! And at what a moment this treachery on the part of Maurice had been discovered! Maurice must be made to suffer!

Muttering in this fashion to himself, André rubbed his belly briskly to soak up the oil, then his stiff part – utterly without regard for the condition it was in! At once a spasm of ecstasy flashed through him like a lightning-bolt. He jerked the towel away, contracted the muscles of his belly tightly to arrest the process that he knew was beginning – but it was too late! There was a roaring in his ears and his heart pounded – his fleshy staff bounded and André doubled over helplessly as it spat its essence into the bath-tub in long jets. Yet even in this moment of humiliation, in his mind's eye he saw a vision of Lucette as she had been in the bedroom, naked and magnificent, pointing at him in her fury, her pretty breasts heaving with the vehemence of her denunciation of him.

When, after a visit to his own home for a bath and change of clothes, André confronted his cousin, his mood was one of implacable hatred. He spoke loudly and with malign intensity, accusing Maurice of double-dealing, perjury, deception, fraud – whatever came into his mind. His mood grew even blacker when Maurice burst into laughter.

'My dear André – do sit down,' said Maurice, regaining control of himself, 'there are things I must explain to you.'

'I want no explanations from you – I want justice!' André told him.

'Very well, you shall have justice then. What do you regard as justice?'

'An apology to me for the disgraceful way you have used my good nature for your own questionable purposes. And for Mademoiselle Cabuchon, full restitution of whatever she has lost in this affair.'

'Ah,' said Maurice, 'but would that be justice? Before we decide, let me tell you of one or two details in Mademoiselle Cabuchon's background of which you are obviously unaware. I am sure that you remember your history lessons at school, in particular, the manner in which Catherine de Medici ruled when she was Queen Mother of France during the infancy of her children.'

'We may dispense with the history and fables and legends,' said André, 'get to the point.'

'But it is the point. Queen Catherine hit upon an excellent device for keeping herself informed of the activities of her political opponents. She recruited and supervised the training of what came to be known as her "flying squad" – now do you remember?'

'No I do not,' said André angrily, 'What the devil have I to do with political espionage and intrigue?'

'Nothing, I hope, but the principle is the same. The "flying squad" was composed of pretty young women selected from the families of impoverished small gentry. If my memory serves me well, the ages of these volunteers ranged from fifteen to about twenty-five. They were infiltrated into the houses of persons known to be enemies of the Queen Mother and her policies, by the simple device of becoming the cherished mistresses of her opponents. They remained loyal to Catherine and reported to her the pillow-talk of the men she most distrusted. Now do you understand?'

'You are suggesting that Mademoiselle Cabuchon is playing a similar part for some other person? I find that offensive in the extreme!'

190

'I am not suggesting, André. I am telling you as a matter of established fact that she does precisely that.'

'Who is the monstrous person involved? I shall kill him!'

'Ask yourself – who brought you and Mademoiselle together?'

'Lacoste!'

'You have your answer.'

'I do not believe you – this is all a fabrication,' said André, the fight going out of him so that at last he sank into a chair.

'Consider then, who was it who had the honour of being Mademoiselle's most intimate friend before you, André?'

'That is no concern of yours.'

'My question was rhetorical,' said Maurice pleasantly, 'there is no necessity to answer it. It was Jacques Malplaquet, there is no secret about that. Poor Malplaquet suffered a sharp loss in a business arrangement with Lacoste very shortly after Mademoiselle Cabuchon transferred her favours to you. And while I do not wish to distress you by labouring the point, before him there was another who encountered the same unexpected business reversal. I will not name him.'

'Have I been duped?' André asked in dismay.

'There is something else you perhaps ought to know, unpleasant though you may find it. Those favours you esteem so highly – and why not? She is a very beautiful woman – have in the past year or two been offered very discreetly to me and to my brother Charles. Of course, knowing of her allegiance to Lacoste, we declined politely.'

'But this is a nightmare!' André exclaimed faintly.

'When you began to ask questions and display an interest in business,' Maurice went on, 'this was so far out of character that I become interested in your motives. It was easy enough to ascertain that you had become

Mademoiselle Cabuchon's close friend. The connection was clear – Lacoste intended to obtain private information through you which he could use to our disadvantage and to his own gain.'

'So you told me a false story,' said André thoughtfully.

'Not entirely – that would have been seen by Lacoste for what it was. It is well known that my sister Jeanne's husband is not able for reasons of health to look after his business. Since he became indisposed I have been taking care of it in the interests of my sister and her children. I have neither the time nor the inclination to continue like that forever and so it was decided between Jeanne and me, and agreed by her husband, that the business should be sold and the proceeds invested to provide a proper income. All that was required was a buyer at the right price.'

'And that was Lacoste,' said André, suddenly smiling, 'you are clever, Maurice, that I do not deny.'

'He bought it at a very high price because he had a strange idea that Verney's company was about to be awarded an enormous contract from the Army. Where such a thought came from, I find it hard to imagine.'

'You sly devil! You hinted to me that you personally had bribed a high government official to get the contract – you even named him to me!' said André, laughing at last.

'You must have misunderstood whatever I said to you,' Maurice answered suavely but very firmly, 'I have never bribed a government official in my life – the idea is unthinkable.'

'But of course. Tell me then, what has Lacoste really bought?'

'A business which is in difficulty.'

'And the Verneys have secured their position, thanks to your little intrigue! You are most ingenious – I forgive you everything.'

'Most unfortunately Mademoiselle Cabuchon has lost

the commission which Lacoste pays on the deals he arranges on information supplied by her.'

'She is a whore!' exclaimed André viciously, 'She deserves it.'

'That is a cruel word to describe so enchanting a person.'

'Enchanting, yes – but false. I shall go to her apartment and spit in her face!'

'You must do no such ill-mannered thing, André. Go to her apartment and make love to her – that will be far more satisfactory for both of you. I have been told that she has remarkable talents in the bedroom.'

'She threw me out! Can you believe it – *she* threw *me* naked out of her bedroom!'

'A lovers' quarrel – a moment of pique – easily remedied.'

'Do you think so?' André asked, hope rising in his heart.

'Certainly. You may be sure that after this episode which has cost him so very much money Lacoste will want nothing more to do with Mademoiselle Cabuchon. She is alone in the world – except for an aged mother she supports in some distant suburb. When she has reconsidered her position I am sure that she will welcome you back.'

André got up to shake his cousin's hand warmly.

'Maurice, how can I ever thank you?' he said, his voice charged with emotion.

THE FORTUNE-TELLER

It is because women are the most rational of creatures, contrary to what men believe about them, that they pay attention to fortune-tellers. The superficial logic which enslaves male thinking compels them to brush aside the arts of divination by cards, palms, mirrors and other means as nothing more than superstition. But women know that events and situations have a certain knack of repeating themselves and from that there follows the ineluctable conclusion that each person's life forms a particular pattern. If the individual pattern can be discerned in good time, then it can be used to advantage.

Naturally, it is only some bizarre and heretical Protestant sects which suppose that the course of one's life is predetermined from the moment of birth, a belief running contrary to religion, commonsense and experience. The truth of the matter is that we each carry our destiny within us, for destiny is the outcome of character. For this reason alone a skilled and gifted fortune-teller, who can see through the veils behind which we conceal our true selves, can assess character and predict the probable course of an individual's life.

It was therefore to a fortune-teller that Yvonne Daladier had recourse in a time of indecision. At the age of twenty-five she believed that she had endured more than a fair share of disappointment. She was, as all her friends agreed, a beautiful young woman. She dressed well, when she could afford to do so. She was lively and intelligent

194

– and she was a charming lover. Yet with so many qualities to recommend her, she had neither a husband nor a
permanent lover.

The reason for her unfortunate condition, Yvonne had
come to realise, was that she invariably chose unsuitable
men. They fell in love with her, they set her up in well-
furnished apartments and bought fashionable clothes for
her, they entertained her in the very best places and they
made love to her in a satisfactory manner. Not one of the
five who had so far been accorded these privileges had
ever proposed marriage to her, though that was under-
standable in the case of the two who already had wives
and families. But apart from that, these lovers eventually
went off elsewhere, leaving her to pay a rent she could
not afford. Altogether, it was infuriating!

Her latest protector was Paul-Henri Courval, a handsome man only a few years older than Yvonne herself.
He had plenty of money, that went without saying. He
was not very clever and not at all witty, but that was of
no importance. In some ways it was a distinct advantage,
in that after a month or so of the enjoyment of Yvonne's
very considerable charms, he declared himself to be madly
in love with her. Yvonne found that most satisfactory, not
merely because it made Paul-Henri especially generous
towards her but because it held the promise of a longer
relationship between them and made it possible for her
to nudge him imperceptibly towards the idea of marriage.

At the same time, she felt it would be sensible to seek
advice from one who could read the secrets of the human
heart. If Paul-Henri was going to prove unsuitable eventually, then the sooner she knew the truth, the better. On
the other hand, if she had made a sensible choice this
time, then she could go ahead with the steps necessary to
bring him to a proposal of marriage and thereby guarantee
her own future comfort and happiness.

One night, as they lay naked together on her bed after
a tempestuous act of love which left Yvonne feeling

somewhat exhausted, she stroked his chest gently while she introduced the topic that had been in her mind all day. Paul-Henri, resting comfortably on his back after his amorous exertions, was in a very good humour – as well he might be – and disposed to listen to her. Even so, he was surprised.

'A fortune-teller!' he exclaimed. 'But why?'

'She's very good,' Yvonne assured him, her finger-tips gliding over his flat nipples in a way calculated to soothe him.

'When did you see her?'

'This morning. A friend recommended her to me. It was very strange – she told me things which she couldn't possibly have known about.'

'But evidently she did know – she probably got a few facts about you from your friend – they're clever at wheedling information out of unsuspecting customers.'

'Not even my friend knew some of the things.'

'Friends often know, or guess, more than you think. They are all charlatans, these fortune-tellers – they make a living out of gullibility.'

'That may be true of most of them, but this one is different. She upset me.'

'But that's dreadful!' said Paul-Henri, taking her into his arms to comfort her, 'what did she say?'

'I can't tell you that – I gave my word. But if she is right, then our love will not last long.'

'What nonsense! I adore you, chérie, and you know that. This person is a fraud who should be brought to the attention of the police.'

'Perhaps – but promise me one thing first.'

'Anything,' he said expansively, his hands fondling the smooth cheeks of her bottom, 'you have only to ask.'

'Go and see her yourself tomorrow. If you tell me afterwards that she is wrong, then I will believe you and that will be the end of my worries.'

Paul-Henri hadn't expected that, but he rose to the occasion.

'To please you, dear Yvonne, I will go and see this lying fraud and tell her that to her face.'

As is well known, promises made in bed often lead to unfortunate results. Be that as it may, on the next day at eleven in the morning Paul-Henri made his way by taxi to the Butte Montmartre to confront the fortune-teller who had given anxiety to the woman he loved. The address he sought was not to be found in the Montmartre known to foreign tourists – the Montmartre of entertainment and music and small restaurants – but in a narrow back-street of shabby houses that seemed not to have been painted or cleaned since they were built in the previous century. On the ground floor of the number he had been given he discovered a small bar with a dirty floor and a zinc-topped counter at which stood two or three scruffy men he judged to be of the petty criminal class.

The bar-tender, collarless, unshaven and with only one eye, sold him a small glass of abominable cognac and told him that Mademoiselle Marie lived on tne top top floor. Paul-Henri was amazed that the fastidious Yvonne should have visited so squalid a place and he regarded it as one more proof of the irrationality of women. If Fate is to speak to us, he thought, it will not be in a filthy den like this.

The men at the bar were whispering together and occasionally glancing at him. His expensive clothes marked him as a target for larceny, he realised, and he already knew what he would do if attacked. He would fling the wretched spirit in his glass into the eyes of the leading assailant, instantly blinding him for life, kick the second one very hard between the legs to incapacitate him permanently, then snatch the cognac bottle from the bar where One-Eye had placed it in the hope that he would order a second drink and smash it over the head of the third man, breaking his skull at the very least and possibly

197

killing him outright. The bar-tender by then would be cowering behind his unwiped bar and would offer no resistance as Paul-Henri left the thieves' rat-hole and strolled down the narrow street to find a representative of the law – if any were to be found in this district.

Nothing of the sort occurred, of course, and he had no opportunity to demonstrate his courage. He left his unfinished drink on the bar and climbed the creaking stairs to the top floor. There was no landing – the stairs ended abruptly at a wooden door from which the green paint of fifty years ago was peeling. He knocked and went in.

The room in which he found himself was made smaller by a shabby grey curtain stretched from wall to wall to divide it in two. The only illumination was that of a sky-light in the sloping roof, the floor was bare and unswept – all this Paul-Henri saw in a glance of distaste that wrinkled his nose. But then he saw the fortune-teller.

She sat, this Mademoiselle Marie, with her back to the curtain, at a small square table on which she was laying out playing cards in parallel rows. She looked up as the door closed behind him and he stood still. He had expected to meet an old woman, though he could not have explained why. Mademoiselle Marie was not yet thirty – hardly older than Yvonne, he thought.

She had a flowered scarf tied round her head and, from under it, her long black hair hung down to well below her shoulders. Paul-Henri had never seen such long hair on a woman in all his life and it held him spell-bound for a moment. It was hopelessly unstylish, but it was magnificent, he thought. Marie's face was broad, with high cheek-bones, a strong nose and a broad mouth. But it was her eyes that compelled attention. They were set wide apart, they were black, they shone – and they were unblinking.

'Sit down, M'sieu,' she said, breaking the silence.

On the near side of the table stood a rickety chair that

looked to have been bought in the Flea Market for a few centimes. Paul-Henri sat and looked at Marie across the table, suddenly aware of her perfume. It was a heavy and sensual fragrance that hinted at . . . but he closed his mind to thoughts of that kind and concentrated on the reason for his visit.

'You wish to consult me?' she prompted him.

'Yes . . . that is to say, no . . . the fact is, Mademoiselle, a very dear friend of mine came to see you yesterday and was disturbed by some nonsense or other you told her. I must make my position clear – I refuse to allow her to be upset like this. What did you say to her?'

Marie was wearing a short-sleeved frock of shiny black satin that buttoned down the bodice. That is to say, more precisely, it could be buttoned down the bodice for, as Paul-Henri saw, the buttons were open from the scalloped neckline to between her breasts. More than that, as she moved her arm to lay another card from the pack face-down on one of the rows on the table, her breasts rolled under the frock to give a view extensive enough to inform Paul-Henri that they were large and bare beneath the thin black material. He found the sight very distracting and almost missed what she said.

'Several clients consulted me yesterday. Which one of them was your dear, dear friend, M'sieu?'

'Mademoiselle Daladier,' Paul-Henri replied, offended by the impertinent way in which she had phrased the question.

'Ah, the pretty one – yes, I might have guessed that a distinguished man like you would be interested in her.'

'If you please,' said Paul-Henri curtly, 'I do not wish to have my personal affairs discussed. I am here to clear up what may have been a misunderstanding.'

He took out his note-case, thinking that the sight of money would inspire the fortune-teller to a prediction of good fortune, long life and happiness which he could carry back triumphantly to Yvonne. But Marie shook her head slowly from side to side.

'Put your money away, M'sieu. My clients pay me after I have told them what I see, not before.'

'As you wish. What did you see for Mademoiselle Daladier?'

'That is confidential between her and me. But I'll tell you this much – she came to consult me about you.'

'About me? That's ridiculous!'

'Perhaps. I could tell her nothing about you because I'd never seen you. But now you're here – let me see your palms, M'sieu.'

'I didn't come here to have my hands read.'

'Maybe not – but it will give you something to tell your friend to ease her mind.'

'Oh, very well then,' Paul-Henri agreed impatiently.

He put his forearms on the table with his palms upwards. Marie studied them carefully, comparing the lines on his left hand with those on his right hand, tracing them with her finger-tip. It took a long time, during which she said nothing to him.

Her touch had an unexpected effect on Paul-Henri. In spite of the extreme inappropriateness of the circumstances, his male part grew stiff and long and he found himself trying to see more of Marie's breasts as she leaned over the table to look at his hands.

But this is terrible, he said to himself. Last night I loved myself to a standstill with my beautiful Yvonne – and here I am getting excited over an overweight gypsy! It's that damned perfume of hers – I must get out of here at once before I am tempted to do something stupid.

Marie settled the matter by laying her own hands flat on his. Her palms were warm and dry and it was as if an electric current passed through Paul-Henri – from his palms, up his arms, down through his spine and up his erect part! He gasped at the sensation, certain that he would discharge into his underwear unless the contact with Marie was broken at once. But her eyes held him – her unblinking stare kept him in his seat, trembling on the brink of an involuntary climax of passion.

'Your hands tell me that you are as honest as any, as selfish as most, open-handed to those you love, deaf to the rest – in short, an average normal man, though with more money than most have.'

'Is that all?' he managed to say through the hot emotions that both delighted and appalled him as he trembled under her touch.

Not being a complete fool, he was by then wondering how much Marie would ask to take her clothes off and let him relieve the monstrous desire she had aroused. After all, his experience was that all women of her sort – gypsies, vagabonds, cafe singers, circus folk and the rest – they were readily available to the man who had money in his pocket and was not afraid to spend it. Marie looked into his flushed face and nodded, as if reading his thoughts – no great feat, and one requiring no particular powers of clairvoyance, for one look at him in that condition would have told any woman what was in his mind.

'Come with me,' she said, releasing his hands.

When she stood up from the table Paul-Henri saw that her shiny black frock was held in tightly at her waist by a broad belt of black leather with a big silver buckle, so emphasising the outward swell of her bosom and hips. With one hand she pulled aside the dingy curtain behind her, making the wooden rings on which it hung rattle together, and with the other hand she gestured him through. With a sigh of relief, he got up and walked past her, so close that his arm brushed lightly against her breasts. She made no move to avoid the contact.

There was no window in the back of the room and, when the curtain was drawn back into place again, it was half-dark in there. The space divided off for Marie's private apartment was tiny and most of the space in it was occupied by a low divan pushed up close to the wall.

There was only one touch of colour in this unprepossessing cubicle – a marvellously embroidered Spanish shawl in crimson and black spread over the divan.

Marie stood with her back to the curtain, seeming hardly to breathe, an enigmatic expression on her face as she waited for Paul-Henri's reaction. He was momentarily at a loss and awaited a sign from her.

'Not what you expected?' she asked casually.

He shrugged, not wanting to give offence.

'You must remember, M'sieu, that I am not a whore. I don't take men to a comfortable bedroom to sell my body. I tell fortunes.'

All the same, Paul-Henri thought, here we are in her sleeping-quarters and money will assuredly pass between us before I depart – so what does that make her?

'You seem a little confused,' Marie said. 'You've never met anyone like me before, have you?'

She took a step towards him as she spoke and again he was aware of the musky perfume she wore. It seemed to affect the nerves and make him breathe a little faster. Her hand reached up to touch his cheek.

'Put yourself in my hands,' she said, 'do not be afraid – unless you are afraid of the truth.'

'Whatever the truth may be,' he said, as jauntily as possible, 'I am sure that I can face it with equanimity.'

'Good, good,' she said, almost absent-mindedly.

Her hand left his cheek to trail down his chest and belly until she could trace the outline of his hardness through his trousers.

'Yes, that's as it should be,' she said, as if to herself, 'otherwise I can achieve nothing.'

'Nor I,' Paul-Henri said with a nervous smile.

Her fingers were busy with his trouser buttons, but she frowned at his little joke.

'This is not a process to be laughed at,' she reproached him.

'Forgive me – I have never had my fortune told before. At least, not like this.'

'No, but *this* has been in a woman's hand before.'

She had the emblem of his virility out of his trousers and was gripping it firmly, her touch increasing its rigidity. Paul-Henri sighed with pleasure.

'You must answer all my questions if I am to be of service to you, M'sieu.'

'I took your question to be rhetorical, Mademoiselle. But yes, as you say, that part of me has been in a woman's hand before – and in more delectable parts of her body.'

'Just answer my questions – I don't need to know your life history. You have been with more than one woman, naturally. Your pretty friend was not the first to play with this, was she?'

'No, nor the second – I am nearly thirty years old – what do you expect?'

'I didn't ask you that,' and she tugged sharply at his swollen projection.

'My apologies, Mademoiselle.'

'That's better. Do you know where a man's heart is to be found?'

'Why, in his chest, I suppose.'

'Wrong – it is lower down. This is your heart I am holding in my hand – this length of stiff flesh you think of by another name. This is what guides your affections and passions.'

Paul-Henri was beginning to tremble at the knees as a result of her attentions to what he must now learn to think of as his *heart*.

'And where are a man's brains to be found,' she asked, 'do you know that?'

'You must tell me,' he murmured.

One of her hands unclasped itself from his *heart*, burrowed inside his open trousers and took hold of his dependents.

'Here,' she said, 'your brains are in these. Does that surprise you?'

'Your words astonish me,' Paul-Henri sighed.

In his mind was the thought that in a few more moments it would be Marie's turn to be surprised when her vigorous manipulation caused him to pour out his excitement onto her black frock.

'Do not mock me or it will be the worse for you,' she warned him, the hand clasping his *brains* tightening to the point where it was almost painful. 'These are what control your actions, and what is in your head merely complies – that is the truth of the matter.'

He gasped as her hands left him suddenly. He swayed as he stood, his male part sticking stiffly out of his trousers. Marie unfastened the silver buckle at her waist and let the belt fall to the floor. In another moment her frock was up and over her head. Without it she was completely naked, Paul-Henri noted with delight – but he was treated to the briefest of glimpses of her full breasts before she stepped past him towards the divan. He had a moment or two to admire the firm round cheeks of her bottom as she flicked the gorgeous Spanish shawl out of the way and then she seated herself on the divan, facing him again, her knees apart and her bare feet solidly on the dusty floor.

Paul-Henri was very nearly at the apex of excitement from her fondling and the sight of her naked body fired him to action. He stepped forward to fling himself on her, carry her over onto her back and drive straight in to assuage the incredible desire she had aroused. But it was not to be so – Marie moved as quickly as a cat, one strong leg bending upwards between them so that the sole of her foot stopped him, planted against his quivering projection and holding it flat to his belly.

'You're not here to do that,' she informed him sharply, 'you are here to have your fortune told.'

'For God's sake!' he gasped, 'I'm desperate! I can't stop now – I'll give you whatever you want!'

'I told you that I am not a whore for sale,' she reminded him. 'Do you think that you can rape me?'

He stared at her sturdy arms and legs, at the muscles of her thighs and her confident expression. Perhaps he could and perhaps not – either way it would be a long and noisy struggle that would surely bring the criminals up from the bar below to her aid.

'I implore you!' he said.

'That's better. Down on your knees!'

She removed her foot and Paul-Henri sank to his knees between her parted legs.

How desirable she was, he thought feverishly, her skin a rich olive-brown colour – ah, with a gasp of surprise he noticed for the first time that she had a little five-pointed star tattooed in blue on the upper curve of one breast.

'What does that mean?' he asked, trying to touch it, but she pushed his hand away.

'That's none of your business. Put your hands on my hips – and otherwise don't move at all, understand?'

Paul-Henri nodded and did as she said. Her fleshy hips were warm and yielding under his hands and he groaned in frustration. To achieve his goal meant that he would have to go along with her ludicrous mystification and to pretend that he fully believed her claim not to be for sale – but he hoped with every fibre of his being that she would not spin out this farce too long before allowing him to proceed to the natural culmination of his passion. Her perfume was heavy in his nostrils – it seemed to emanate from every part of her body, as if she soaked herself in it from head to foot. He could scent it in her long black hair hanging down over her shoulders, on her meaty breasts – it even rose from her thighs and groin! He looked down at the mat of coarse black hair which covered the lower part of her belly – and while he was staring, she raised her legs and wrapped them tightly round his waist.

'Keep your hands on my hips,' she warned him.

She took a firm grasp of his engorged part once more and for a delicious moment he believed that she intended to insert its swollen head into the plump lips between her legs, now exposed to him by the position of her thighs around his middle. But his hope was dashed – she laid his projection the length of those warm lips and, with the flat of her hand, pressed it against her crinkly fur. Inadequate though this arrangement was, Paul-Henri still found a fierce excitement in the contact between their most intimate parts.

'Look into my eyes,' Marie instructed him.

He forced himself to look away from his baulked pride, so very close to where he wanted it to be, yet trapped under her hand. His gaze travelled slowly up her broad belly, up to her breasts and paused at the tattoo mark, then up to her unsmiling face at last. The eyes he looked into gleamed with an emotion he found it impossible to identify.

'Tell me your name,' she said.

'You know it already.'

'Tell me your full name!'

'Paul-Henri Courval.'

'Good, keep looking into my eyes.'

He had no choice – her compelling stare held him immobile.'

'What do you see?' she asked.

'In your eyes? A certain darkness – but it has depth . . . there is a sense of an impending revelation . . . I can't describe it.'

'Look through my eyes into my soul. In a moment the clouds will part and you will understand.'

Paul-Henri was held almost as if in a trance by her bright and unblinking stare. His state of arousal had dulled his critical faculties and, even while he trembled with pleasurable sensation, he was unaware that the hand that pressed his erection to her mat of hair was moving insidiously. His only thought was that his whole body was hot and shaking and that some overwhelming event was about to take place.

'What do you see?' Marie repeated.

'I see . . . I see . . . '

Before he could determine what it was that he believed he could see in her eyes, his body convulsed in a paroxysm of gratification and his tormented passion gushed out beneath her hand.

'No!' he exclaimed in consternation, 'No!'

' . . . four, five, six, seven . . . ' he heard her counting aloud as the spasms shook him.

Then he was still, an angry discontent in his heart at the way in which this so-called fortune-teller had led him to expect much and then tricked him. He tried to pull away from her, his intention to leave at once with an appropriately rude remark or two about fraudulent practices. But she held him fast between her strong legs, her hand still clamping his disappointed part to her.

'Wait,' she said, 'I have it now.'

'Whatever it is that you have,' Paul-Henri said curtly, 'it is not where I expected you to have it. Release me – or is it part of your scheme to provoke me into forcing you to let me go?'

'Don't you want to hear your fortune? You find my methods unusual, perhaps, but they are effective.'

'I wish this entire transaction to end now.'

'As you wish,' and she removed her legs from his waist.

He was on his feet at once, buttoning his trousers. Marie remained seated on the divan, the evidence of his passion visible on the thick black hair which adorned her belly.

'Your fee?' Paul-Henri demanded.

'You owe me nothing, M'sieu, since I haven't told you anything.'

He had not the least intention of letting this creature extend her victory over him by a display of generosity. He delved into his pocket for all his loose change and flung the handful of coins onto the floor between her bare feet. She smiled in mockery at his gesture and, as he left abruptly, she called after him:

'You'll be back – we'll talk about payment then.'

Paul-Henri was in an extremely bad temper as he strode through the narrow streets until he found himself in a part of Montmartre he recognised. He went into the first decent bar he could find and drunk a glass of good cognac – not the rot-gut he had been offered before – while he set his chaotic thoughts in order.

What could have been the fortune-teller's purpose in leading him into so wretched a substitute for an act of love? That was the question he found impossible to answer to his satisfaction. She had not done it for gain, evidently, for she had refused to take money from him. She had not done it to tell his fortune through some bizarre form of bodily contact, as she had hinted, for that was too absurd an idea to contemplate at all. Unless she was in some way deranged, perhaps . . . ? But that seemed unlikely. She had given every indication of intelligence and purpose. Did she suffer from some type of perversion that gave her pleasure from handling men in that particular way? That seemed the most probable hypothesis, even though he had not observed any signs of pleasure in her demeanour during the episode or afterwards. The whole affair was an enigma for a doctor or a priest to resolve!

When Paul-Henri left the bar and strolled on, he was more puzzled than angry. He came eventually to the Place du Tertre, where the usual crowd of hopeful but penniless artists were exhibiting their paintings under the trees in the middle of the square. At first glance the pictures appeared to be about equally divided between views of old Montmartre, views of the white-domed church of

Sacré-Coeur and views of naked women in various poses. Painters, Paul-Henri reflected, seemed to be much devoted to naked women as a subject for their work. One or two of them were passably painted, many were not. He almost grunted with surprise at the sight of one that depicted a big-breasted woman sitting on the side of a bed in almost exactly the position the fortune-teller was in when he left her room. But closer examination showed it to be a portrait of a different woman, with light-brown hair arranged in a fringe over her forehead and a somewhat stupid expression. And without the strange blue star tattoo on her breast, needless to say!

When he had seen as much of the exhibition as he found interesting, Paul-Henri decided that he was hungry. He lunched well in one of the little restaurants for which Montmartre is known – an excellent piece of filet de boeuf and a bottle of good red burgundy. He was unable to dismiss from his mind the fortune-teller's parting words to him: 'You'll be back.' She had said it with such confidence! To a man she had just tricked in the most despicable manner!

There is, as everyone knows, no better or more certain way to banish a man's annoyance and to reconcile him to the world than good food and good wine. As his spirits were raised, Paul-Henri found himself dwelling upon the memory of Mademoiselle Marie's very obvious physical advantages – all of which had been presented to his view, if to no other part of him. The clasp of her legs about his waist was, in retrospect, very enjoyable. It would without question be an exceptionally gratifying experience to feel those legs round his waist again while he lay on her broad belly and flattened her breasts under him in the pleasant exertion of discharging his passion into her secret recess!

More than that, not only would it be gratifying, but he owed it to himself to even the score between them.

For all Marie's talk of not selling her body, Paul-Henri was still convinced that it was only a matter of how much money she was offered. He would return to her rat-hole of a room and place on the table before her more money than she had ever seen before at one time in her life – and then she would agree to do anything he wanted. After all, she had made it clear that she expected him to return. She had gone so far as to say that they would then discuss her fee. Paul-Henri's mind was made up – he called for his bill and was soon on his way back to where she lived.

Through the street-level window he saw that the same two or three idlers were in the bar – well, what else could one expect from that type of person? He climbed the dusty stairs to the top floor and, without knocking, entered Marie's room. The reason for not knocking was one of pride. To knock is to seek permission to enter – and Paul-Henri was not here as a supplicant but as a man come to purchase a certain service.

The fortune-teller was not there. Her cards were spread carelessly on the table as if she had completed a reading and then swept her hand across the rows to break up the pattern. A faint trace of her perfume lingered in the air and made his nostrils dilate as he sought to savour this evanescent memory.

It was decidedly strange, of course, that a man of his subtle tastes and refined pleasures should find anything to interest him in a woman he regarded as coarse. He found it difficult to explain to himself why he was on fire for her and in what lay the appeal of her earthy sensuality. But the simple truth is that men, however delicate their tastes become, remain part animal in their nature, most especially in all matters relating to the appendage between their thighs – to which they ascribe a ridiculously inflated importance. Let a man be without the company of the woman he loves for a day or two and even a washer-woman, so long as she is not grotesque of appearance, has the power to stiffen his male part. And if he has been without the intimate friendship of a woman for a week or more, then even a washerwoman of grotesque appearance

210

will serve his turn. Any harbour in a storm, as seafarers say! Marie, though not beautiful by any stretch of the imagination, was not ugly.

How long Paul-Henri stood by the table in the dimly-lit room, his homburg hat on his head, his lemon yellow gloved hands clasped in front of him, he could never afterwards determine. His reverie was disturbed by a sound from behind the grey curtain which divided the room – the sound of a long sigh.

It was unmistakable that sigh – the sound of a woman with her lover! Marie was at home, after all! And more than that, she was lying on the divan behind the curtain in the throes of pleasure! The realisation aroused Paul-Henri immediately – his face flushed red and in three sudden jerks his male part stood erect. He also experienced an overwhelming curiosity as to what sort of man Marie allowed these intimacies. One of her own type, he thought, probably one of the ruffians he had earlier seen drinking rum in the bar below. But not necessarily – it might be someone like himself, a man of intelligence and status.

He put his hat on the table and took a few silent steps to the wall, where the curtain met it. With the greatest caution, so that the wooden rings should not rattle and give him away, he moved the curtain just enough to see into the alcove.

Marie's broad back was towards him as she lay on the divan, propped on one elbow, her head scarf removed and her mane of black hair hanging loosely down almost like a wimple. She had one knee up to part her thighs lasciviously and her companion, who was hidden from Paul-Henri, was evidently caressing her between those strong thighs, for at that moment Marie sighed again – a long exhalation that expressed the keenest pleasure.

Paul-Henri had only to wait, he knew, and before long Marie would be on her back with her partner on top of her – and he would see what sort of lover she preferred.

211

That he was intruding unpardonably into the private concerns of another person never entered his mind – he was too aroused for niceties of conscience to mean anything to him just then. Perhaps too, though of this one cannot be certain, he did not regard Marie the fortune-teller as a person worthy enough in relation to himself to be accorded the ordinary courtesies of social behaviour. And when one cannot be sure, one must be charitable – and attribute his spying to his condition of acute excitement.

Still sighing pleasurably, Marie's big body moved languorously and her head descended towards her lover. It was then that Paul-Henri received the second surprise since he had entered, uninvited, her room. The other person on the divan with Marie was also a woman!

He stared in total amazement, hardly able to accept what he saw. But it was true – Marie's new position revealed to him the thighs and belly of her companion – soft, rounded thighs between which lay a small patch of curly brown hair, and not the slightest indication of a hard stem like that which quivered inside his own trousers. Even as he watched, Marie's hand covered the patch and her fingers parted the lips they found there and probed within. She had bowed her head, he realised, to kiss the tips of her lover's breasts, which were still concealed from him.

After the initial shock of seeing two women engaged in pleasuring each other Paul-Henri experienced a state of arousal that made him shiver so violently that he found it necessary to lean against the wall to support himself on his trembling legs. His erect part was fluttering in his underwear – a sensation painful, delicious and intolerable at the same time. He was unable to stop himself from ripping open his trousers to let his monstrously swollen stem jut out.

'That's good, that's good!' Marie moaned to her friend, 'faster now!'

212

With the back of his glove Paul-Henri wiped from his forehead the drops of perspiration which were threatening to trickle down into his staring eyes. The movement of his arm made the curtain rings click together a little, but fortunately for him the two women on the divan were far too engrossed in each other and their own emotions to take note of so small a sound. Marie's friend was gasping without pause as the hand between her thighs continued its impetuous ministrations. Soon, very soon now . . . Paul-Henri would observe both women attain the climax of their passion! The thought was overwhelming!

It was almost too overwhelming! His hand was clutching the hard-standing part he had released from his trousers, squeezing it tightly. Two or three fast flicks would be enough to spray the dusty grey curtain with a climactic release of his own! But no, he insisted to his raging desire – wait! Very soon now there will be a choice of two warm receptacles for this throbbing part!

Marie's friend screamed briefly and her bottom lifted off the divan as her critical moments arrived. And immediately afterwards Marie's body jerked furiously for a moment or two – Paul-Henri's eyes were bulging almost out of his head! The engorged stem in his hand was shaking so furiously that he knew what was about to happen to him!

The fortune-teller's ecstasy was brief. While her friend was still gasping and kicking her heels against the mattress, Marie was off the divan and, with a sweep of her arm, flung back the curtains to reveal Paul-Henri! Unlike the first two surprises of the last quarter of an hour, this third great shock was extremely disagreeable. Paul-Henri leaned against the wall, open-mouthed, petrified with the horror of the situation and unable to move a muscle.

Marie was within arm's reach of him, her big round breasts heaving from her recent exertions on the divan, a drop or two of perspiration running down her belly towards the expanse of black fur that concealed her secret treasure.

'M'sieu Courval,' she said, a smile on her broad face, 'I knew you'd be back.'

It was the most ghastly moment of Paul-Henri's life and he could do no more than babble incoherently.

'You've arrived at a good time,' said Marie, 'in fact, you couldn't have chosen a better time.'

'But . . . but . . . '

'And you're all prepared for it,' she added, looking down at his bared and distended part, still firmly grasped in his yellow-gloved hand.

'But . . . but . . . '

'Come and join us,' she said with a grin.

She brushed his arm aside and took him by his projection as if it were a handle and pulled him towards the divan. The warmth of her body accentuated her perfume and Paul-Henri was dizzy from its effect. Perhaps it was that, perhaps it was the grasp of her hand on his male part – but it was too much! What he had feared a moment or two ago now happened – his legs felt like rubber, his loins twitched convulsively and he fountained his pent-up desire onto the divan!

The fourth shock of the afternoon was a coup-de-grâce! As he tottered on unsteady legs, spattering the mattress, there before him he saw, still trembling in the aftermath of passion – Yvonne!

THE EMANCIPATED MADAME
DELAROQUE

The very first time that Laurence saw her he was absolutely sure that she had just been making love. She was coming down the stairs from a second floor apartment in the Boulevard Beaumarchais and he was going up. Her clothes were distinctly elegant – a neat little summer suit in pale green silk, with an exquisitely pleated skirt. Under a pull-down hat in a matching shade her face was beautifully serene, yet to Laurence's perceptive eye there was about her an air of satisfied desire that left no room for doubt as to what she had been doing.

He stood aside politely to let her pass and raised his hat to her. She was no more than twenty-five years old and extremely attractive. She acknowledged his courtesy with a nod but did not return his smile – perhaps she read in his eyes his instinctive awareness of her recent pleasures. The subtlety of her expensive perfume was not lost on Laurence as she passed close to him and he thought he could even detect a hint of the exciting natural fragrance of a woman who has just been loved, but that might have been his imagination. Her white gloves were very fine, he noted, with criss-cross stitching on the backs in a contrasting colour.

In short, he desired her greatly from the moment he saw her. If she had returned his smile he would have tried to engage her in conversation then and there, with a view to persuading her to meet him at some later date. But she did no more than nod graciously and went on down the stairs.

It was almost six in the evening and Laurence was on his way to call upon a friend to invite him out to dinner and an evening of whatever entertainment presented itself as suitable to two young and unmarried men. There was also a little matter of business of the most interesting sort to be discussed between them. The friend, Jean-Claude Sorbier, greeted him warmly and settled him down with a drink while they debated which of the scores of restaurants they knew and liked should be their starting-point for the evening. Eventually Laurence could contain his curiosity no longer.

'On the way up the stairs I passed a most enchanting lady,' he said, 'does she have an apartment in this building?'

'I don't really know any of my neighbours,' Jean-Claude replied, 'I'm out so much, you know.'

'You couldn't possibly live in the same building as this one and not know about it,' Laurence protested. 'About twenty-five, wearing a light green suit – quite magnificent in every way. You must have seen her.'

'I don't think anyone like that lives here,' Jean-Claude said vaguely.

'But you've been here for years – you must have passed all your neighbours on the stairs at some time!'

Jean-Claude shrugged and Laurence guessed the truth at last.

'You devil!' he said with a grin. 'She was here to visit you – I might have known it! You lucky dog – she is superb! Who is she?'

'Well, since you've found me out, her name is Marcelle Delaroque. But please don't breath a word to anyone – her husband is a jealous man from what I hear and I don't want to cause any problems for her.'

'Naturally,' said Laurence, 'but Delaroque – the name seems familiar, though I can't place it. Who is he?'

'No one of importance – he's one of our representatives at the League of Nations. But surely you've heard of Marcelle Delaroque?'

'Of course – she's the woman who campaigns for education for women! The newspapers always have articles by her. I started to read one of them once but I couldn't get through it. But she's a perfect beauty – and I'd imagined that the writer of those articles must be a plain old maid. She can't be Delaroque's first wife – he's at least sixty.'

'His third.'

Laurence tried to question Jean-Claude further about his charming friend, but achieved nothing. Discretion was of the utmost importance, Jean-Claude insisted, and they returned to the question of where they should have dinner.

The little matter of business which Laurence raised over dinner was an opportunity which had come his way of acquiring for a reasonable sum of money the lease of a cottage in the country, not much more than an hour's drive out of Paris. In the nature of things, the ladies who became intimate friends of gallant young men like Laurence and Jean-Claude were frequently married and therefore the greatest of discretion was necessary to preserve the social decencies. This occasioned short and sometimes hurried encounters, when the pleasures of love really required more time and security from interruption by inconsiderate visitors or observation by servants.

From time to time it was possible for married ladies to explain to their husbands why they would be away for a night or two, staying with their sisters outside Paris, or some other convenient relative – and it was especially easy to explain such absences to husbands who had urgent preoccupations of their own with other married women, and easiest of all if a husband was conducting an intimate friendship with an unmarried woman he was also supporting. To provide for assignations arising from considerations like these, there were a number of small but very comfortable hotels within an hour or two of the city. They were well-frequented, particularly at week-ends.

The problem was that one might meet inconvenient acquaintances in these places, engaged in the same activities. More than one story was told of married couples each accompanied by someone else, meeting by chance in a small country hotel – with disastrous results! Whether these stories had any basis in fact or were merely idle gossip to amuse was neither here nor there – the possibility, however remote, of an unwanted encounter was enough to give rise to a certain nervousness.

To have a small house of one's own in the country – that was a proposition of real merit. The cost was fairly high, of course, since the owners of suitable properties were no fools and knew the value of what they had to offer. But shared between two good friends who trusted each other, the cost was reasonable and the advantages obvious. In a cottage of one's own there would be space and privacy to play love-games which were not practical in a hotel room. Jean-Claude congratulated Laurence on finding such a place and said that an opportunity like that must not be missed. They would take the cottage at once and divide the costs equally.

After that the evening continued merrily, with a visit to the Moulin Rouge to see the last show, then visits to numerous low dance halls with accordion music and singers in sequins who claimed to be Spanish, until they found their way towards dawn to a café near Les Halles, to round off the night with thick onion soup and a little glass of marc.

So the arrangements were completed, the cottage leased and plans made for the inaugural visit. At that time Laurence was on grounds of close amity with Marie-Véronique Blois, the charming cousin of another of his friends, Charles Brissard, through whom he had met her. To say that Marie-Véronique was charming was true, up to a point. She was pretty, she dressed well, she enjoyed the pleasures of love – all the qualities a man looks for in a woman with whom he intends to maintain an intimate relationship. But sadly, Marie-Véronique had proved to be an uninteresting conversationalist. She had a tendency, which Laurence found boring, to talk about domestic matters – and this to a lover!

In the tender throes of love-making Marie-Véronique always remained silent, even at the supreme moment itself. At first Laurence had attributed this rare characteristic to the profundity of her passion, but on longer acquaintance with her he began to ask himself if it might perhaps be because she was silently planning tomorrow's meals for her family. At all events, it seemed to him that their close friendship was not destined to last for very long. Nevertheless, for the present – that is, until someone else appeared in his life – he was content to leave things as they were and to enjoy what Marie-Véronique had to offer.

It was therefore Marie-Véronique that he drove into the country to assist in putting the newly acquired cottage to its proposed use. She had no great difficulty in absenting herself from her family for a day or two – one of her complaints against her husband was that he no longer loved her and was away too much. It was no secret to Laurence and most of the people he knew that Marie-Véronique's husband had for the past two or three years been conducting a tempestuous love-affair with a Polish opera singer, but Marie-Véronique herself never made any reference to that. Either she did not know or she chose not to believe it.

Naturally, Jean-Claude invited Marcelle Delaroque. According to what he told Laurence, she had declined outright when she heard that others would be present. But Jean-Claude had eventually succeeded in overcoming her objections by assuring her that his life-long friend Laurence was completely trustworthy. As for Marie-

Véronique, she was clearly in no position to reveal to anyone who she might have met at a place she should not herself have been in.

Both the women were delighted by the cottage itself when they saw it. It had evidently been built originally as a superior type of farm-house and much improved by its present owner. Running water had been installed, and even a bath-room, but the rustic touch had been preserved in the heavy wooden furniture and white-washed walls. The kitchen floor was stone-flagged and had a big open range for cooking – and this room also served as a dining-room. Upstairs there were two bed-rooms, each furnished with an old-fashioned high bed, sturdily built of wood and ideal for amorous cavortings.

There was no telephone or electricity, of course, which added to the rural charm. An excellent dinner, prepared by the ladies themselves, with plenty of good wine, was enjoyed in the soft glow of an oil-lamp suspended from the kitchen ceiling. The entire scenario was romantic in the extreme and even Marie-Véronique was able to forget her domestic preoccupations. Indeed, stimulated by Marcelle Delaroque, who was a witty and lively talker, Marie-Véronique positively blossomed. All in all, it was a most enjoyable evening.

Well before midnight the two couples retired to their bedrooms for the most important part of their expedition into the country. Laurence undressed Marie-Véronique in the golden candle-light which was the only illumination upstairs, kissing her breasts as he uncovered them. Once in bed, her unaccustomed vivacity continued and their love-making had a greater degree of exhilaration than ever before. She sighed and gasped as he embraced her – something she had never ventured previously, and when he mounted her, her legs clasped him boldly! Oh, the marvels that are wrought by good country air, lively companionship and enough excellent wine! Laurence rode her proudly and was rewarded at the critical moment by hearing her gasp his name lovingly as he delivered his passionate offering into the shrine of love.

He lay trembling on her warm body, holding her close and delighted by what had happened. He had judged her too harshly, he thought; he had been unkind and over-critical. In truth, she was a marvellous woman to have as a mistress.

Through the wall that separated them from the room into which Jean-Claude and Marcelle had retired, he heard a woman's voice exclaim '*Ah! Ah! Ah!*' – the excla-mation rising in crescendo to a long wail of ecstasy. It was Marcelle in a devastating climax of love, there could be no doubt of that.

'She's very noisy,' Marie-Véronique whispered beneath him.

Laurence's pleasure in his own love-making was destroyed like a toy balloon pricked by a pin. He had thought Marie-Véronique exceptionally responsive that night – yet here thrust upon his attention was a contrast which made him realise how timid her responses really were. What he wanted was a woman like Marcelle – one who plunged so completely into love-making that all else was forgotten in her orgasmic release. In short, he wanted Marcelle in bed with him, not Marie-Véronique.

How strangely self-defeating are the whims of men! The plain fact of the matter was that Laurence was in bed with a most amiable young woman who had just given him the supreme satisfaction of love. Even now her warm breasts were cushioning his chest and her tender prize still clasped his shrinking male pride. A reasonable man would have been well content – yet Laurence was fretting silently because he wanted a different woman beneath him. The emotions of affection and gratitude which he should by rights be experiencing towards Marie-Véronique were not in his heart. By this example it may be seen that men are, for the most part, idiots.

He moved to lie beside Marie-Véronique and hold her

221

in his arms – for the sake of appearances rather than for the proper reasons – while he contemplated his situation. Now that he considered the matter, he had wanted Marcelle ever since the moment he saw her coming down the stairs from Jean-Claude's apartment.

'Do you want to do it again?' Marie-Véronique asked in a whisper.

She had never asked that before – it had been understood without words that their pleasures would be repeated. Perhaps she felt with feminine intuition that all was not well – that he had turned away from her in his heart.

'Are you tired, chérie?' he asked, as graciously as he was able.

'Yes – it must be the fresh air. Would you mind very much if I went to sleep now? We have all day tomorrow.'

'Of course – go to sleep in my arms.'

No more was said and in only a few minutes her regular breathing told him that she was asleep. Laurence lay awake for a very long time, thoroughly miserable because of the cry of delight he had heard through the wall. His misery deepened when, in due course, that cry was repeated, this time with even more abandon than before. Laurence's male equipment stirred and stood erect at the sound, but he had no heart to make love to Marie-Véronique again – and besides, she was sound asleep. What was he going to do? he asked himself. To free himself from his affair with Marie-Véronique was easy enough – but how to win Marcelle away from Jean-Claude? Evidently she was devoted to him, or she would not be here. No doubt she could be persuaded to transfer her affections – Laurence never under-estimated his own abilities to please women of the world – but Jean-Claude would then be mortally offended by what he would surely regard as treachery by his oldest friend.

In a dilemma of this kind, friendship loses every time. Laurence resolved to win Marcelle for himself and, if

Jean-Claude never spoke to him again, so much the worse for him. The priorities were self-evident!

The excitement he was experiencing made him picture her – with what pangs of gnawing jealousy – in Jean-Claude's bed and the events that had led up to that cry of ecstasy. Naked, stretched out on her back, Jean-Claude's hand busy between her thighs and his mouth at her breasts! Or Marcelle sprawled in abandon across Jean-Claude, her fingers playing with his upright part! Oh, it was too much – it was intolerable to lie here in the dark while all that he desired most in the world was separated from him by the thickness of a wall!

Marie-Véronique had turned away from him in her sleep and was breathing peacefully – while he lay in a fever of frustrated desire, his erect part pushing up the sheet like a tent-pole. He had never known such torment in his life before. But there was worse to come – a repetition of Marcelle's long cry of delight, this time prolonged beyond the point of credibility.

For Laurence in his state of acute arousal it was too much. His trembling hand seized his hard projection and rubbed frantically. The echo of Marcelle's wailing cry still sounded inside his head and in seconds his frustrated part jerked mightily and poured its wasted passion in a stream onto his bare belly. After that, though he was not contented, he was at least fatigued by the strength of the despairing emotions he had experienced and eventually he drifted off to sleep.

The unfamiliar sound of birds singing in the trees about the cottage to greet a new day awoke him some hours later. He had no idea what time it was and through the bedroom window the sky looked pale – presumably it was very early indeed. Marie-Véronique slept on, lying on her back with one slender arm above her head on the pillow. Her pretty face was calm and she looked no more than twenty, innocent and vulnerable. Laurence's conscience began to trouble him when he recalled his unworthy

223

emotions of the night before. After all, this dear woman had taken a deliberate risk with her domestic happiness to be with him. She had responded warmly to his love-making, putting herself utterly at his disposal – and how had he repaid her trust and affection? Laurence was ashamed of himself, most of all when he remembered his furious act of self-gratification while she slept at his side.

He drew the covers down gently so as not to disturb her and contemplated her captivating little breasts. In truth, Marie-Véronique was a very desirable woman and he had behaved towards her with unforgivable ingratitude. He touched the tip of his tongue lightly to the rose-bud that adorned one of her breasts and inhaled the delicate perfume of her skin. He had been much to blame, he freely confessed that to himself. Between his legs there stirred the part that demonstrated his masculinity and, by the time he turned his attention to her other delicious breast, he was at full stretch.

Marie-Véronique sighed in her sleep, dreaming of love, no doubt, as a result of the enjoyable sensations which Laurence's gentle ministrations were giving her. He pushed the covers down further to admire her smooth belly and then he stroked it very lightly. She is beautiful, he thought – a verdict which was confirmed enthusiastically by his quivering male part.

She was lying with her legs slightly apart. Laurence's finger-tips brushed through the dark brown fleece between them and came to rest on her secret lips. So warm, so tender! Laurence sighed in appreciation, his heart overflowing now with profound affection for Marie-Véronique, whom only the night before he had spurned. She sighed too as the growing sensations of delight urged her towards wakefulness. Laurence's questing finger inserted itself with delicate skill between the soft lips he had been caressing and – ah, yes, the dew of arousal was already manifesting itself within her luxurious little alcove! He touched her hidden bud as lightly as a butterfly settling itself with fragile beating wings on a summer flower. She sighed again, almost awake now, and her elegant legs moved slowly apart in a most touching gesture of surrender. Laurence's finger caressed a little more firmly until, with a gasp of pleasure, she became fully awake, her deep brown eyes opening to gaze at him in rapture.

'Oh, Laurence!' she whispered in delight.

Her arm went about his neck, pulling him towards her. He rolled lightly onto her and, as her knees bent upwards, the head of his ready projection found of its own accord the entrance to her warm grotto of Venus and an easy push lodged him within. Laurence's heart was full of the tenderest emotions towards her – he made love to her with deeply affectionate passion, intent on her pleasure as much as his own. In circumstances such as these, when mutual esteem and desire are equally matched, the outcome is guaranteed to be enormously satisfactory to both partners. The pace quickened, became urgent – and at the moment when Laurence paid his respects to her in a passionate flood, Marie-Véronique arched her back in delight and gasped out that she adored him.

After many murmured declarations of mutual love, they at last lay in each other's arms and, because it was still ridiculously early in the morning, Marie-Véronique soon fell asleep again, an expression of utter content on her face. Laurence also tried to sleep, but his gratification at his renewed affection for Marie-Véronique did not permit him to do so. He lay awake, happy and pleased with himself, at peace with the world. In due course a growing awareness of the need to visit the bathroom to ease the pressure of the wine he had drunk the night before compelled him to get out of bed. He moved cautiously, not wishing to disturb his darling Marie-Véronique and, still naked, went to the bedroom door and lifted the old-fashioned iron latch without a sound.

The door to the bathroom was opposite and to the

right. At the very moment that Laurence pulled open his bedroom door – at the instant he stood there with one bare foot over the threshold – the bathroom door opened and Marcelle came out. She too was naked, evidently not thinking it worthwhile to put on a peignoir for the short journey from bed to bathroom. Laurence stood frozen in mid-step, staring at her, his new-found content gone in an instant. That she was beautiful was obvious to everyone – but Laurence had not realised how entrancingly beautiful she was until this moment when he saw her naked. His heart stood still and he forgot to breathe.

She was of middle height, neither too tall nor too short, and gracefully slender of form. Her hair had been dishevelled by the loving exertions of the night and, as yet uncombed and unbrushed, floated about her head in a silky haze of light brown, with strands of an even lighter hue, almost blonde, in it. Her eyes were wide-set and large – their tint a fascinating grey-green. Her mouth was wide and generous, her little chin had the delicate squareness of a woman who knew her own mind.

All this, of course, Laurence had seen before and admired greatly – her ready smile as she talked over dinner, the way her eyes shone when she became animated in discussion. What held his attention during this unexpected encounter at dawn was what he had not seen before – her exquisite naked body. He stared and stared and could not believe what he was privileged to see.

Beauty, it is said, is in the eye of the beholder. Perhaps it was so with Laurence. Marcelle's breasts were stylishly small and perfectly round, decorated with pink buds – and this description can be applied to many thousands of young women. Her waist was narrow, her hips broadened out in curves of restrained voluptuousness. An anatomist would have regarded her as a good specimen of adult womanhood, but to Laurence she was the most alluring person he had ever seen in his entire life. Her belly, for example, was a masterpiece whose subtle shape was accentuated by a round and shallow navel – a subject for a poet rather than an anatomist!

Descriptions in words are banal and futile to a man in so emotional a condition as Laurence was at that moment. *Impression* is all, not detail – and the impression he received was one of richness of visual and tactile beauty. Still there was more – a fleshy and luxurious mound adorned with neatly clipped and curly hair – dark brown – much darker than the hair of her head! This luscious treasure was set between thighs and legs the sight of which would have made the most talented of sculptors shed tears of despair at the thought of attempting to reproduce their perfection of line.

The passage of time was suspended for Laurence. He had lived through a lifetime, and seen Marcelle and received so powerful an impression of her beauty that, given pencil and paper, he could have drawn her from memory with the utmost accuracy – all in the space of perhaps a second and a half. For Marcelle glimpsed him from the corner of her eye and turned her head to look fully at him, without the least sign of embarrassment at being caught naked and unaware. How she interpreted the expression on his face at that moment, who can say? Her grey-green eyes flickered downwards briefly to take note of his male equipment, hanging limply after its recent attentions to Marie-Véronique, then she looked up to his face again and smiled in a way that was both friendly and casual. There was also a hint of amusement in that smile – and a touch of conspiracy – as if to say: *I know what you've been doing, and I've been doing the same.*

She turned away and went to her bedroom, leaving Laurence with a last glimpse of her long and slender back and the firm little cheeks of her bottom.

He let out his pent-up breath in a long sigh and a great truth forced itself upon him – he was in love with Marcelle Delaroque.

If anyone had been curious enough to ask him *why*?

he could not have answered the question. Even if some rational part of his own mind had induced him to make a comparison between Marcelle and Marie-Véronique, he would have been unable to exercise the detachment necessary to consider the differences and the likenesses. Certainly he could never have been brought to see that the likenesses were greater than the differences. Yet the facts were that Marcelle and Marie-Véronique were of much the same age, give a year or so, of about the same height, of the same social class. They were both attractive and amiable, they were both marvellously well designed by Providence for the uses and delights of love. In comparison to all that, a reasonable man would have found the differences trifling. Marie-Véronique's hair was a darker shade of brown than Marcelle's, that was true, and her breasts were a little fuller – an advantage in the eyes of many men. The most important point of difference was also in her favour – she loved Laurence, and Marcelle did not.

When all that is said, when the rational mind has enumerated all the excellent reasons why Laurence should cling to Marie-Véronique and pay no more attention to Marcelle than courtesy required, the truth was that Laurence did not love the charming woman to whom, only a quarter of an hour before, he had made love most tenderly. He stood like a naked statue in the doorway of his bedroom staring down an empty passage, struck dumb by the amazing discovery that he was hopelessly in love with a woman whose ecstasies in the arms of Jean-Claude had disturbed his sleep.

A further thought made his blood run cold – he would hear those sounds of ecstasy again in the night to come! Last night was bad enough, but now that he was fully aware of his feelings towards Marcelle, it was impossible! Separated from him by only a thin wall, that superb body would be bared for the kisses of Jean-Claude! And horrible to contemplate – it would be Jean-Claude gasping out his passion as he burrowed into Marcelle's plump little mound! Ah no, that was intolerable!

Laurence decided then and there to return to Paris immediately after breakfast, to spare himself so much agony. He must think of an excuse — some remembered appointment — anything to remove himself urgently from the country cottage which had been acquired as a place of pleasure and had so quickly become a place of torment for him.

To be fair to him, he was not a bad sort of fellow, this Laurence. He was handsome, well-liked and, in the normal course of events, he behaved with consideration for others. He had been the intimate friend of innumerable pretty women, some married, some not, and he treated them all well. Needless to say, he had never before been in love. At the age of almost thirty he was utterly unprepared for the formidable impact of that emotion!

In the weeks that followed the visit to the country Laurence found that it was excessively difficult to speak to Marcelle, either in person or by telephone. For he was obsessed by his passion and thought of little else but the pursuit of it. Alas, Marcelle proved to be extraordinarily busy, it seemed, and almost never at home, except when she and her husband were entertaining guests. Her presence was required in Geneva when her husband was at meetings of the League of Nations, and that seemed to account for half her time. As for the rest, her interest in promoting the cause of education for women took her to speaking engagements in cities all over France. When she was in Paris without her husband, her servants never seemed to know where she was — which indicated to Laurence that she was with Jean-Claude.

Weeks passed in this infuriating way. From time to time Laurence called upon Jean-Claude and, after some general talk, asked casually about Marcelle. The answers he received were never very satisfactory.

'She was here yesterday afternoon. She left for Geneva this morning.'

Or even worse:

'Marcelle? We were down at the cottage for a couple of nights and came back yesterday. She's off to Marseilles to address some worthy group of people on her favourite subject.'

And even more frustrating:

'Marcelle – oh, she becomes more beautiful every day! How is Marie-Véronique – have you taken her to the country recently?'

Truth to tell, Laurence had invited Marie-Véronique once more to the country cottage after the first fateful visit and she had accepted. After all, because a man is dying of love for a woman he cannot possess, his natural instincts do not disappear! In the absence of Marcelle, the visit had been, one might say, a success. Laurence enjoyed Marie-Véronique's compliance in bed and she appeared to be well content. Yet, even as he enjoyed himself, Laurence could not prevent the thought flitting through his mind that this, in some manner, was not the real thing, only a second-best. And on getting up in the morning, he found himself staring at the bathroom door, where once he had seen Marcelle in her naked beauty, foolishly hoping that the door would open and she appear to him – and knowing full well that she was a long way away and certainly not thinking of him.

The problem was to arrange to meet Marcelle when she was not with her husband and not with Jean-Claude. Laurence gave the matter some prolonged thought and made a plan. He telephoned to the office of the newspaper in which Marcelle's articles on education were most often published and acquired the information that she was to make a speech to an audience in Bordeaux in three days time. A few more telephone calls to the best hotels in that city produced the further information as to where a reservation had been made for Madame Delaroque.

230

Laurence reserved a suite for himself in the same hotel and congratulated himself upon his sagacity. Marcelle would be alone in a hotel, far from her home and friends. She would be surprised and pleased to meet someone she knew, apparently by chance. They would talk, Laurence would remind her subtly of the circumstances in which they had accidentally viewed each other naked. The rest would follow naturally.

On the due day, he took the train to Bordeaux, dined alone in the hotel and then sat with a glass of cognac where he could watch the entrance and be seen by her when she returned from her meeting. Time passed very slowly, because of his eagerness to see her. He ordered another cognac and rehearsed in his mind the explanation he had concocted for his presence in Bordeaux.

It was after ten o'clock when at last Marcelle came into the hotel – accompanied by two other women, all of them talking at the same time. Laurence stood up, an expression of false surprise on his face.

'Madame Delaroque – how very pleasant to meet you again! And how unexpected!'

'Monsieur Callot – what are you doing here?' she said, smiling at him.

There was a babble of introductions and Laurence kissed hands – his story about being in Bordeaux on a business matter completely lost in the fuss. At last he succeeded in getting the ladies seated and drinking champagne while he listened to Marcelle's account of her speech and the enthusiasm of her two companions. One of the ladies was a school-teacher, he gathered, the other a librarian. They were both devoted to Marcelle – they admired her courage, her intellect, her clothes, everything about her! She was what they would both have wanted to have been if they had had the inestimable privilege of being born in Paris – and of having her looks and position, of course!

Laurence judged that things were going well and he

ordered more champagne. The two disciples would decide that it was time for them to go home before long – for surely no one stayed up until midnight in Bordeaux! He would be alone with Marcelle! The moment would arrive when he persuaded her to accompany him to his suite! Or perhaps she would prefer to invite him to her room, who could say? Not long after that she would be in his arms! He would assist her out of her clothes and cover that beautiful body with hot kisses! After that – ah, the imagination could not reach far enough to encompass the felicities of what would happen then! But he would hear that orgasmic cry of hers and know that it was his doing – and, he promised himself as the champagne bubbled through him, he would hear that cry of hers at least three times before he let her sleep! At least three!

Quite suddenly, the plan changed entirely. Marcelle stood up and said 'Goodnight' to them all and offered her hand to Laurence.

'I must leave you,' she said. 'It is late and I am catching an early train to Geneva tomorrow.'

Then she was gone! Laurence sat down again, thunderstruck. This wasn't his plan at all! The two friends were supposed to leave – but here he was, left with them – both of them chatting away and drinking his champagne – the third bottle!

After a while his normal good nature reasserted itself and he accepted the fact that the situation was ridiculous. But the hours of anticipation of the pleasures of love could not be dismissed easily. He looked at the two women he had been left with and gave them his most charming smile.

They were a contrasting pair. Mademoiselle Bergerac was well over thirty – nearer forty, perhaps – a plump woman in a dark blue summer suit that had obviously been bought in a department store. She was a teacher, he had been told, a vocation which Laurence did not esteem highly, but above her round and pink cheeks there was a certain sparkle in her brown eyes that suggested she might know more interesting things than those she taught to children in the class-room. Her friend, Mademoiselle Clavel, was younger – about thirty, perhaps – and, by comparison, thin. She wore rimless spectacles and gave an impression of seriousness when she spoke – even when she laughed. For all that, her skirt had crept above her knees as she sat, revealing a hint of green garter.

In ordinary circumstances Laurence would not have given these ladies a second glance, of course. But situated as he was, alone in a strange city, bereft of the object of his desire, his blood up – why not? He did not expect to meet them ever again. There was nothing to lose.

'Ladies,' he said, 'it would be a pity to end our conversation. May I make a suggestion?'

'Of course, Monsieur Callot,' said Mademoiselle Bergerac, eyeing him cautiously.

'We could continue our most interesting discussion in my suite, over another glass of champagne.'

Mademoiselle Clavel and Mademoiselle Bergerac looked at each other in silence for a moment or two. It was plump Mademoiselle Bergerac who spoke eventually.

'You are very kind, Monsieur, but this is not Paris, you must understand. Things are very different here. It is out of the question for a woman to accept an invitation to a hotel room – unless she is of a certain type, if you follow me. Since you are a stranger here, we take no offence at your suggestion, since it was surely made in good faith and friendship and with no intention of being insulting.'

'My most profound apologies,' said Laurence in his most gracious manner, 'I assure you that I have the greatest of respect for you.'

'Because you are a friend of Madame Delaroque,' Mademoiselle Bergerac continued, 'that alters the circumstances. We both have the highest regard for her.'

So do I,' Laurence assured her, 'I admire her greatly.'

'It is because of these special circumstances that we feel

able to accept your invitation,' Mademoiselle Bergerac concluded.

In the expectation of entertaining Marcelle, Laurence had reserved for himself a fine suite in the hotel. Mademoiselle Bergerac was impressed when she saw it, and said so at length. So was Mademoiselle Clavel, though she said less. The conversation continued, becoming even more vivacious after another glass or two of champagne. At some point the formal titles of Monsieur and Mademoiselle were abandoned in favour of Laurence, Brigitte and Marianne. Not long after that Brigitte, the plump one, declared that she was hot and removed the jacket of her summer suit to reveal a white satin blouse well filled out in front. Thus encouraged, Marianne took off the short jacket she wore over her striped frock. She seemed to have very little bosom but, as Laurence could not help but notice, her skirt kept riding up as she twisted about in her chair until a gleam of bare flesh appeared above her stocking-top.

Laurence asked permission to shed his jacket, agreeing that it was a warm night – a marvellous night – a night made for love, dare he say? At once the conversation turned to love and the ladies explained to him at some length how exceptionally difficult it was in their home-town for a woman possessed of education and taste to meet, in the right circumstances, a man worthy enough to be entrusted with their tender emotions. Laurence commiserated with them, his sincerity so apparent that, without anyone appearing to move, all three found themselves on the sofa together, Laurence in the middle, with an arm round each of them.

Naturally, they were all a little drunk by now and in very good spirits. So much so that when Laurence's arms slid a little down their shoulders and his hands eased their way under their arms until each hand rested on a breast, neither Brigitte nor Marianne was in the least shocked. On the contrary, they seemed to regard this development as perfectly natural. Laurence sat in great comfort, a big soft breast in his left hand and a small flat one in his right. He too found it quite natural and not in the least outrageous when Brigitte's hand found its way inside his shirt to stroke his chest and Marianne's warm palm rested on his thigh, about midway between knee and the source of his pride. On the contrary, his extensible part was puffed up with pride at that time.

Marianne seemed content to leave her hand where it was and make no further advance but Brigitte's fingers had begun to tease Laurence's nipples slowly. Yet it was Marianne, her spectacles glinting, who insisted in all seriousness that between good friends there should be no secrets. As soon as Laurence agreed with her proposition of frankness, Marianne stood up and pulled her frock over her head to show herself in plain pink camiknickers. These too she removed to let Laurence view plainly her thin body and childish breasts – but her belly was enticing, he thought, very smooth and flat – and her lean thighs had a sinewy look about them that was interesting. She sat down again within his arm and pressed herself closely to him, her palm moving a little higher up his thigh as he caressed one of her tiny rosebuds with the ball of his thumb.

'There!' she whispered, 'I have no secrets from you, Laurence.'

'I admire your strength of character,' he said. 'You have demonstrated with total clarity that you are a person of principle – you mean what you say. Do you not agree, Brigitte?'

'But of course,' Brigitte exclaimed. 'Her courage is to be admired also. She believes that men do not think her truly feminine because her breasts are so small. But she displays them to you and that requires real courage.'

'I am honoured,' said Laurence, 'I praise your courage as well as your principles, Marianne, and I assure you that I have no doubts whatsoever of your femininity. Nor do I think that your breasts are too small – I think they are enchanting.'

To prove his assertion he continued to play with the one he could reach until the little rosebud was standing up firmly.

'Fine words,' said Brigitte on his other side, 'but words are cheap enough. What of your secrets, Laurence, are they to remain concealed from us?'

'As a man of honour I can do no less than follow the example set by Marianne,' he answered cheerfully.

He rose to his feet and stripped himself recklessly, hurling clothes and shoes to the furthest corners of the room. When he sat down again between the two women both stared at his bare muscular thighs and the strong stem which rose from between them. A hand crept up each thigh – one with short and plump fingers and one narrow hand with long thin fingers – until they met and both took hold of the part of him created to give pleasure to women. It felt strange, and very exciting, to be handled by two women at the same time.

'Now, Brigitte,' he murmured, 'you are the only one still hiding secrets from your friends. This raises serious doubts as to your sincerity and friendship – don't you agree, Marianne?'

'She is always like that,' Marianne declared, 'quick to speak but slow to act. Come on, Brigitte, what are you waiting for? Off with your clothes and let's see those big fat breasts of yours, even if they do dangle more than they should.'

Stung by the gibe, Brigitte unbuttoned her blouse, then stood up to drop her skirt. She was wearing a full-length chemise, embroidered over the bosom and plain at the hem. She hoisted it over her head and, as she bent over to remove her matching knickers, Laurence stared in fascination at the immense round cheeks of her bottom.

'Ah!' said Marianne, 'the sight of your backside made

him jerk in my hand. Look out for yourself, Brigitte, he might be one of those who prefer the back door!'

'Have no fear,' said Laurence, amused by the suggestion, 'my tastes in these matters are orthodox. I have always found the front entrance adequate for my purpose.'

'As to that,' said Marianne, 'We shall see.'

Brigitte was still on her feet and had turned to present to him her frontal aspect. The big bouncy breasts she had boasted in her youth had indeed become somewhat slack with time, but they were still most presentable. Laurence reached out to squeeze one of them appreciatively.

'My dears,' he said, 'the moment has surely come, now that we have exchanged secrets, to move ourselves into a more appropriate part of the suite so that we can investigate these secrets more thoroughly in a comfortable position.'

'The horizontal position,' Marianne suggested.

'Exactly.'

Laurence, wearing nothing at all, led the women – wearing only their stockings and garters – to the bedroom, each of his arms round a bare waist. He was wondering how the decision could be made as to which of them would first receive his tribute without the other one becoming offended. It was an engrossing and amusing train of thought.

His concern proved unnecessary. The instant that the three of them were on the bed, Marianne's spectacles removed at last, matters arranged themselves. The only light was that of the moon through the open windows – a most suitable setting for what was enacted there! As they rolled about together on the broad bed they ceased in some strange manner to be three distinct and separate persons. There was warm flesh, wet mouths and caressing hands – and that was all! There were hands between Laurence's legs, hands stroking his chest and belly, hands manipulating his upright part, mouths pressed to his

237

mouth, mouths pressed to his body and thighs. His own hands grasped and fondled breasts, bottoms, soft-haired little mounds!

Together they writhed, sighed and gasped – now Laurence was on his back with a warm belly across his, a breast squeezed down over his mouth as he worried at its firm bud with his lips. Then he was face-down on a yielding body, his head between open thighs, darting his tongue into smooth groins, while above him a warm and wet mound was being rubbed against his back and fingernails were digging pleasurably into the cheeks of his bottom. The woman beneath him rolled and he was on his side, his face pressed into a hot belly, a pair of thighs clamped round his waist and his fingers deep within a wet little aperture.

These frenetic exercises and the sensations they induced brought Laurence very nearly to the point of climactic release. His whole body was trembling, as if in delirium, and he tried to grasp a pair of hips – any pair – to force one of the women onto her back and get between her legs urgently. But even as he tried, four hands seized him, one under the chin, one by his hair, one by the ankle and one by his fluttering stem. He was rolled onto his back, a leg was thrown over his chest and, an instant later, one of the women was sitting astride his chest. He raised his head to nip playfully at the bottom pinning him down and even as he did so, he became aware of certain voluptuous sensations elsewhere that informed him that the other woman had taken her seat astride his loins and that his engorged pride had been expertly guided into a tunnel of warm flesh.

Laurence sighed and shook, his hands over the thighs so near his face to get at the tender lips between them – only to discover that other hands were there before him! He rubbed urgently at the busy hands, half-wondering whose they were, until the jolting of the woman astride his belly, who had taken his hard-standing part into her tender care – this jolting produced the desired explosion and he cried out '*Ah, ah, ah!*' as his spasms fountained his passion upwards into its destined receptacle. The woman seated across his chest wailed in exquisite pleasure as the fingers rubbing between her legs brought her to a climax of sensation – the jolting over his loins increased in speed, halted abruptly for the length of an in-drawn breath, then resumed furiously for a few more strokes, accompanied by a long sobbing wail of ecstasy.

Soon after that the two women sagged slowly sideways, pulling Laurence onto his side. There were adjustments of limbs, then all three lay quietly for a while, Laurence with his head on a smooth thigh and a head pillowed on his belly.

'My dears,' he said eventually, 'that was astonishing.'

'I suppose that in Paris you have little amusements like that every day,' said a voice in the near-darkness, 'it wasn't too boring for you, was it?'

He recognised the voice as Marianne's.

'It was magnificent,' he sighed, his hand moving gently over a big soft breast which must be Brigitte's.

'It is good of you to say so,' said the owner of the breast he was fondling, 'but we realise that here in the provinces we cannot hope to equal the pleasures taken for granted by a man of the world like you. I mean, after Madame Delaroque Marianne and I must seem extremely ordinary to you.'

'You do yourself an injustice,' Laurence protested.

He wished with all his heart that she had not reminded him that the divine Marcelle was in another bed in the hotel. To some extent it spoiled the pleasure he had just enjoyed by making his companions seem to him, as Brigitte herself had said, extremely ordinary. He sighed, and it was not with pleasure.

But there was a hand caressing his limp part affectionately and, as it began to respond, the memory of Marcelle faded from Laurence's thoughts. After all, it is impossible

239

for a man to be remembering and sighing over the love of his life at every moment of the day and night – especially when he is in bed with two other women totally unrestrained in their enjoyment of the delights of love. With the hand that was not fondling Brigitte's breasts he reached out to touch Marianne's belly in the dark and let his fingers move to the secret place between her slim thighs. How deliciously wet it was there! In this way – muted and gentle – there commenced the second movement of the symphony. Naturally it became livelier and more energetic as it proceeded, the tempo quickened and a delightful *agitato* made itself apparent.

At the height of it, Laurence found himself sitting upright on his heels, a woman across his thighs and his baton enclosed within the soft container intended for it. It was the plump Brigitte who was affording him this accomodation – he knew that by the feel of her breasts squashed against his chest – and from that fact he guessed that it had been Marianne who had received his first offering. Not that she was content to be left out of things – she was kneeling behind Brigitte and rubbing her little breasts against her friend's broad back! Nor was that the limit of her participation – as Laurence's hands moved everywhere over feverishly hot flesh, he found that one of Brigitte's arms was behind her, in a position, as far as he could judge, to put her hand between Marianne's splayed thighs!

Brigitte responded very quickly to the thrilling stimulus of Laurence's hard appurtenance within her. She moaned and shook violently in her ecstasy, the pulsating grip of her inner muscles causing him to attain the culmination of desire much earlier than he had expected. But the pleasure was none the less for that – he forced his hands between their bodies and squeezed her breasts tightly throughout his critical moments, enravished by sensation. Marianne was a little slower – presumably impaled on Brigitte's fingers – but she too at last uttered the sobbing cry that denoted her arrival at the supreme peak of pleasure.

'*Mesdemoiselles* – you are a delight!' said Laurence. 'I don't know when I last enjoyed myself so much! But if one may ask – do you always seek your amusements together in this way?'

'Of course not!' Brigitte exclaimed, unseating herself from his thighs. 'What must you think of us! This is the first time we've ever been together with a man!'

'Then I am very greatly honoured. I beg you not to be offended by questions meant only in a spirit of friendly curiosity about two persons for whom I have the very highest regard. What made you decide this evening to, so to speak, share your diversions?'

'We both liked the look of you,' said Marianne, entering the conversation at last, 'neither of us could bear to let the other have you to herself when you invited us to your suite, so here we both are.'

'That is very flattering! I hope most sincerely that you are not disappointed by the outcome of your decision.'

'I think you're marvellous,' said Marianne, reaching over to stroke his thigh tenderly, 'don't you, Brigitte?'

'Superb!' Brigitte sighed.

In the traditional manner, the symphony of love had four movements and, after an appropriate pause for the players to recover from their exertions, the third movement got under way. And then the fourth, by which time it was late into the night and the moon was down and the room in almost total darkness. When the final chords were sounded at last, all three were fatigued and content. Laurence drifted off to sleep, pleased with his night's work.

He was awakened some time later by a persistent shaking of the mattress beneath him. His eyes opened lazily to see, in the half-light which heralds dawn, plump Brigitte sprawled on her back and Marianne crouching over her. Laurence's eyes opened wider and with a sudden shock of excitement he understood what he was seeing. One of Marianne's hands was between Brigitte's parted thighs, moving rhythmically, while her mouth was at Brigitte's breasts. The shaking that had woken him was caused by Brigitte's legs trembling hard against the mattress as delightful sensations coursed through her. Laurence propped himself up on one elbow to observe more closely – Marianne glanced up from the breasts to which she was ministering and her eyes met his for a moment. Or more exactly, his eyes met hers, for without her spectacles she stared myopically at him for an instant, then bowed her head to resume her labour of love, her nimble fingers moving swiftly between Brigitte's thighs.

Brigitte cried out in orgasmic delight, her legs thrashing at the mattress. Before her convulsions were finished, before her legs were still, Marianne turned as quickly as a cat and spread herself the length of Brigitte's trembling body, her slender legs between her friend's plump legs. She pressed her soft-haired little mound tightly against the one beneath her and rode it furiously, as if she were a man! Brigitte lay still at last, her ecstasy over, letting her friend have her way with her until in a final fury of thrusting Marianne achieved her aim and moaned loudly in release, her open mouth over Brigitte's mouth.

The observation of this strange proceeding aroused Laurence mightily. His male extension was at full stretch long before Marianne reached her moments of culmination. Hardly had her throes of delight faded to a delicious nervous twitching as she lay on Brigitte than Laurence took her by her narrow hips and pulled her off her friend and towards him, until she lay on her side with her back to him. It was the work of a moment to lift her topmost leg and burrow his stiffness between the soft lips still pouting from her climactic pleasure of not five seconds ago. Marianne cried out in surprise as she felt herself invaded in this manner, then jerked her little bottom against his belly to make him begin.

242

He held her by her waist and thrust easily, enchanted by this unexpected turn of events. Brigitte rolled over to face Marianne and squeezed her fat breasts against her friend's flat little breasts. Her arm was over Marianne, to grasp Laurence by the hip and pull him closer, so that he felt that he was making love to both women at the same time.

It was in Laurence's mind that this charming little interlude would be of considerable duration, given his supreme exertions of an hour or two earlier and for this reason he set himself a gentle pace that could be sustained to a satisfactory conclusion. In this he was mistaken. He had been extremely aroused by the sight of Marianne lying on Brigitte's plump belly and utilising it in so masculine a fashion that he found himself soon plunging hard and fast into Marianne's very moist convenience. As for Marianne herself, her most tender parts were evidently very sensitive from the pleasure they had just received and she returned his thrusts most firmly – and the instant that Laurence sighed and delivered his offering within her, she too cried out and hugged Brigitte to her.

He fell asleep again at once, still joined intimately to Marianne, an arm over her waist and his hand resting between Brigitte's warm thighs. When he awoke it was broad daylight and he was alone – his companions of the night had departed without disturbing his rest. He lay in the incredibly rumpled bed, content with the world, recalling with the greatest of pleasure the escapades of the night. When he looked at his watch it was after ten o'clock and he was very hungry.

He found a scribbled note in the sitting-room of his suite when he sat down to the breakfast a waiter brought him. The note thanked him for a most enjoyable occasion and gave an address at which he was requested to call when he was next in Bordeaux. It was unsigned and Laurence smiled and put it into his wallet as a souvenir of a memorable encounter.

On the train back to Paris his thoughts turned to Marcelle Delaroque. She, after all, was the cause of his long journey – and his plan to get her alone had proved to be totally futile. Naturally, his tremendous passion for her had not been diminished in the slightest degree by his adventure with her acquaintances. He loved her madly and desired her to distraction! There was only one thing for it, he decided – no more subterfuges! He would go to her and explain frankly his emotions towards her, in the hope that she would be moved to take pity on him.

In the event, to find Marcelle at home and alone for the simple purpose of declaring his passion proved to be exceedingly difficult to achieve. It was always the same when he called at her apartment or telephoned: *Madame is away. Madame is out.* But Laurence persevered and, after seemingly endless attempts, he succeeded, about ten days after his return from Bordeaux, in speaking to her on the telephone.

He told her that there was a matter of the utmost importance and discretion that he must discuss with her immediately! Marcelle seemed not disposed to take this completely seriously – certainly not as seriously as he would have wished – and made half a dozen excuses to put him off. But Laurence was not to be put off any longer, having reached this point. To settle things, he said that he would call at her apartment in a quarter of an hour – and put the telephone down before she had time to say no.

There was no time to change his clothes, visit his barber – no time for anything at all except to find a taxi and bribe the driver to get through the traffic at high speed. Even then, it took rather longer than the quarter of an hour he had specified.

A maid opened the door to him – no doubt the one who had been dashing his hopes for so long by her constant reiteration of *Madame is not at home*. Laurence told her his name and she ushered him into Marcelle's salon. How

244

his heart was beating at this moment – he was alone with Marcelle at last!

She was sitting in a large arm-chair and was dressed most elegantly in a close-fitting frock of moiré silk in a delicate shade of moss-rose, a belt of the same material very low round her hips, with a round silver buckle in front.

Laurence sped across the room to bow over her hand and kiss it.

'You can only stay for a moment,' she said, 'I'm going out. There is something you want to say to me – can it be that urgent?'

'You cannot imagine how urgent,' said Laurence, at a loss how to begin in these unauspicious circumstances.

'Then tell me and I shall know.'

'Marcelle – since the first moment I saw you there has been growing in my heart a certain emotion, though it may be that you are unaware of this.'

'Of what should I be aware?'

There was nothing to be done but blurt it out and hope for the best – and this he did.

'I am in love with you, Marcelle.'

'Are you?' she said calmly, 'you've given no signs of it. Have you been drinking? You look a little flushed.'

'No, I assure you that I am sober. The agitation you see comes from the very powerful emotions I am experiencing.'

'And you have been in love with me since the first time you saw me – not just since lunch-time, is that what I am to believe?'

'Exactly that! At first I did not understand my own feelings. But then it struck me like a blow. Since then I have not been able to get you out of my mind.'

'When did this blow strike you?'

'That early morning when I saw you coming out of the bathroom of the cottage.'

'By chance you saw me with nothing on,' Marcelle said.

'Do you fall in love with every woman you see like that – Marie-Véronique, for example?'

'No, I do not love her!'

'I am sorry to hear it – she is devoted to you, from what I observed.'

'These things can't be regulated. I have an affection for her, but that is another matter entirely.'

'Well, you have told me your urgent news,' said Marcelle, 'I must go now or I shall be late.'

'Please – don't go yet!'

'I must. There are people waiting for me.'

'You cannot leave before I have an answer!' he said in great distress of mind.

'You haven't asked a question, so how can I answer it? What is it that you want?'

'You.'

Marcelle looked slightly puzzled.

'Are you suggesting that I should break off my friendship with Jean-Claude and . . . ' she left the sentence unfinished and shrugged.

'Yes, yes, yes! Forget Jean-Claude and think only of me.'

'But I thought that you and he were old friends.'

'We are, but nothing matters to me except to obtain your love – nothing!'

'Such vehemence! But as you said a moment ago, these things can't be regulated.'

'You don't love him, I know that.'

'You sound very sure,' she answered, smiling a little.

'I am.'

'All this talk of love is beginning to become faintly tiresome. I really must go now.'

'One word before you do – unless I make love to you very soon I shall either go mad or die – that's the state I'm in.'

'Is *that* all you want!' Marcelle exclaimed. 'Heavens, why didn't you say so before instead of sitting there talking about love? Well, it will have to be quick – I have an appointment in ten minutes.'

Before Laurence had fully grasped the implications of her words Marcelle was on her feet and raising the hem of her frock. He saw the embroidered garters which held up her fine silk stockings – then, a sight to make him gasp aloud in delight – her bare thighs above her stocking-tops. He stared in disbelief at the lace edge of her knickers and he broke out into perspiration as she slipped the knickers down her legs and to her ankles!

How could it be possible that a hunger that had gnawed away at him for so long should be so easily appeased? Yet there she was, hopping from left foot to right foot as she removed that intimate garment completely and dropped it casually onto the chair where she had been sitting.

'You are not to crease my frock,' she said, 'I haven't time to change and make up again.'

Laurence nodded, dumb with amazement.

'Open your trousers,' she said, a touch of impatience in her tone.

He fumbled with his buttons awkwardly. This was not at all how he imagined the scene would be played between them. He had envisaged a lengthy – but interesting – dialogue in which he advanced his cause and she was at first modest, then more responsive – and finally welcoming, won over by his respectful fervour. Then kisses, dozens of them, on her mouth and face! That would be followed by the leisurely and completely intriguing process of undressing her to fondle her breasts – and so on! That was the usual procedure, as Laurence understood it, from his past experience. It was a shock to see Marcelle standing before him, her underwear discarded at almost his first word.

Impatient with his fumbling, she reached down into his lap, flicked open his trouser buttons and pulled out his stiff part.

'At least that's ready for action!' she said with a chuckle.

She raised her skirt with one hand – up to her navel – uncovering the neat tuft of brown hair between her legs. Her other hand was at her mouth – she licked her fingers and passed them between the lips hidden in her tuft, to moisten the entrance for him. A moment later she was astride his lap and he felt himself guided into place by her hand, then jammed inside her as she sat down forcefully across his thighs.

'There we are!' she said cheerfully. 'Now you've got what you wanted. Why didn't you tell me before? Today is very inconvenient.'

'Oh Marcelle!' he gasped, not knowing what to reply.

She rode up and down sharply on his embedded spike of flesh, very adept at the task.

'Does that feel good?' she asked. 'No, you mustn't touch my breasts – you'll ruin my frock. Sit still and let things take their course.'

However unprepared spiritually Laurence was for the event which was taking place with him as a participant, his body responded to the stimulus in a natural way. Marcelle's brisk up and down motion produced sensations of the keenest pleasure that made his emotions surge. Something else too surged and he uttered a final gasp of surprise as Marcelle drained him of his passion.

'There now!' she said, her movements ceasing at once, 'now I've made you happy! And you've made me late for my appointment – I must fly! Call for me at about twelve tomorrow and you can take me to lunch – and then we can go to your apartment for the whole afternoon – I shall be free until dinner.'

Before Laurence could say a word, she was off him and out of the room, snatching up her pretty silk underwear from the chair as she went.

MORE EROTIC CLASSICS FROM CARROLL & GRAF

☐ Anonymous/ALTAR OF VENUS $3.95
☐ Anonymous/AUTOBIOGRAPHY OF A FLEA $3.95
☐ Anonymous/CONFESSIONS OF AN ENGLISH
    MAID $3.95
☐ Anonymous/THE DIARY OF MATA HARI $3.95
☐ Anonymous/DOLLY MORTON $3.95
☐ Anonymous/FANNY HILL'S DAUGHTER $3.95
☐ Anonymous/FLORENTINE AND JULIA $3.95
☐ Anonymous/THE LUSTFUL TURK $3.95
☐ Anonymous/MADELEINE $3.95
☐ Anonymous/A MAID'S JOURNEY $3.95
☐ Anonymous/THE MEMOIRS OF JOSEPHINE$3.95
☐ Anonymous/PRIMA DONNA $3.95
☐ Anonymous/ROSA FIELDING: VICTIM OF LUST
                                $3.95
☐ Anonymous/SECRET LIVES $3.95
☐ Anonymous/THREE TIMES A WOMAN $3.95
☐ Anonymous/VENUS REMEMBERED $3.95
☐ Anonymous/VENUS UNBOUND $3.95
☐ Perez, Faustino/LA LOLITA $3.95
☐ van Heller, Marcus/ADAM & EVE $3.95
☐ van Heller, Marcus/HOUSE OF BORGIA $3.95
☐ van Heller, Marcus/THE LOINS OF AMON $3.95
☐ van Heller, Marcus/ROMAN ORGY $3.95
☐ van Heller, Marcus/VENUS IN LACE $3.95
☐ Villefranche, Anne-Marie/FOLIES D'AMOUR
                              Cloth $13.95

☐ Villefranche, Anne-Marie/JOIE D'AMOUR
$3.95 Cloth $13.95
☐ Villefranche, Anne-Marie/PLAISIR D'AMOUR
$3.95 Cloth $12.95

Available at fine bookstores everywhere or use this coupon for ordering:

Carroll & Graf Publishers, Inc., 260 Fifth Avenue, N.Y., N.Y. 10001

Please send me the books I have checked above. I am enclosing $_____ (please add $1.75 per title to cover postage and handling.) Send check or money order—no cash or C.O.D.'s please. N.Y residents please add 8¼% sales tax.

Mr/Mrs/Miss _____

Address _____

City _____ State/Zip _____
Please allow four to six weeks for delivery.